DWELLING

a novel

by Doug Karr

Illustrations by Ophelia Fu

DWELLING

A NOVEL

Copyright © 2018 by Doug Karr

ISBN-13: 978-0692133750
ISBN-10: 0692133755

Written by Doug Karr
Illustrations by Ophelia Fu

Cover art by Ester Chuang
Edited by Masie Cochran

www.dougkarr.com
www.opheliafu.co.uk

Give feedback on the book at:
doug@piefacepictures.com

Twitter
@Doug_Karr
@ophelia_fu

Steemit
@dougkarr
@opheliafu

First Edition

Printed in the U.S.A

To Aimee, Travis and Wesley

PART I
TIGHT QUARTERS

"We are from the Lower East Side
We don't give a damn if we live or die"
— David Peel and The Lower East Side

CHAPTER ONE
THE TENEMENT

Mioko moved frantically about her apartment, her milky legs covered in Japanese horimono tattoos. The distant towers speckling the darkness outside her windows were the only reminder she wasn't entirely alone.

She ruffled through old vertical files, the photographic evidence of her existence. A frenzied leap boosted her onto a chair. She fished the forgotten space above her closet. It had to be here somewhere.

Dumping a pile of photographs onto her kitchen table, she quickly shuffled images to the floor. And then—there it was, emulsion, the snap of a shutter, tactile in black and white. The faintest whiff of light and chemicals gleaned off the photo paper. The edges curved slightly. Analogue perfection, despite her subject.

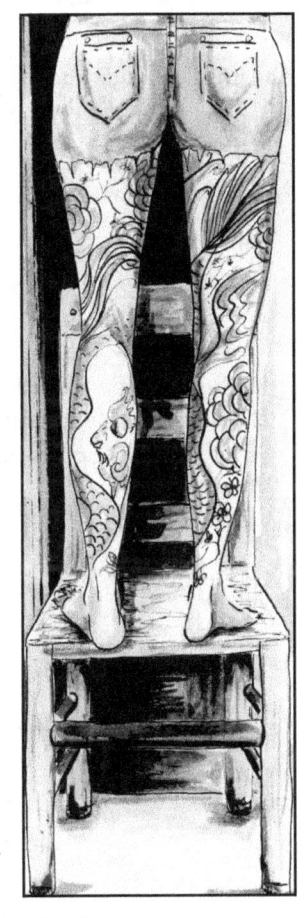

Wildly cranking kitchen drawers, Mioko found a pen and leaned to scrawl a note. She grabbed a roll of tape on her way out the apartment door.

The six-story tenement's ground floor was all bare light bulbs, paint-caked moldings and pressed-tin wainscoting.

In the front foyer, Mioko taped the photograph against the cool inner vestibule glass. She could still feel his hands on her. Despite the fact that the photo was inanimate, incapable of inflicting pain beyond a paper-cut, her stress responses were firing white-hot waves down her spine. In the picture a shirtless hispanic kid had one arm leaning against a metal gate, the other reaching for the lens. She tried to keep her eyes off his face. Negotiating between her adrenalized rush and abject repulsion, she affixed her note below, before opening the foyer door and hurrying back down the hall.

WARNING. This is Rube Carbia and he is stalking me. He was waiting outside the bldg. today and SHOULD NOT be let in under any circumstances. Hopefully he will not come back. Please be aware.

— Mioko.

The door clicked shut as Mioko Kimura disappeared up six flights.

Outside the Lower East Side tenement, Ludlow Street was clearing out. The motley haze of formative singer-songwriter hyphenates, hipster fanboys and junior stock market tycoons had tripped back down the block to their respective chic hovels and phallic glass towers. The last of a ceaseless line of honking taxis had managed to squeeze out of the Ludlow trench onto Delancey, heading home empty as they crossed the bridge for Queens.

An unripe blonde leaned against the doorway as Dorian Teasdale, the picture of maturity at twice her age, slipped his key in the six-story walkup lock.

The drunken artist dragged the blonde into the foyer from the street. Her eyes met Mioko's sign as Dorian struggled to fit his key into the second door lock.

Squinting at the scrawled out cry for help, the blonde struggled to finish reading, but Dorian unceremoniously yanked her inside.

"What's the rush?"

He ignored the question as they rounded the first of many stairwell turns.

On the fifth floor in apartment 19, Morris Hacking, a large ogre of a man sat on his toilet. He stared blankly through the open door at the cavernous mess of his one-bedroom. Morris was incapable of appreciating the depths of his apartment's disheveled state; the encrusted surfaces, the pockmarked ceiling. His mind was too busy wandering into much darker caverns.

This evening's preoccupation: his increasing sense that the bedroom shadows were shifting of their own accord every time his gaze drifted. Had they somehow taken on mortal qualities? But more importantly, would they try to butcher him in his sleep? He crushed the end of a pencil into the wall. If only he could draw the shadows properly, he might stand a chance of measuring their movements.

The sound of footsteps brought Morris back to his oval perch.

He stood up, his hulking frame towering as he leaned over the toilet, pressing his nose into the marked up wall.

He peered out through a timeworn relic of a peephole in the sealed wooden door. A pair of communal latrines on each floor had once been shared by apartments bursting with tenants, but were now sloppily coupled to each living quarter in a string of slapdash late seventies renovations. Yet Morris's keyhole remained.

Through the glass ring, he caught the slightest waft of the artist and the blonde stumbling up the stairs. He'd missed his opportunity at a proper glimpse by mere seconds. The sheen of the blonde's soft skin was painfully elusive in its rapid exit from sight.

Dorian pushed the rusty rooftop door, yanking the blonde out into the cool spring night. Kissing her, he peeled off her top as they crossed the tar-covered roof.

Dorian watched the blonde's sizable breasts push against the sheer of her strapless bra as she looked down at the blinding street below. Leaning with her, the angle made him woozy, but his usual fear of heights was dulled by blood alcohol count.

"It's kinda cold out here, isn't it? "

Her nasal twang was killing Dorian's vibe. Time to get on with the show.

Dorian pushed her against the edge, unbuckling his pants. He spreads her legs, licking his fingers and dragging them along her crease. He shoved his pelvis towards her open skirt. She squealed a little. Despite herself, she got into the rhythm for a moment, but then started to frown. He moved in for a kiss, but she hooked a finger in his mouth, and shoved his head away.

"Dorian."

The nasal screech of his name made his entire being cringe.

"This isn't what I call *treating me like a lady.*"

The words had a familiar ring. Which made sense considering they'd had a lengthy discussion on what treating her like a lady meant just hours prior, but seven Stoli and Sodas' and the first half of a joint seemed to be dulling his brain's ability to recognize patterns.

"*Dorian*, let's go inside," she said, her hands pushing his chest away.

Typically a little mild resistance would just have encouraged him, but his trusted brush, wilted by too much turpentine and rough handling, had gone soft.

Dorian pulled out.

Reaching into his pocket, he extricated the second half of the joint and lit up. The slender blonde stared at him, working to muster as much offense as she possibly could.

"You're such an ass."

He smiled back with ample condescension, offering her the roach. She adjusted her skirt, waiting for something else. But something else didn't come.

"Don't bother calling," she said as she finally turned and strutted away.

He took a long haul off his smoke, enjoying the night, as the blonde struggled with the rooftop door.

She guided herself down the stairs, relying on the banister for balance. Reaching the last step, her heel hooked and she tripped forward, slamming headlong into the first floor apartment door.

A loud thud forced open the eyes of Ndusen Muluzi, an African man who lay in bed with his wife, Kondwani.

"Ndusen. Did you hear something?" Kondwani asked in their Malawian tribal language of Chichewa.

Ndusen closed his eyes again, hoping she would follow suit.

"Go back to sleep," he said.

"Go and check."

Ndusen didn't move. His wife dug her knee right above the bone of his pelvis. How did that confounded woman know exactly where his bladder was located? The need for sleep was suddenly in stiff competition with the urge to urinate. He sat up, climbed out of bed and felt his way through the doorway in his boxer shorts.

Ndusen walked past his three children sleeping on rolled out mats in the tiny living room and another Malawian woman who occupied a folding cot.

Opening his apartment door, he peered out into the first floor hallway, now completely empty. The building silent.

Groggy, taking in the hallway, Ndusen looked out past the doors of the timeworn foyer.

Outside, only two sounds were audible in the twilight hours, the clip of the slender blonde's high heels fading into the distance and the metal shutter of *Rosarita's Pizza* slamming to the pavement.

Rube Carbia stood down the block outside *Rosarita's*, clicking a padlock on the restaurant's grate. His eyes were locked in the direction of the slender blonde. Her broken heel amplified her already offset balance, so that she walked at a gravity-defying angle down the center of Ludlow. Her fingers probed a growing forehead welt from her stairwell tumble. Rube's tongue pushed up against the inside wall of his cheek as he scrutinized her.

Apart from the surgical enhancements up top, she was all jagged edges. Rube was partial to juicy curves. As the clicks of her heels receded, he turned his gaze slowly back towards the old six-story tenement.

Crossing the street, he peeked inside the front door—only to find his own image staring back at him.

Oh shit.

Rube didn't hate the way his bare chest looked in the pic, but he wasn't too eager about the sign next to it. He knew he shouldn't linger, but he moved a few steps back all the same, taking in the giant vertical of the tenement. Gazing up at her window, the faintest of glows was visible inside. A few more steps and he felt the far curb underfoot. Another hour, she'd be up. On her way to work.

But that sign. It had to go.

He looked about for something blunt to smash the glass.

Blunt.

It was about that time.

The call of lulling himself to sleep with a good blunting put his feet in gear.

Sign could wait a night or two.

CHAPTER TWO
KICKING PAINT

Standing in his eight-foot studio share, Dorian defocused his eyes at the blackened tenement painted on his canvas. The building began to lose shape, fogging out in a pixelated haze.

He could almost stand the canvas when it was this blurry, the image beyond recognition.

Almost.

In truth, he felt like pissing on it. Would have been a superior expression than the work. Instead, he drove his fist through it, piercing clear through canvas into the drywall behind.

"OWWWWWWWWWWFUCK!"

Pulling his hand out from inside the plasterboard, Dorian grabbed at the hunk of screaming nerve endings. Had he really just punched through a wall?

He ripped the painting down. That felt better. Dorian moved along, yanking down every other piece, shoving canvases into dragon fruit packaging. He was even more disgusted than he'd been at the Chinese grocery that morning begging for the discarded boxes.

Shoving the art out the door, he kicked an open can of orange paint. The wall was a garish stripe of liquid latex. It was the best work he'd done in months.

In the hall he passed a studio-mate. The one who handcrafted porcelain dolls with reproduced Mattel molds to make his fucked up Barbie and Ken rip offs, then posed them in queer positive positions, fusing their privates with a glue gun. Was that what they taught the kids at Pratt these days?

Eyes met as paths crossed, but they were well beyond pleasantries by now. Dorian was tempted to smash into the little corporate plagiarizer with the corner of his box art, but why add insult to injury.

"Godspeed pal," was all Dorian could muster.

Spotting the latex carnage inside the room, his studio-mate pivoted.

"DUDE?" the little twerp managed to squeak out.

Dorian ignored this, prompting his studio mate's balls to drop an octave.

"HEY ASSHOLE! It's not my fault you can't afford the goddamn rent!"

A self-satisfied grin crept onto Dorian's face as the gate clicked.

Dorian jammed his boxes into the back seat of a cab and climbed in. As the yellow Prius sped towards the Williamsburg Bridge, Dorian felt the full throb of his knuckles and yearned for an ice-filled bodega freezer. He knew in a few minutes he'd be back at the tenement, hustling boxes 6 floors up. The foreknowledge of each successive trip was enough for Dorian to start looking at every curb flying past as a possible dumpsite for his entire year's work.

Dorian stood at his tiny stove, upending vodka and cream into a sizzle of overdone onions with his bruised hand.

A southern belle, the latest in a lengthy string of Dorian's on-again, off-agains, held a glass of merlot inches from her face. Althea Pittman surveyed Dorian's artistic wreckage. Half-unpacked supplies, canvases, and giant stereo speakers were now strewn about the space—just past the warped floor fissure, which demarcated the living room area.

Dorian poured pasta into a strainer. He could smell it oozing off her. The disgust. His wretched failures complicating her carefree existence. Another looser in her life scheduled for the scrapyard.

"I think my friend Gregor still wants to come take a look at your work," Althea said.

"Where am I gonna show him my work?

Dorian plated sticky linguini strands.

"Bring a couple over to my loft," she said. "I'm sure he'll buy something."

"Sure if it gets him closer to slipping it in, probably take the whole lot."

"Not interested," she said. "How many paintings a month do you have to sell to cover a four hundred dollar studio share anyways? One?"

Dorian closed his eyes.

The plate slipped from his fingers. Plummeting, it jammed the floor sideways with more splatter than smash.

Five feet down, Morris sat slumped in his threadbare easy chair. Ice Road Truckers glared his old cathode ray, a half-eaten microwave dinner on a side folding table. Dorian's dinnerware thundered above. Morris squinted in the direction of follow up footsteps. They were just getting started. Another surefire ruined evening.

He jammed the volume till eighteen-wheelers drowned out the steps. He'd wait till his show ended before trudging upstairs to give Dorian a piece of mind. If Morris was lucky, whatever whore that loser had up there'd get restless and start demanding a night on the town. Although that would likely just delay the inevitable. A drunken four am return was always a hell of a lot worse. Best case, a preemptive roar through the artist's door might send her packing.

Still Morris was at least a couple commercial breaks from the show's tail credits, and now that he'd set himself a goal, he was damn sure gonna prove his staying power.

Eleven feet up, Dorian knelt, sopping vodka sauce off the floor.

"I just want to help you figure some options out, so you don't have to live like this, sugar"

I can't stand the sight of you, how can you live like this, fucking loser.

Dorian flopped into a chair, dowsing his glass and the table in merlot. Squeezed out of his own life.

Althea took an exploratory first bite. Chewing slowly, she tried to swallow.

"That bad, huh?"

He wasn't sure why he was even asking. The look on her face dispelled what little had remained of his own appetite. Dorian pulled an American Spirit from Althea's pack and lit up. He leaned away from the table, kicking off with his feet until the back of his chair hit the bathtub, a prominent kitchen fixture in the two-room tenement. Three if you counted the tiny ensuite bathroom just past the loft bed, he'd had built in the early Octies.

He inhaled the Spirit slowly. Why on earth had he ever tried to quit these wonderful things?

CHAPTER THREE
NSIMA

D ark water rushed towards the gutter.
Ndusen stood outside the tenement building spraying down the sidewalk with a garden hose.

He paused to watch the expensively dressed youth as they passed him by on the sidewalk. They seemed so determined to get somewhere. Their eyes never left the stream of Ndusen's sprayer, their only concern was the possibility of an accidental discharge on their top dollar designer jeans.

As they shuffled past, it gave Ndusen a deep sense of his own utter invisibility.

Inside their cramped first floor apartment, Ndusen's wife, Kondwani, the consummate matriarch, stood at the tiny counter packing porridge-like maise-meal into handfuls of Nsima. Her hands moved the very same as her mother, and mother's mother before that. Only Kondwani had exchanged a straw hut filled with coal smoke for a plaster box permeated with the faint rotten-egg smell of leaking natural gas.

The beautiful young Malawian in her late twenties, Stella Muluzi, stood at the stove next to Kondwani. The older woman handed Stella maize patties as she finished shaping. Kondwani knew full well she was distracting the young woman from the rapeseed and pumpkin leaves that were Stella's responsibility to prepare. Nsima was the main attraction, so naturally that was Kondwani's domain, but the side dishes were in truth what gave the textured porridge much taste, and both women knew that Stella's dishes were starting to burn.

Kondwani turned her neck to a degree that she was yelling directly through her young companion's head. As if the sound would gain amplification by traveling in one of Stella's earlobes and out the other.

"Ndusen the nsima is ready," she bellowed in Chichewa, waves of tinnitus reverberating through Stella's eardrum.

Ndusen stood in the cramped bedroom, peeling off his coveralls.

"I will be there in a moment," he called back in response.

Ndusen's daughters Dziko, Alile and his little seven-year-old son Chisulo, sat around the table waiting patiently for the meal. No coloring books, or plastic toy clusters anywhere in sight, let alone the typical western array of electronic distraction.

Ndusen entered the kitchen area, buttoning his shirt.

"Mika's family is having hamburgers for dinner tonight," Chisulo announced as their father joined the children at the table. "Can we have hamburgers sometime?"

"Is there a cow someplace that you are hiding from me?" Ndusen asked. "Under your bed perhaps?"

"No." Chisulo said.

"Then how do you propose we make this hamburger?"

"From the meat at the store."

"Ah yes, the store. How silly, I must have forgotten. But if we begin to eat the store's hamburger, might they not run out? Then will Mika be forced to be eating our Nsima? And who will be blamed for pilfering his hamburger?"

His son was stumped with this circular logic.

"And let me ask you, where did this store animal of which you speak come from? Did it walk to the store all by itself?"

"No, in a truck."

"A truck? A cow raised in a truck?"

Presiding over the table, Kondwani turned an impatient eye towards Stella who still stood by the counter working to rescue her scorched garnishes.

"Stella, bring the nsima to the table," Kondwani said, putting the strictest of schoolmarms to shame.

Knowing better than to ask one of the children for help, Stella began to place the serving dishes in front of each member of the family.

"On a farm. It came from a farm," Chisulo said.

"Aha. Have you seen this farm?" His father asked.

"No."

"Then how do you know if it is safe to eat their cattle?"

Chisulo scrunched his already compact face.

"It's not safe?"

"Perhaps."

Kondwani took her seat across from her husband.

"But then again," Ndusen said, "perhaps not."

Stella moved round the table with a pitcher and bowl. Starting with Ndusen, Stella poured water over his hands so that he could rinse. Ndusen looked up and smiled at Stella with his kind eyes.

"Thank you," he said.

It was negligible attentiveness, but it was all he could risk without a skirmish beginning across the table.

"You are welcome," she spoke back with deliberate English elocution. Stella's command of the language was finally bearing fruit and with every new sentence she crafted, Ndusen could sense a cloud brewing in Kondwani. Even after seven years in New York, Kondwani was unable to pronounce but the simplest of phrases through her own thick Malawian accent. Kondwani eyed Stella closely as she poured rinse water for her family.

Foregoing English completely, Kondwani addressed her husband in their native tongue, "Do you have more work in the building tonight?"

"Do I ever not have work in this building?" he asked in Chichewa.

Kondwani kept her eyes on her husband, while Ndusen rolled his nsima into tiny orbs with his fingers, hoping to finish the meal without a battle.

Ndusen climbed the stairs, the meal swishing in his gullet. A uniformed City Marshal trailed behind him. This was Ndusen's building and the Marshal let him take the lead.

As they passed the third floor, Ndusen could not help but wonder yet again what had really become of Sal Agnelli. A decades long resident, Sal had reminded Ndusen of one of his village elders back at home, a lethargic cat, always leaning in close to convey some worldly insight through sour breath and an easy smile.

The Wall Street type and his decoration girlfriend that had since moved into number eleven were oblivious to the previous tenant's unexplained disappearance. Which was how the owner, Moshe Axlerod preferred it.

When Ndusen had asked if he should mention anything to the new tenants, on the off chance Sal returned, his boss had replied that, "No one wants to live in an *Unsolved Mysteries* episode." Ndusen had never seen the show, but had little trouble interpreting his boss's meaning. Mr. Axlerod, the purportedly devout Orthodox Jew, who from Ndusen's vantage seemed to care about little other than showing off his affluence with expensive clothes and fast cars. Who'd left the old neighborhood for "Strong Island when the Lower East Side went down the shitter." Who commuted a few times weekly to his multiple properties in his loathsome old neighborhood in order to bark orders and slowly enact the machinations of his true passion: underhanded trickery.

But as with most of the building's predicaments, the weight of the disappearance matter had fallen on Ndusen. In the absence of anyone else even taking notice, Ndusen had been the one to file the missing person's report down at the 7th precinct. The hardest part had been overseeing Sal's daughters when they came to pick up his belongings. Not much had remained by way of a legacy. The furniture was mostly laid to rot, but they did find a few antique books that they seemed pleased with. Little solace for the mysterious loss of a father.

Reaching the fourth floor, Ndusen pointed out apartment eleven to the Marshal, who quickly began taping an "Unconditional Quit Notice" of eviction on the door.

The Marshal turned to leave as a grizzly packrat in her late fifties, opened the door and looked at the notice, suddenly furious at Ndusen.

"What the hell do you think you're doing?" demanded the packrat.

"Posting a notice," Ndusen said, wishing he could find words that might be of some comfort to this woman.

"I pay my rent. Piss off," she said.

"Not according to our records you don't." The Marshal was already halfway down the stairs, and didn't turn back with his closing instruction, "You got six days, lady."

The packrat looked to Ndsuen for a second opinion. He strained for his most solicitous timbre. "I am very sorry," he said.

A distasteful business to be sure, but Ndusen had his orders. Decrees that were on the rise of late. It seemed that every wealthy young person in the country suddenly wanted to live in these little one-bedroom flats. To hear the old lady at the Economy Candy Market tell it, back when the neighborhood was called 'Klein Doitchland,' upwards of six hundred people lived in Ndusen's building, which now leased to a measly forty-two. What started as the Gateway to America gradually descended into the heroin infested Lower East Side, which was now resurging as the trendy L.E.S. The rents on Axlerod's apartment would triple, in some cases quadruple, every time he flipped an older residence, lifting the apartments from their rent-stabilized restrictions. Axlerod liked flipping apartments.

The packrat wasn't interested in apologies. "Listen here you little suck-egg dog. If you think illegal harassment, suing me repeatedly for unpaid rent that's already been received, three baseless dates in housing court and a piece of goddamn paper's gonna make me vacate my apartment, you got another thing coming!"

The packrat spat on the ground by Ndusen's feet.

"Get out of my sight."

This Ndusen could do. He turned, taking a deep breath as he walked back down the stairs.

Just as he cleared the packrat's sight, boring down into the back of his shirt, Ndusen spotted an even more dreadful interaction in the making.

He hugged the wall to avoid contact at all cost with Morris Hacking, trudging up the stairs in construction clothes, his hard hat swinging by his side.

CHAPTER FOUR
MOTHER

I nside his dingy fifth floor cave, Morris changed from his construction gear. Another shit day on the lawless site, but he knew he'd be back in the morning, for Mom's sake.

He pulled off his sweat drenched t-shirt and jeans. A crumbling plastic suit bag lay on the kitchen table. Reaching inside, he jerked out a wrinkled shirt that at one time in history had been a bleached white. He quickly buttoned the shirt, hoping she wouldn't notice the wrinkles then pushed his arms into the badly worn suit jacket.

He nearly felt like a real person.

Slogging down Avenue A in his scuffed dress shoes, Morris was a wholly different species than the rest on the busting sidewalk. An invertebrate in a sea of creatures joint of spine. A porous sponge, lacking the complexity of every other being he saw.

Passing a corner bodega, Morris was drawn to a cellophane wrapped bouquet of purple daisies. He tried to stop his hand but couldn't halt the inevitable. His fingers gripped crinkly plastic squishing the petals. They were weightless, and free, the stems dripping a line of telltale circles on the concrete. Shuffling faster, he weaved through pedestrians before the bodega clerk reemerged.

"Get back here you motherfuck!"

Morris sped with his pilfered cone of discount blossoms.

Shame. Fear. Hope.

Hope that she wouldn't be able to guess at how he'd gotten them... but mom always said never to arrive anywhere empty-handed.

Reaching Demetrakas, Morris shoved open the funeral home doors.

There he waited.

He scraped at his shoulder pad.

Then waited some more.

After too many minutes being ignored, standing in the wood-paneled front vestibule, Morris's anxiety level was starting to spike. He paid these bastard's salaries; you'd think they'd show a little respect.

A funeral service assistant finally stalled out in the hall, pretending to notice Morris for the first time. The overt recognition and false grin he could have done without.

"Right this way, sir."

Morris followed down a corridor and into The Chapel of Rest.

Morris felt his shoulders relax; the large brightly colored viewing room was the closest he came to that feeling.

Home.

Despite the hideous chandelier above the pulpit.

"Have a seat, Mr. Hacking."

The assistant disappeared into a side door.

Morris occupied his usual hover by the front row.

In the rear prepping area, the service assistant found his trainee staring stupefied at the contents of an open casket. Inside was an ancient corpse; little more than a skeleton with stretched leathery skin.

"I finished cleaning the drainage tubes and aspirators, but couldn't find the mouth formers for the blue haired lady with the missing teeth," the trainee said, thoroughly distracted by the ancient corpse. He looked to his supervisor, "What's the deal here?"

"Geraldine Hacking," the service assistant said. "Every Tuesday for almost a decade. Forty dollars a week in fees, three replacement coffins, and only the good Lord knows how much he's spent on makeup."

The trainee looked seriously disturbed.

"Well... it's perfectly legal. And a faithful repeat client is a rarity in this business..." he said, hoping he'd closed the book on the unpleasant subject of Geraldine Hacking.

They wheeled the casket out. The trainee nodded, another bullshit grin added to the tally as the service assistant brought over a folding chair.

Morris stepped forward. The assistants stepped away.

He opened his plastic bag of ladies cosmetics. Lifting the lid on some powder, he leaned in and began to paint the face of the remains inside.

"That's better isn't it?" Morris asked.

The trainee stood at the back of the viewing room, transfixed by the unwholesome display.

Morris moved on to the lipstick as he began to quietly confide in the withered corpse.

"I can't stand the guys anymore, Mom. Last week they hooked a crane to a port-a-potty with Alvarez inside, pretending they didn't know, and lifted it thirty feet into the air. Bunch of damn jerks. It's not safe there. Horsing around like that. Screwing tools together and pissing in the cement. At least they fired Steinlicht's ass on the spot. It screwed with the PH levels, so the cement didn't harden properly."

Morris knew he had to get this stuff off his chest, but he hated burdening her with all the nasty details. Why couldn't he ever come prepared with something nice to say? He made a mental note to come up with a few pieces of pleasant news for his next visit. Maybe he'd call aunt Riana and find out how she was doing. But then he'd have to hear about her hip, the old scags at her home, the staff that never let up with their socialize this and do crafts that.

Not necessarily much positivity to be mined there.

Reaching back into her makeup bag a thought occurred: he could go see a movie before his next visit. A comedy. That way he could tell her something funny, since nothing funny ever happened in his own life.

"You'd like that wouldn't you?" he said. "You used to love the pictures. Next time I'll bring a picture for you in my head, something to laugh about."

Morris finished with the lipstick, placing it back inside its crystal *Things Remembered* case, the engraved letters spelling out *Geraldine* above the polished silver heart and cubic zirconias.

Morris clicked shut last year's mother's day gift. He rolled the cellophane flower cone closer with his shoe.

Was he such a bad son after all?

CHAPTER FIVE
WHERE THE HELL IS MIOKO?

I n a swank studio towering the no man's land between Chelsea and Meatpacking, a half-dozen emaciated models stood scantily clad in tribal tropes. A tarted-up Polynesian warrior, an anorexic Asian hill tribe whore, and an attempt at a Samburu from the foothills of Mount Kenya represented by a six-foot-five fresh-faced beaut wearing only strings of beads. English art rock blared from the stereo. A mishmash of straw huts and brick slapped before the white cyclorama badly in need of post retouching leaned behind them. A photographer's third assistant balanced on a ladder hanging a soft lamp.

"No. Not like that. I said I wanted a toppee glow behind the jungle bunny, you fucking twit."

Jake Perry, an effeminate elf of a man, sat on a cushy leather couch, eating cereal, dictating notes from the unintelligible scrawl in his precious moleskin.

The third assistant turned to his exponentially grizzlier counterpart on the ground.

"Which one's the jungle bunny?"

The second assistant shrugged, equally confused by the order.

"Where the hell is Mioko?" Jake demanded as he tossed his cereal carelessly at the table.

"Oh just move the spot back to the left three feet, for fuck's sake," he hissed as he strutted past the digital techs and agency producers at the monitor. Jake glanced at the stylists working a busty Andean hunter-gatherer by the clothing racks. Both the model and the stylist smiled back.

"Just five more minutes Jake," the stylist apologized.

But by then Jake was already out in the client lobby.

Sweeping to the espresso bar, Jake found Mioko debasing a latté with artificial sweetener.

"Goddamn it, Mioko, I need you with me at all times," Jake said. "That's why I pay you."

Mioko tried for a smile, but her lips didn't particularly cooperate.

"I was getting you a coffee."

"I didn't ask for a goddamn coffee!"

"Yes, you did."

"Listen, sweetheart. You think I need a forty-three year old burnout as my bloody assistant? I throw you a fucking bone, and what do I get?"

A bone.

Was that what he'd thrown her?

Four years of answering the phone. Of doing his dishes. His laundry. His dog-sitting. Hauling cameras and lights and computers and hardware from rental house to shoot, from apartment to office, from airport to hotel, from location to studio, from Manhattan to Brooklyn to Rome to the damn volcanic mountaintops of the Azores islands. A thousand promises to help her with her own work, to facilitate her someday pulling the trigger for a client herself, if becoming a commercial photographer was even what she wanted anymore this far down Jake's poisoned well. And even if she did still have aspirations, she was just as far from a finished commercial book as the day she serendipitously snuck Jake a peak at her portfolio in the elevator at Milk.

"I'm sorry, Jake." Mioko put down the empty sweetener. "You can always just call my name, or text if you need—"

"If what? I need to come to you?"

"I get it Jake, I'm sorry."

"Do you? Do you really?"

Jake snatched the coffee from her hands and pivoted back to the studio.

If Mioko looked as much the shrunken mess from the outside as she felt on the inside, the studio barista deserved an Oscar in pretending not to notice.

"Last warning!" She heard Jake call as he headed back to his camera.

Mioko looked at the floor, exhaling slowly, before retrieving her phone. It was 8:15am.

Alone on a subway car, Mioko ached from the endless pile of returns and emotional abuse. Was it only Tuesday? A deep hankering for an old pharmacological pal hit her, but she did her best to breathe through. Reaching into her bag, she retrieved a miniature bacon chocolate bar saved from the client-only craft table. She popped the paper top, but was distracted by a rush of air and sound. An MTA conductor pushed through the door connecting her car to the next.

She did her best not to look up at the conductor as he approached. She didn't want to put a face to it.

As he moved down the length of the car, she could feel it coming. He was veering in close to her, and as the pant leg of his uniform accidentally brushed the bare skin of her knee, Mioko's back straightened with a little jerk. Her face filled with a flush of exhilaration.

Mioko sped her stride as she passed the housing projects. Her eyes darted round the shadowy corners of Eldridge.

Not tonight, she implored in a loop till it started to echo like a mantra.

Please, not tonight. Not tonight.

The words were as familiar as an old show tune, her brain itching to remember the rest of the lyrics.

In her tiny converted darkroom, Mioko was secure. Her hands worked the enlarger and chemicals. The womblike glow of her red safelight. All concept of time and space dissolved as she clipped prints of Suffolk night-crawlers and Stanton Street junkies up on strings to dry. A well-dressed kid laying facedown on a plush sidewalk mattress, twiggy girlfriend wrenching his arm, trying to coax him from his comatose state. A crazed viking-haired man-child streaking past in a shiny blue prom dress. A wheelchair-bound junkie, applying dental glue to his upper partial.

Washing away exposed silver halide crystals from the negative, that woozy off-gassing glow enveloped her. She watched each image materialize, then halted development in the stop bath.

Even when she suffered the occasional acetic acid chemical burn, her darkroom was the only place where Mioko felt any control. She often wished someone would shut a padlock on the door from the outside. That she could wind away her days in dim red light, drifting from one exposure to the next.

She imagined the look on Jake's face when he found out she was dead and couldn't thumb his lunch order.

Mioko could only imagine herself missing one other person less than Jake from the shelter of her favorite entombed fantasy.

And that was Rube Carbia.

CHAPTER SIX
CAGE O' RAGE

R ube reigned supreme, backing the counter of *Rosarita's* in a soiled apron. Hair grease swayed under his ultimate b-boy championship cap, his head bumping as he flattened a ball of dough under palm. Deuce Biggn'Low was representing through pudgy cheeks, beat-boxing furiously from a stool by the window, his tight cornrows and bargain-basement bling almost pulling off his hustler steez. For now, they owned the joint. Rube freestyled as he pinched and stretched his disk of dough.

> *"Fill your cup, and empty your cupboards,*
> *My man Deuce is on the scene, and he ain't wearing rubbers.*
> *Like an animal trapped in a cage o' rage,*
> *Rosarita's pizza parlor be the Deuce man's stage.*
> *If you be littering the streets with your message of hope,*
> *He gonna crush your dreams with a bag full o' dope.*
> *The Deuce-o-meter thermometer be here to measure,*
> *D's got the mercury rising for your bitch's pleasure."*

Deuce was lovin' it like a triple stack Big Mac. But with jubilation came the rhyme's ruin. The vocal percussion throw-down turned to blunder with a flurry of piercingly, arythmic turntable effects jutting from Deuce's lips.

Giving up on his rhymes Rube humored his lesser counterpart. Spreading his fists, Rube stretched the dough as he started popping and locking his elbows.

"Yeah son!" Deuce leapt up, "the Rube is enforcin' with the 'za he be bakin', mozza and sauce he be makin' to bring home da bacon!"

Far from lyrics to go. He wanted to tell fat ass to button his abysmal trap and stick to the beats. But Rube made nice, busting a pimp walk behind the counter to the heinous train-wreck of rhyme.

"The beats in the streets from his head to his feets, hos' can't get enough of his Nuyorican treats."

"Enough." Rube B Lethal a.k.a. Def Killah grabbed back the mike.

"Back on the 808, 'fore I bust your plate.
You failed hip hop class.
I give crack to the mass.
Hood loves it when I warm the hits.
Cum behind as I swarm the tits..."

A bantam crew of black kids strolled past *Rosarita's* open door. The stage lights dimmed.

Rube knew those scrubby midgets. He wasn't a fan. And he most definitely didn't appreciate the bitch-ass snark on their faces, trying to diss his hip-hop stylings. But Rube had already puffed a dozen vape hits this shift and as tempting as going buck wild might be—*blastin' ass and robbing their stash*—he didn't quite have it in him tonight.

"Wass 'appenin?" he managed.

The loud-mouthiest of the midgets, scrawny in a blue camouflage hoodie, responded to Rube's efforts at humanitarianism with verbal gunfire: "Pop Pop POP."

Rube lunged for the doorway, fronting. Just because he was in an apron flipping pie, didn't mean he would stand for any whack bitches and their fugly slut's derision.

"COME BY L.E.S. ONE MOTHAFUCKER! Come by the PJs later on and say that shit. Pussy ass motherfuckers!"

Rube spun the dough like an NCAA game ball. He and Deuce stared down their foe from *Rosarita's* glass box as the midgets paraded off, whooping it up. They kept busting a gut right at him. Or at the very least throwing a chuckle at the self-styled Puerto Rican Gigolo weighing down the stool next to him. Either way, Rube wanted to curb their teeth. He'd show them some pop, pop, pop. Set the hammer, round in the chamber—Rube whipped the doughy disk at the window, missing Deuce's fat face by a half inch. Didn't even realize he'd done it till he saw the midgets jump back, tripping like little bitches. Immediately pretending it wasn't shit.

This killed Deuce and Rube. Hysterical. Sleighed by an uncooked pie.

"Pussy ass motherfuckers."

That useless, tubby, garlic-knot vacuum never hung round the night shift long enough. A few minutes of agonizing flow, with occasional *boom-boom-clack* repose to bolster Rube's off-the-chain freestyle and that half-stepping *saramanbiche cabrón* was out. And that's why chickenhead didn't get a cut. Deuce the sucker.

Rube wasn't some newjack hustler neither, sure he dealt piff and eightballs of ice right over the register—ignorant pizza parlor owning giuseppe motherfuckers—selling his goods to dumbass wannabe-players, and rich scummy white bitches ordering gourmet ricotta slices, dropping quarters in the tip jar through hundred-dollar nails, their Prada hanging open. Sometimes when they reached in their leather, it was all he could do not to jump the register and hightail it with a fistful of guap and plastic. But he had some big game in his scope he wasn't about to jeopardize. Some rhinoceros hustle shit.

But despite his imminent rise, once the droves thinned from boredom and burnout, Rube had nothing left to do but bust out the Ajax.

After a halfhearted once-over with the mop, Rube stood in the skanky bathroom smoking more vape. He puffed steam, then grabbed up the mop he'd bequeathed 'Little Ho' to push more cornmeal and kalamata. Devin The Dude's, "Broccoli & Cheese" distorted on the stereo. A decent track, but Rube's mold was more the pure *Baricuas* with non-stop attack-the-track-flow. Fat Joe, Cuban Link, Tony Touch, Hurricane G. But Rube's true hero was Big Pun, the South Bronx Punisher, the late 90's king of verbs, killer of words, the giant sumo *papi chulo* of Puerto Rican rappers. Big Pun even sweat sauce in a Bronx pizza shop, back when he was Dirty Chris Lee Rios, selling crack with a sawed off beneath his trench. The first solo Latin rapper to go platinum, dead before reaching his third decade. Rube liked to imagine the Pun sharing a VIP table in hell with Biggie and Tupac. Sadly his quintessential lyrical masterpeice *I'M NOT A PLAYER (I just Fuck a lot)* was the Pun's downfall rotation on *Rosarita's* stereo, *"Climbin up the walls, with my balls, bangin off your hymen, I'm a diamond in the rough bustin in your face, taste the sweetness of my dick, rip your fetus out of place, yo"*. Turned out, the old grape-stoping moolies who owned the place didn't have any understanding of satirical hilarity. They banned the Pun outright, which Rube felt was a loss to every pizza patron in the L.E.S.

And that was how lesser MC's came to dominate the parlor's speakers.

That said, The Dude filled the blankness of dead air boredom nicely, making Rube's jock hard, willing every fly girl south of 14th Street to come in for a slice. He imagined sniffing all that quiff as he belted Devin's baller lyrics:

"Girl, this dick is so clean. This dick is so clean, that you can boil it in some collard greens."

The front door chimed.

The slickly dressed Orthodox walking to the counter with his scraggy slick-back full of product didn't look like much, but Rube knew better. Little fazed Rube, but being caught blasting The

Dude's *pendejo* lyrics in front of the Heeb was pure humiliation. The Jew weren't no La Perla gangster from back San Juan way, but this *Caco* had some serious heat on Ludlow. From *Rosarita's* own muttonhead owners who he jacked monthly for the exorbitant rent to Axlerod's pull with the Five-O (the exception of course being that Barney Fife undercover neck tattoo hard-on who pepper sprayed Deuce and him that night on Eldrige yelling). Didn't seem to have much pull with that pig. But then again nobody did.

"Kid," the Yid dropped a bulging envelope on the counter. "I brought you something."

Rube knew it was best not to marvel. Nor to snatch the prize. He heard the words "Oh. A'ight then, Mr. Axlerod. Thanks," trickle out as he steadied, peeling his eyes off the envelope.

Moshe Axlerod gave a nod and turned on his heels.

Rube peered inside the envelope. A stubby stack of green stared back at him.

O.G. money.

He nearly dropped the mop, but he didn't let on. A MAC-10 motherfucker. The *Baricua* son of L.E.S. ONE. Rube knew just the play. Even Big Pun would have waxed poetic on the irony. His hometown of the Bronx in the Seventies—every building on whole blocks burning because the *caseros* that owned the hood did better off torching their own properties than charging rent. Of course the LES was far from kindling. These days shit was insane, the rents straight up stratospheric. No, he wasn't about to burn no prized tenement to the curb. Just give that hoe a taste.

But Rube had to admit he felt different about Mioko than any girl he'd trailed before. No doubt he wanted her, but something more. Something deep of the gut. She made him uncomfortable in a way that was unique. He spent late nights pondering if that pussy would taste as sweet as the thousand-dollar Cristal bottle-service he could now throw down for. Shit was conflicted. Besides, what had the fair photographer ever done to deserve the Axlerod's special attention?

Never mind that. Rube had to look past his inflamed genitalia. Stay on target. He had shit to research online. Plus he had to hit up that obeast porker Deuce and bribe his tubby ass with a jumbo pack of Kennedy fried fowl, get a ride to Home Depot tomorrow and outlay some of his new scratch.

Rube could already smell that Roly Poly flatulating behind the wheel. Shameful motherfucker.

Useless as he was, though… at least he owned a whip.

CHAPTER SEVEN
LIFE'S WORK

n the tenement hallway, smoke particles wafted underneath the door to apartment #9.

Mioko lay in REM cycle as the room became thick with grey. A detector in the hallway began to bleat. She was stuck, still disembodied inside a dream. After what had seemed like days of intense and prolonged pain, a tiny object which looked more like an heirloom tomato than a human being had spewed from her uterus. Overwhelming her with waves of joy. Her intense delight cut short when she noticed the needle in her arm. Months of the drug routing her veins, crossing the placental lining, had filled the tiny fetus with euphoric waves of transcendent bliss before this being even had a chance to experience daylight. The minuscule preemie lay at her breast, peering into her eyes, longing with junk-sickness—as a series of nurses and doctors chastised Mioko on low birth weight, hypoglycemia, intracranial hemorrhaging, the likelihood of imminent infant death. Their words bounced off delivery room tile. None of it mattered. Mioko was in love.

"Are you awake?" she asked her neonatal son. His tiny hazel eyes peered open, staring up at her with an ancient wisdom.

"Yes," he whispered back.

She inhaled a rich cloud of fulfillment—but her breath filled with black carbon. Her abdomen pulled taut as her lungs exploded. Her newborn was gone. Her bed was engulfed in a think grey fog. Another coughing wave hit before she knew for certain where she was.

She stood, but her knee joints buckled. Her lizard brain pleaded for attention, supplicating one leg in front of the other, to move away from oblivion. But her evolved mind invited a little lie down; breathe in a few more lungfuls of monoxide. She'd heard that death from drowning was the best way to go. How bad would asphyxiation be?

And then she saw the flickering glow of flames. She pictured them sucking her chalky white remains up with an industrial vacuum. And then an entirely more gruesome thought occurred: the photographs.

Mioko leapt to find her life's work already half consumed. She cursed herself for never buying a fire extinguisher. Too late for the prints. All that mattered now where the negatives.

Wrenching the front door open, Mioko jammed her key into the neighboring apartment. So far her darkroom was untouched, the air arctic in comparison to her roasting living room. She ripped open drawers, prioritizing eras, unfinished projects, lovers, friends, family, and endless streets filled with strangers; a long overdue spring cleaning in the space of a few life threatening seconds.

She grabbed up as many binders and sheets as she could. Thousands of hours of work spilled from her arms as Mioko ran for her life.

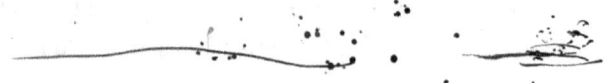

In #21, Dorian cautiously opened his door. Thick smoke poured up from the stairs. He hacked a cloud of alveoli cells before slamming the door.

"Althea, get up. We gotta go."

Climbing from Dorian's loft bed, Althea slowly came to.

With another devastating cough, Dorian stumbled towards the windows and yanked up the bamboo blinds, revealing the retractable concertina grille secured to the sill. He grabbed at the padlock, suddenly panicked.

"Baby, where's the goddamn key?"

She pointed in the vague direction of the other window.

Despite his dread, Dorian couldn't help but use up precious seconds to pass judgement on his sporadic consort. Not only could her tar-caked lungs withstand this carbon onslaught, but in her latest homicidal exercise in chain smoking, she'd misplaced the key to their escape.

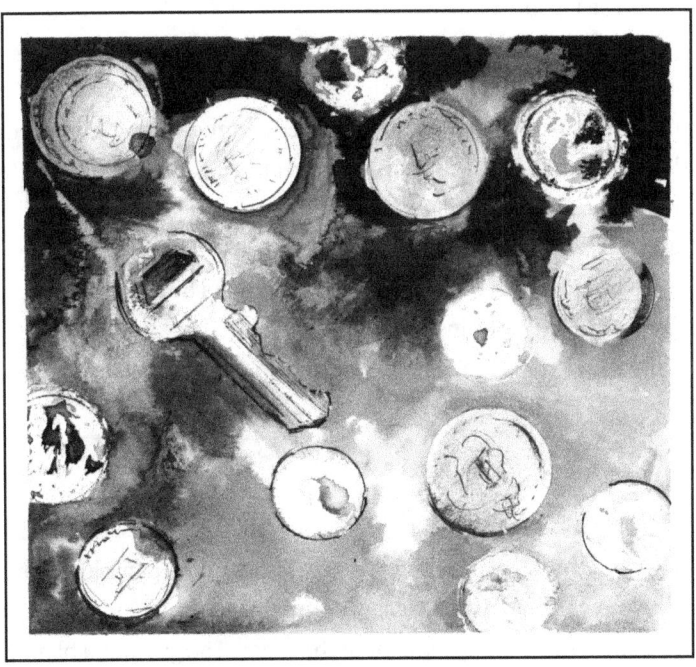

Dorian grabbed at a change bowl on the far ledge and dumped it. Dropping to his knees, he fished through the nickels and dimes.

Althea knelt over in spasmodic contractions. Maybe her hardened lungs weren't so unsusceptible after all.

Dorian finally produced a key and leapt up. He tested it in the padlock, but it took solid seconds for him to realize that he was trying to push it in upside-down. Pulling apart the lock, he wrenched the grille aside.

The fresh air recharged his heroism, so he helped Althea climb out the window first onto the rickety bars of the ancient egress. As his eyes struggled to absorb shape in the black air, Dorian became aware of the sirens blasting all around.

"What about the art?" Althea asked as they wound their way down the layers of metal stairs.

"Let it burn," he said.

Letting go of the ladder, it shot upwards, slamming into the metal platform above. Dorian wheeled around to find himself in the abandoned garbage heap at the rear base of the building. He was surprised by the mass of it, the countless years of trash piled in a towering jigsaw. He realized that he'd been looking down into this mountain of detritus for twelve years but never properly seen it. Maybe it was just the adrenaline, but there was something oddly satisfying about experiencing it up close for the first time.

That fucker Ivan had finally done it. Morris just knew. Hoarding eight foot piles of ancient newspapers, religious pamphlets and who knows what else in foot-wide trenches, squirreling his way from one end of the apartment to the other. The guy was a blatant fire code violation. This jackass with an entire pulp and paper mill jammed into four hundred square feet on the top floor of a residential structure. The hell was he thinking?

Morris stood in a damp nightgown outside Cake Shop, staring up at the smoke funneling off the roof.

He'd even complained to the landlord, that useless fucker, Moshe Axlerod. In writing no less. Quoting him the Uniform Fire Code. Detailing the many ways the contents of Ivan's apartment could obstruct, delay and hinder the operations of the fire department with language he'd taken the time to look up on library computers.

Bottom line is, from a safety perspective, the combustible loading in Ivan Hershber's dwelling is a clear hazard.

But did Axlerod listen? And now look. The fucking building was up in flames.

Well good riddance, he thought.

Morris wondered where he'd go if the fire reached his and mom's place. He'd rather haul up at the Bowery Mission than stay with The Lawyer—that cocksucker of a brother, on the Upper East. Even if Brent's legion of asshole qualities weren't all his own creation. Their hyper critical shit of a father hadn't done either of either of them any favors before he got himself locked up for wire fraud. Of course he didn't do their mother any favors either, with 208 bones in the human body, he'd manage to break ten percent of hers on six separate occasions. And even when their father did finally get released, he climbed into a bottle and was never heard from again, till he turned up frozen one night in a ditch off route 95, a half-mile from Stamford.

Morris had been wide-awake when the alarms had started sounding. He could never nod off when his upstairs tormentor had a female over. Dorian, that sexual deviant. Morris could hear every torrid squeak, every nail in the artist's loft loosening as he pounded his latest pushover. Morris had taken to submerging his head in the bath, face first, and exhaling slowly as possible till the sounds of bubble exploded on the surface drowned out the foul business above. He stayed like that till he choked on a mouthful of dirty bath water or till the water got so cold and his skin so pruned that he felt his entire hide begin to dissolve off. But he knew he wasn't supposed to think like that.

A couple hours in the tub, and the lewd sounds upstairs had finally abated. But the vanished waves of Dorian grunts and female screamscapes had suddenly been replaced with an even more highly-pitched menace; the shrieking alarms.

It appeared now that Morris had been one of the first ones out of the building. How difficult would it have been to wedge a beam in the front door and trap his neighbors inside? His shoulder started to tingle, which he recognized as a warning, and he tried to ignore the new thought that was vying for the front page now. His breathing quickened. He stated to count... *One, two, three, four, five, six, seven, eight, nine, ten. One, two, three, four, five...* but he couldn't stop the thought...

Six, seven, eight... your place burns, even if you didn't do shit, who are they're gonna blame? They'll lock you up again ...*nine... ten...* They'll dose you. *five.* Chlorpromazine. *six.* Haloperidol. *seven.* Perphenazine. *eight.* Fluphenazine. *nine.* Risperidone. *ten.* Ziprasidone. *one.* Therapy art. *two.* And giant shared birthday cakes. *three.* As they prod you. *four.* And make endless belittling insinuations. *five.* And Brent won't pay his share of the Demetrakas fees. *six.* And mommy. *seven.* Mommy. *EIGHT.* MOMMY WILL BE DESTROYED FOR ETERNITY JUST LIKE EVERYTHING ELSE THAT WAS GOOD IN THIS GODFORSAKEN *NINE...* HELL... *TEN...* HOLE...

That's when he saw Mioko come out the font doors of the building. *ELEVEN...* Her hands filled with a pile of her photography crap.

She looked even more unglued than usual.

Morris stared at her as she crossed the street, then followed her eyes as she craned her neck up, and he realized that it wasn't Ivan at all.

The smoke was seeping out from a third floor window.

Her window.

The goddamn junky had done it.

CHAPTER EIGHT
MACHINE CITY

Mioko sat at the back of *Machine City*, surrounded by her negatives. She could still smell the acrid airborne particles. Flash the other pajama-clad tenants. The pair of red fuzzy dice swinging from the top of the Chinatown Dragon Fighters ladder as it nudged its way upwards towards the scorching 3rd floor hole.

This third coffee was finally allowing her to keep her eyes open for minutes at a time now. She knew a bar was the last place she should seek refuge, but she couldn't help it.

"She lit it herself." Morris had tapped two fingers to the crook of his elbow, making a *shhhhh* sound as he pushed down an imaginary plunger.

"Hey fuck you Hacking, I've been clean four and a half years."

Yes, her confederate addict ex-lover still managed *Machine City*, but Wednesdays were his night off. Besides, she and Trey had a strictly business relationship now. It'd taken her all to climb from that bottomless pit of co-dependence in the first place.

And *Machine* was one of the last establishments in the LES Mioko still recognized. For the longest time the dive had even managed to repel the droves of glassholes, knowing they'd just as likely get spit on as served by the hardened barmaids, but these days seedy was à la mode, and the pair of juiced-up Jersey bros in dress shirts fawning over their blonde counterparts looked right at home. Mioko watched one of the blowhards fondle a designer hole in his Barbie's skinny-jeans, wondering if he'd go all the way. But then Mioko couldn't help recoil the second he did.

Her gaze snagged on the bathroom door. She'd spiked more needles sitting on that dirty little hole of a toilet than she cared to count.

"Listen. You need to answer my questions, ma'am," the firefighter had said.

"I could smell something. Gasoline maybe…"

"Rotten eggs? Or, did you leave a burner on?"

"I'm not… "

"You close your window before you went to bed?"

"I can't remember."

Not a soul to turn to in her blackest hour since she'd kicked the junk. Only a charbroiled wreck in a city she'd come to loath. Even the bridge and tunnel foursome were making a break for the door. Mioko's pair of rent controlled apartments and whatever ashes remained of their contents were the only proof she even existed.

She'd been twenty-one years old the day she'd moved in. Her first apartment in New York. It didn't matter that taxi drivers refused to drive down her street. It was the only place she could afford, and she was steeled by the hopeful notions young ladies dream when they decide to go it alone in the big city.

Foolish notions it turned out. Mioko had emerged from her new place that first morning to find dozens of emaciated junk-fiends lining the corner of Stanton and Ludlow, a bucket lowering from an apartment window above; a hundred thousand dollars of smack being moved on her corner at a drop, with two drops daily.

It was barely a week before she chased the dragon that first time.

Another month before she snorted a line.

Six months in, she was shooting china up her veins at every opportunity.

The bartender looked across at her. The only customer left. He was ready to close.

"Another coffee?"

She looked down at her mug.

Yes, the apartment was a piss hole, but it was her piss hole. Surrounded by a community of artists and drug dealers and bowery bums. Back when even the building landlord, Moshe's father, Cyrus Axlerod, was a part of the scene. He'd let the drunks sweep the buildings for a buck, and was even chummy with Fatso and TJ, the dealers moving most of the junk on the block. That was before Cyrus's heir-apparent took over, and the whole real estate game went nuts. The trust fund bitches moved in and started opening cute little dress shops. Ludlow became just like every other street in the city: loud and corporate and overwrought.

And for some reason that's when she and Trey had finally decided to stop using—which turned out to be a terrible idea, considering what they had to sober up to.

How long had she held her death grip on this mug of congealing brown upper?

"No, that's alright. Thanks."

At first it had felt just like getting a cold, mucus building up until she was incessantly clearing her throat. But soon she was shitting, spitting and pissing all the fluids out of her body. She'd never felt like an addict. It was just something she did to get off. Like rubbing out an orgasm. Only worlds better. But ten years of banging crystalline alkaloid into her body had taken it's toll. She had no idea what to do with her new clearheaded reality. Except wallow in self-hate. Till one night Trey had brought home that old plastic camera. An eyelevel Brownie 127 someone had left at the bar, which barely even cranked negative without ripping the roll in half. Yet for some reason, every snap of the shutter had helped her feel again.

It was clear to her now that she'd simply substituted one addiction for another.

Rousing herself, Mioko carried her salvaged negatives out into the spring morning air. It somehow felt strangely like the beginning of any other arduous day.

As she opened her apartment door, twenty years of history stared back at her, charred and blackened. She couldn't help herself; she sat down at her table and wept. She wept for every inch of furniture she'd pulled off the streets. For every painting. Every note from a lost lover. For the Brownie camera that was now a puddle of plastic on the shelf. The Japanese fan her neighbor, old Sal, had given her before he disappeared, saying it reminded him of her tattoos. For every unsent letter to her parents. Even for the antique Bush/Cheney bumper sticker on her fridge she so loved to hate, which had been transfigured from a faded pink and turquoise to an illegible brown sheen. She couldn't help it, a smile started to curl the edges of her lips. Those bastards just refused to burn.

Her eyes moved along the charred walls, the crisp blinds, the blackened spiral on the floor where the flames had eaten most deeply into the linoleum. The pattern evoked the coiled shell of a pet snail she'd had as a child.

It took all her effort, but pressing down, her thigh muscles engaged and Mioko managed to stand. She wasn't a hopeful twenty-one-year-old anymore. But she'd been through worse. Pulling open the charred cabinet door, she reached for a roll of industrial garbage bags—at least one thing had made it through the fire intact.

CHAPTER NINE
I'M STICKING WITH YOU

very aspect of old people gave Rube the crawls. Over sharing
and funky smells. Codgers sitting on benches chatting up
gnarly blue haired old ladies like they were peacocking at
the club. Little blue pills in their pockets. Ready to partay.

The entrance hall of the geezer drop-in at the corner of
Stanton and Allen, was one of Rube's hunting blinds. Perfect
concealment. His targets, clueless. And Grandma and her fuddy-
duddy perpetual hard-on pals couldn't whiteness a perp through
their clouded cataracts. Like the man at Coney Island's *Shoot the
Freak* used to yell down the boardwalk (till they shuttered the
bitch and turned Coney plastic), "Shoooot Da Freak! You c'shoot
him, an 'e won shoot back." Perfect.

Spotting her crossing the median, Rube's heart kicked up.
He waited till she cornered, twenty more steps, then he jogged
in behind.

The Velvet Underground's "I'm Sticking With You" kicked off
in his earbuds. Those childish pitched vocals were almost sinister,
and that grimy tape-deck quality sound mesmerized. Even if Lou
Reed also sang about sucking dick in bathroom stalls. If Rube
B Lethal a.k.a. Def Killah was gonna level a rise to universal
master of flow and skill—an uncontested champion MC blessing
the mic—any chumpchange industry hack knew, influences
were sourced from all places. And if some fool ever dared jack

his player and claimed Rube's listening choices weren't legit, he'd puncture their eardrums with a screwdriver. He flicked the Velvet track to loop.

Traversing Roosevelt Park, he eased up as Mioko passed the basketball courts. Some *pendejo* might holler out, blow Rube's cover. Not that he was sweating. Twenty steps more to the other side of the fence, a group of wrinkly Chinese practiced Tai Chi under the open hoops, their sagging limbs slicing air like Jello.

Lou Reed harmonized with that eerie androgynite, Moe Tucker, *"I'm sticking with you, cos I'm made out of glue. Anything that you might do, I'm gonna do too..."*

The far side of the court, Mioko stopped. Rube made a lateral shuffle. She was perching in front of some horizontal laying park bench homeless twat, her hand still clutching last night's brown-bag. Rube circled wide as Mioko brought her camera up and snapped. She wound that jack in the box relic like it was some prize, then walked on.

"...You held up a stage coach in the rain. And I'm doing the same..."

Circling in, he tried to imagine what the picture might look like, framing up for it with a finger cube. Puzzling. Where Rube stood, it looked like squandered film.

"...*Saw you hanging from a tree. And I made believe it was me...*"

Up from the bench skank, Rube scanned the sidewalk on the park's far side.

His toes wrinkled in his kicks. He'd lost the bitch.

"Fucking amateur hour."

He moved out past the courts still cursing. Then scoped south.

There she was—a block and a half already. Heading towards China Town. Rube was master of her routine, but she wasn't on it. He bounced across the street, she hooked a right, picking up speed.

"...*People going to the stratosphere. Soldiers fighting with the cong...*"

Blocks flew by, then SoHo. He tailed her as she darted through the packed streets.

"...*but with you by my side I can do anything. When we swing, we hang past right or wrong...*"

Shuffling past tourist mobs, cunt models putting on airs, Rube kept pace with her. Any other day he would have been whispering "ecstasy, cocaine, crystal?" down sidewalks this jammed, but today was a more high-priority business.

Rube broke off as Mioko ducked into some home decorating outlet. Paint & Wallpaper. He knew he better cross and wait till she re-emerged. Maybe chug a Coke by the halal cart. Just another Puerto can-kicker on a liquid lunch break. Invisible to the privileged horde. Cast sideways by the waves of white wealth. But Rube couldn't help himself. "*Naah na-na na-na. Cos I'm made out of glue.*" Slipping inside, itching his sack, he ducked to the right, pushed to the back. A sixth sense on that shit. He sniffed her out like hot pink between thighs.

She was loading up on half-priced wallpaper. Rube wondered what her pad must look like post burn. As if some chinzy markdown wall decor was really gonna make char-broiled feel homey again. Besides, he couldn't possibly imagine that mishmash of gaudy patterns in her hands working together— maybe Velvet was starting to rub off. She headed to the register and Rube pulled up his hoodie and bounced.

That scratchy-sweet piano persisted, *"...anything that you might do, I'm gonna do too..."*

A century later, she poked her fine self through the doorway, and for a beat Rube thought she made his ass. But nahh. Those Japanese eyes were fierce, always scanning the streets for a photo occasion—but the Rube's skills were fiercer.

Back in the hood, Mioko hoofed home at a clip, loaded down with discount wallpaper. A piece of him was inclined to help her with the load. That maybe they could have a conversation, bridge the gap between their diverse lives, he could slide in beside, pull her up in his arms, and kiss her lips. Rube worked to squash that pussy ass bullshit. But in the deepest recesses of his consciousness Moe and Lou were in agreement, *"...I'll do anything for you... Anything you want me too..."*

As they narrowed the all too familiar sidewalk lining the projects, Rube sidestepped into a doorway. Precise, professional. Back on his game. A second later, Mioko checked her shoulder to see if she was being followed. Tick tock, Clockwork.

Rube ducked out of the corner almost hoping she'd double back and find him coming out what she'd no doubt take to be his front door. But she was already half sized, crossing Essex, balancing wallpaper, fumbling for her keys.

"Ohwoahhhh, I'm sticking with you. Ohwoahhh, I'm sticking with you. Ohwoahhhhh..."

The words reverberated, robust and clear, vying for attention in Rube's cortex... but the rest of his brain simmered overtime, sorting and connecting memories and future plans as he imagined her cornering Ludlow, inserting her key, before watching the door slowly inch shut behind her, a foot in the jam, then slipping in upstairs, unseen, unlocking her crib, slamming her to the ground, his tongue licking the sweltering pores of her tattooed skin, as her flesh dissolved piecemeal, limbs, head and torso, into the inner bowls of darkness in the most macabre regions of Rube's mind.

CHAPTER TEN
BOOZY DESSERTS

D orian stood at the takeout window at the side of El Sombrero. The busy bartender finally came to take his order.

Dorian gave her a knowing little nod, a signal of their history together, the solidarity of years sharing the same street. "Yeah, three frozen lime, please."

The bartender shook her head. Dorian could feel their fraternity slipping.

"We don't do that no more."

"Come on. I'm not one of these fucking interlopers. You know me. How long have I been coming here? I ain't police."

The bartender hesitated, squinting at him, then disappeared back towards the kitchen. He talked the talk. He was old school. While he waited Dorian surveyed the carousing droves milling about Ludlow. What used to be arguably the coolest neighborhood in Manhattan was now overrun with a plethora of dooshbagery: neocons, theocons, pluto-cons, grab-assing models, spending countless piles on booze and cocaine.

These days Dorian's fantasy life had narrowed to a thin scope of mental amusements. Of course there was always the imaginary pleasures of tightly cropped pubic regions between his sheets to do with as he pleased, or the envisioned gratification of finishing a painting (when had that last happened?), but what really colored his rainbow was the fantasy of unleashing a pack of mythological three-headed Cerberean dogs on lower Manhattan, guards of the infernal regions, able to kill with their breath and a dirty look, their teeth gnarling down Ludlow, ripping into the moneyed scumery cramming up his once beloved streets.

Maybe he should paint that.

The El Sombrero bartender shoved a trifecta of frozen green slushies through the window. He took a slurp, pleased to find his maw filled with sugary lime and cheap tequila. With or without the mythic beasties, he could always count on El Hat to lighten the late afternoon doldrums.

"thirty six dollars."

"Are you fucking serious? It's me."

"To-go price."

Dorian shelled forty, and waited for change.

Althea and her curly haired business partner, Dwyer, sat on the front bench outside their boutique garment shop, 'A&D Dress Co'.

Dwyer perked up when she saw Dorian walking up.

"Boozy desserts! Sweet."

Dorian had to close Althea's fingers in around her margarita.

"This supposed to be a peace offering?" Althea asked.

Dorian shrugged, he couldn't even fully remember the offense. He took a seat on the bench between them. Snatching a cigarette from Althea's pack, he lit up. He knew he was slipping, but he didn't care.

Dorian peered inside the shop, "How's biz?"

"The bitches want their dresses."

He liked Dwyer's style. Always had. Even the self-congratulatory note in her blasé report. He wondered if trying to get them both in the sack tonight would be too firm a twist of the knife for her already wounded counterpart. He let himself drift for a moment with the image of them ripping his pants off with their teeth in perfect synchronicity, and wondered what it was exactly that had made him gravitate to the one pretty girl over the other that first time he'd ducked his head into their shop five years before.

Dorian's beautiful erotic vision vanished as an intoxicated yuppy branched from his Saturday night crew and veered in their direction.

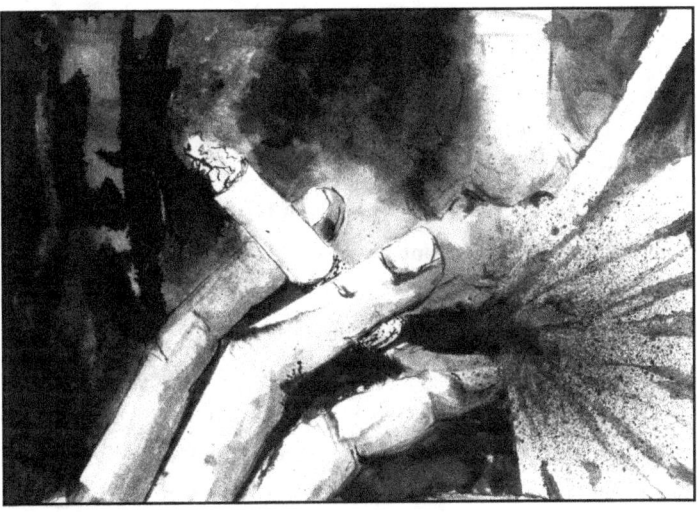

"Hey, can I buy a cigarette off you guys?"

The yuppie was trying for casual but only managing mild abrasiveness. Dorian greeted the stiff's handful of change with a huge phony grin, then took a slow, satisfying drag.

"Let me ask you something, friend," Dorian said, "If you walked out your front door every Friday night and found droves of guys dressed just like me crowding your picket fence, or picking fights with your doorman, would you sell me a cigarette?"

"What's your problem, pal?"

He wasn't trying for casual anymore.

"That I used to like my neighborhood," Dorian said.

Dwyer smirked. The yuppy shook his head and moved off to rejoin his crew, but not before yelling "FUCKING HIPSTER, FAGGOT!" back in Dorian's direction.

"There you go!" Dorian called right back after him. "Let your true colors shine bright!"

He was hit with a dense twinge of satisfaction, delighted to have forced the dooche's hand, eliciting the urban professional's shadowy inner truth within moments of making contact.

"You sure do know how to make new friends, hon," Althea said.

Dorian flashed her a devilish grin. She clearly hadn't meant it as a compliment, but he would take what he could get.

His levity was short lived though, as he spotted Morris walking past with a bag of takeout. Dorian sucked at his margarita, his eyes fixed on his neighbor.

"Isn't that your ogre below the floorboards?" Dwyer said, her eyes lighting up.

She loved it when he told tales of the man downstairs who slammed his broomstick into the ceiling at all hours. Who walked the streets with a box cutter. Who yelled anti-Semitic hate at the hoarder next door. The beast who tossed glasses of piss in his neighbor's faces unprovoked. But Dorian wasn't in the mood for story time.

"Look at that guy," Dwyer said, rubbernecking with what almost resembled a sexual charge. "I find him fascinating."

Dorian's boner was gone for good now.

"He's all yours."

CHAPTER ELEVEN
FRANK

Using his brown takeout bag as a plate, Morris messily sucked up a pulled pork sandwich, perched at his two-seat table in a pair of tighty-whities. It wasn't the best meal he'd ever had, but after another horrendous day on the midtown site, it was the closest Morris could get to some kind of satisfaction. And then his jaw made a minor miscalculation driving his lateral incisor clean through the flesh of his lower lip.

"SON OF A GODDAMN WHORE!"

He touched the soft wet inside his mouth, his own plasma coalescing with the tangy barbecue. His last savored bites nauseatingly contaminated by his own metallic undertones.

Yet again, the world conspired against him.

Much to his displeasure, Morris was back on 6th Avenue site the next morning, balancing precariously with a welding torch near the top of the steel skeleton. Sparks flew off the I-beams of the mammoth structure towering over the delis and bars below.

"That's lunch!" the foreman's assistant yelled up from the staging floor.

Morris turned off his torch and climbed down from the I-beam.

In line at the gut wagon, Morris watched his fellow crew members chum it up. Being this close to the other guys made his shoulders tighten. He wore the same steel-toed boots, the yellow mesh breakaway vest, the white hardhat, but he felt like an impostor.

The Greek husband and wife team inside the belly of the catering truck sizzled egg sandwiches and gyros. Each crewmember got his order and stepped aside. To Morris it was like a grade school square dance. Step up. Order. Cook. Money. Change. Food. Step off. Repeat.

The line got shorter as the beam workers—always the last to get fed—shuffled their way to the window. Jackson, that sack of shit, was next.

Step up.

"Yes?" The Greek wife asked.

Order.

"Two beef empanadas."

Cook.

The Greek husband turned to toss the empanadas in the toaster oven.

Money.

Jackson pulled a twenty from his wallet.

Morris saw his chance. If he was fast enough clear of Jackson's periphery, he could fetch his prize before the Greek wife looked up from her change making. Jackson extended the twenty into her waiting hand. Morris gingerly reached out and snagged a Snickers. Pocketing it, he did a one-eighty and walked off.

Success.

Fuck them all.

He had his lunch in his pocket and he hadn't paid a thing. Cost of living was beyond a bitch. And besides he lived for this. He hoped the couple would count their inventory at the end of the day and notice the discrepancy. Fuck em. Every tool he owned:

the integrated chuck and gearbox driver, the portable tile saw, shock mount radio, lithium-ion LED work light, even his orbital reciprocating saw, he had swiped them all, right out from under the noses of the cretins who ran these nightmare jobs. It was small payback for the years of maltreatment, but it was a start.

"Hey!" the Greek wife yelled after him, "Hey! That guy!"

Morris kept walking, he knew better than to look back.

"Thief. That guy! Thief!" the Greek wife wailed.

"I saw that Hacking, you fuck." Jackson said.

He hadn't seen shit. Morris knew this for fact. Unless Jackson was a freak with superhuman peripheral vision. Morris had done his own extensive visual testing. He'd spent hours mapping the fields of his eyes. He'd even pressed his optometrist about the limits of human periphery—especially at distinguishing color and shape. Jackson was a fucking liar.

"MORRIS. Stop right there." The foreman commanded.

Morris halted. You didn't mess with the foreman.

"Turn around."

Morris slowly complied.

"D' you steal off the gut wagon?"

Morris tried to explain, "Look. It wasn't worth seventy-five cents..."

"That's it, Morris, you're off the job."

Over a measly Snickers bar?

"You gotta be kidding me. You can't fire me for that." He could really feel the tingle in his shoulders now. "You look the other way when Alvarez brings a canteen of whiskey. When Benedicto and Hooks start a fist fight up on the beams."

"Stealing can't be tolerated. Sorry. Goodbye. Off my site."

Morris slammed his hardhat against the ground. "THIS IS BULLSHIT!"

The foreman shook his head, with a micro smile.

Morris grabbed up the hat and stormed towards the gate. He'd be damned if he was going to let them keep their hardhat.

That night Morris sat in his easy chair stewing.

The German Expressionist "Nosferatu" flickered on the television. Soon the young hero would find Count Orlok deep inside his castle crypt, asleep inside his coffin. Morris had seen it a hundred times.

But his eyes weren't on the television. They were locked on the Snickers bar sitting on his kitchen table. He hadn't touched it. Hadn't even peeled back the wrapper for a smell. Instead he vacuumed a bag of microwave popcorn into his mouth, washing it down with pale lager. He dropped the bottle next to the growing row of empties.

Packed with roasted peanuts, nougat, caramel and enrobed in milk chocolate, Morris knew deep down it was the only thing that would really satisfy. But under no circumstances was he going to give in.

The bitter refrain of human voices emanated from the other side of his door.

Morris leapt to his bathroom in time to catch a glimpse through his peephole. He half expected to see the men in black suits again, the ones he knew were watching the building, making sure he didn't deviate from his regular activities. But instead he found Dorian and some floozy climbing the stairs.

"...I'm telling you. Death and profit, babe. Modern-day capitalism adds a whole new dimension to the finality of death. You gotta look at it as a business opportunity. Cut right through the sentimental tear-jerk crap. It's all about scarcity value. You just gotta force the supply of new works to come to an end. Trust me, the last thing a smart artist should ever do is overstay his welcome."

"That's super creepy." Althea said.

"What's creepy is dying of old age, penniless, in nameless obscurity."

Morris squinted through the miniature glass lens. This was just what he needed. Another sleepless night.

Dorian looked up at the tiny closed-circuit camera above his shut-in neighbor, Ivan's door, a red light blinking next to the lens. The lens tracked them with a mechanical whine, as he and Althea walked the hall.

Dorian unlocked his door, eyeing his neighbor's invasive hardware.

"Can you check first?" Althea asked.

"Baby, I don't think Frank's coming back."

She shuddered at the name she herself had given.

Dorian took a cursory look as he stepped inside the dark apartment. He peered at the sink and under the bathtub in his kitchen.

"I put down glue traps and doused everything in folic acid." Dorian said.

Althea took a cautious step inside as Dorian flipped on the lights.

She jumped backwards petrified, "FRANK! Frank! There he is! FRANK!"

Dorian spotted the cause of her hissy fit; a humongous cockroach climbed the wall above the tub.

"Oh fuck!"

He'd been hoping to be done with the unsavory little houseguest by now.

Althea couldn't stop squealing, "Kill him!"

Grabbing a bowl, Dorian stalked his prey, ready to pounce.

"Come here, Frankie boy, I isn't gonna hoit ya."

Down below, in #19, the Snickers bar still sat untouched. Morris had moved on to a more egregious distraction. Two pairs of shoes pounded the floor above.

Morris stood poised with his mop, staring up at the ceiling. A fresh set of thumping was followed by hollering. Morris could hear a girl's voice yell the words "KILL HIM DORIAN!" at the top of her register. Morris's mind filled with the blackest thoughts. A crusade of justice moved his broom handle into the ceiling. Plaster and dust rained down.

He waited a moment.

Two loud thumps came in reply, along with Dorian's muffled voice: "FUCK OFF!"

Morris threw down the broom and bolted for the door.

"He's just gonna crawl back up into the building."

Hanging out his open window, Dorian shushed Althea. He slowly lifted one of his old art show postcards off the bowl's lip, letting Frank the cockroach fall six long flights to the garbage dump below. Despite Frank plaguing him for weeks, Dorian was almost sad to see the little bastard go.

Slamming at the door startled the couple.

"Dorian, I don't give a rat's ass who you're killing in there, you've got to shut the hell up!" Morris yelled from the hallway, continuing to assail the door with his fist.

Althea was petrified. Dorian glanced at the kitchen knives above the sink.

"You better go back downstairs, Morris, or I'm calling the cops."

Morris hated pigs and he knew from past experience Dorian wasn't bluffing. He'd called 911 on him on three separate occasions, and Morris couldn't afford another. "Just open the door, and talk to me like a man," he said, trying to reason with the little fruitcake.

Althea vehemently shook her head, "Don't."

Ignoring her, Dorian opened the door.

"I'M TRYING TO WATCH MY GODDAMN TV!"

"AND WHAT?" Dorian said.

"You're making excessive fucking noise! I can't even hear my show."

"I'm calling the police."

"Dorian, you pussy! Just shut the fuck up. Just be quiet."

Dorian pulled his phone and started dialing. This was good. He knew Axlerod loved nothing more than to flip an apartment, and if Dorian could get the cops out again, he could use it against Morris. Maybe even get him evicted. Maybe even push for a finder's fee.

While he listened to the dial tone, he leaned out the doorway, "This is harassment, Morris. You are harassing me!"

The sight of his massive neighbor in retreat pleased Dorian. You couldn't be a hundred percent sure, but though Morris cut a daunting figure, Dorian had an inkling that deep down, The Ogre was a pussy.

"That's right you curmudgeonly bastard—yes hello, I'd like to report a verbal assault."

Althea dropped to the couch, trying to block the whole distasteful affair. Another ill-advised night at Dorian's place.

Dorian shot a habitual glance down the hall at Mioko's apartment as he climbed past the third floor, hoping to repeat the exceptional sighting three years back of her peering out in a silken robe. But unsurprisingly the door was shut as Dorian led the baddest of badass female police officers up the tenement stairwell. Officer Cochran was a big round ball of a black woman in uniform, her pudgy Asian partner in tow.

"You try wearing a Kevlar vest and thirty pound belt, walking up five flights in this heat."

"I bet that's really uncomfortable." Dorian said.

"Damn right it is."

They turned the banister, arriving at the fifth floor.

Dorian pointed to the tiny glass peephole at the top of the stairs.

"First of all, I'd like to bring your attention to the peephole, right here, that he installed in his bathroom." Dorian said. "Placed in just such a way that he can spy on the rest of us as we come up and down the stairwell."

The officer nodded, unfazed.

Dorian then pointed to the actual doorway of #19, ten feet down the hall. "That's him."

A torn Bollywood movie poster, featuring a buxom Hindi starlet, hung above the bulging trash bags and construction supplies that lined the narrow corridor. The hall light was all but blacked out by a mounted shoebox covered in black electrical tape.

"Not a fan of light, huh?" Officer Cochran said, making sure she had the right door, "This one?"

Dorian nodded his head. Officer Cochran moved in first. At the back of the line Dorian noticed her Asian partner pop a can of pepper spray with a thumb flip. He desperately hoped the volatile little can of solvent would find it's way into Morris's unsuspecting face. Dorian tried to think of something he'd wanted more in the last year. A solo show at Gropius Gallery came to mind, but even that paled in comparison to the image of Morris laying on the floor, crying in a ball of his own snot and tears. One broomstick slam too many. The Ogre deserved everything he had coming.

"What's his name?" Officer Cochran asked.

"Morris." Dorian said, downplaying his contempt.

Officer Cochran knocked on the door forcefully. After a decent interval, Morris answered.

Dorian almost puked at Morris's attempt to present a softer, gentler side, but he wasn't opening the door all the way. Dorian knew his neighbor didn't want the black and whites seeing in.

"I'll tell you what, Officer, Dorian is way off base here—"

"Why don't you tell us what's going on then?" Officer Cochran interrupted him.

"I'm trying to watch television. He's making excessive noise up there."

"I was in my apartment all of two minutes." Dorian chimed in from his perch on the stairs.

Cochran showed Dorian her open palm, without looking back. "Don't say anything, Dorian. We're not going back and forth here." She addressed Morris again, "If you've got a complaint, Norris, you call management. You go to Landlord-Tenant court."

"You kidding me? They don't answer my calls." Morris whined.

"Keep tryin'."

"All Axlerod cares about is top dollar tenants."

"Who's Axlerod?"

"He's making excessive damn noise. We keep different hours—"

"What, walking around the apartment?" She interrupted him again. "That's not excessive."

Morris was getting flustered. He didn't like her tone. The condescending way she craned her neck sideways at him when she talked. "No it is. He's just too damn loud. And when he's making a racket, I tap lightly on the ceiling."

Morris watched the nosy cop's eyes wandering up above his head. She pushed the door forward a few inches. Morris felt the pressure of the door on his chest. He wanted to slam it in her face.

Officer Cochran looked into the apartment past Morris's shower stall. She saw the pock-marked ceiling, the fallen plaster.

"What is that? Did you do that? That's not light tapping."

"That's him, upstairs. The plaster falling down."

"No it ain't! That's anger. You're slamming the ceiling with anger. I see the evidence. That's evidence right there Norris."

She'd said it again. The bitch. His name was Morris. Not Norris. Norris was a barber who'd cut his hair lopsided while making eyes at his mother.

"Morris." He corrected her, all attempts at courtesy drained.

"I see the evidence, *Morris*."

"You've already chosen sides. You're not here to listen to me. You people come up here. You accuse. You blame. He's up there with seven different women a week!"

Upstairs, Althea tightened her eyelids in Dorian's open doorway. This wasn't news, but to hear it from The Ogre's lips. The intricate compartmentalization she'd so successfully built around each element in her makeup started to hemorrhage. The little box she kept her friend, and not so occasional lover, Dorian inside began to bleed into all the other little boxes he wasn't in. She felt desperate and empty. She knew the antidote, but drinking it somehow seemed as painful as passively letting the poison continue to slide down her throat.

"Look you crazy bastard," Dorian yelled.

Her patience evaporated, Officer Cochran held out her arm.

"He's making noise at all hours. I can't watch my television. He's up there with two, three people sometimes. Fucking and sucking and who knows what—" Morris interjected.

"Three people?" Cochran threw up her arms, "25-30 people, that's excessive. Dancing. Dancing, like this."

Cochran demonstrated a loud foot clomp, her knees jamming into the rolls above her holster, the soles of her standard issues pounding the floor.

Dorian couldn't believe his eyes. This was awesome.

Behind them, Althea moved so quickly down the stairs, Dorian nearly missed her whisking past.

"That. That's excessive." Cochran continued "Four, five people that's not excessive. You gotta get yourself some sound proofing. That's it."

"Where are you going?" Dorian asked, abandoning his police action to trail Althea.

"Hey we're not done here." Morris called.

"Yes we are," Cochran said, turning to leave.

"Oh yeah? Well, by the way..." Morris pointed to a commemorative sticker on his door. "9-11. I used to respect you guys."

Morris slammed his door. The cops shook their heads as they continued down the stairs.

Dorian jammed the downstairs door open to find Althea already climbing into a cab.

"What the hell? He had that coming. I thought we were gonna Netflix and—"

The cab door slammed shut. Cochran and her partner smiled knowingly as they waddled past, climbed into their cruiser and slammed theirs too.

Dorian continued to breath fast, realizing one of his bare feet was firmly planted in some kid trader's puke.

CHAPTER TWELVE
CHOICES

A spiral of golden flame burned linoleum. The flames flickered as they lashed at darkness, then shrank with an inverse quiver, extinguishing from the center of the spiral outwards, until there was nothing but a coiled pool of liquid. The liquid defied gravity ascending back up into a canister of gasoline as a faceless figure moved strangely in reverse. The ghoulish apparition worked his circular way around the darkness of a kitchen.

Ndusen's eyelids burst open.

Rattled, he turned to find himself safely in bed next to Kondwani. She was already awake, finely tuned to his nighttime movements.

He spoke to her in muted Chichewa. "There is something about that fire. I cannot stop thinking of it."

"And what is it that you think of?" Kondwani asked.

Ndusen sat up in bed. The nightmare was an ebbing tide. A wave of spiral patterns on Mioko's kitchen floor. Smoke hissing from immense heat.

"Instead of filling my time with fixing this building to make it livable, Mr. Axlerod has me checking every mailbox in the entrance-hall to swipe late payment notices from landlord-tenant court. I did not come to this country to thieve mail."

"But what choice do you have, Ndusen?"

Ndusen looked off into the living room at Stella and his sleeping children. There had to be a choice. He had made the choice to leave his mother, his brothers. Ndusen had come to America craving more, bigger, better. All he had ended up with was modern, faster, and a complete lack of control. All the same unfulfilled cravings. When he looked at his pompous employer he saw a man driven by his own greed. A man with seemingly no scruples whatsoever. Or if Mr. Axlerod did possess any kind of a conscience, he had somehow developed rather an intricate system for justifying the contemptible choices he made on other people's behalf. Ndusen had been out to Mr. Axlerod's Long Island mansion. He had seen the lavishness first hand. The garish entrance hallway framed below a wrap-around banister of fine wood. Giant chrome cookware built into an outdoor bar, nestling a jacuzzi. The neighboring manicured golf course. A trophy wife, and their trophy children. What would he himself do in order to possess such material treasures?

Ndusen knew full well as he pulled on his trousers that for a man like him, these luxuries simply would never be on offer.

Standing on his footstool, Ndusen replaced the hallway overhead on the sixth floor with a long-life bulb. He could not help but notice the sounds of fiery copulation permeating the hall.

A sheepish shut-in emerged from his apartment.

"Good morning, Mr. Ivan." Ndusen said.

Ivan Hershberg wore his standard uniform: a bike helmet and reflective cycling vest so filthy Ndusen wondered if even the brightest of vehicle headlight would catch any glare. Ivan clipped his helmet and closed his door. The copulation sounds were beginning to surge.

Ndusen couldn't help it. He had to know. "Is he always this…"

Ivan raised an overgrown eyebrow. "Disruptive?"

"Yes." Ndusen smiled.

"With Dorian, all depends who's in there with him."

"I see."

"Don't worry about him. Let me give you and your boss some free advice." Ivan moved in a little too close, with a soft conspiratorial tone. "You wanna upscale this place, suck up some more trust fund babies to this shitbox tenement, you oughta drag that guy Hacking—one flight down—to the nuthouse. Guy's a menace. You ain't gonna convince Desiree the Debutante to move in below a guy who's apartment smells like an abattoir."

"My interest is not to rid this building of any tenant." Ndusen said, "I simply do the job of repairing it."

Ivan strapped his vest shut. "Sure it is," he said as he continued down the hall.

Ndusen knew that inch-by-inch the divide had blurred to the point where many of the tenants mistook him, the super, for a cog in the wheel of the system at large. He was just as much a neighbor to them as a minion of their landlord, but every day he felt the increasing withdrawal of trust—never again to be restored.

Ndusen heaved industrial garbage bags out the back courtyard. He would have to have some kind of a talk with Mr. Axlerod about his aggressive tactics. If anyone could give this landlord some idea of the impact his eviction attempts were having, it was Ndusen. Yet each sentence he tried to formulate made him sound ever more a landless man trying in vein to steer a world governed by landlords.

Ndusen's nostrils were filled with the entirety of his powerlessness as he tossed the first trash bag high into the pile. Not even the buzzing flies cared for a garbage man's thoughts. He swung with the second bag but for some reason he hesitated before releasing.

He looked at the forsaken courtyard. How long had it served as a way station for rubbish? Had this long neglected space ever served any other purpose?

Finding himself inexplicably hauling wood and debris through the ground floor hallway, Ndusen tried to block out the weight of powerlessness that bore down on him.

Up the street, he shoved pile upon pile of rubble into the dumpsters. Time suspended into a stream of heavy lifting. Of aching arms, of filthy shoes and broken skin. The sun moved from east to west, and still the lowly laborer wrapped his fingers around discarded items, once new and clean and expensive. With each rusted piece of metallic debris, each broken appliance, discarded stroller, or dissolving refrigerator box, Ndusen summited the mountain of trash. The smell of his sweat brought him back to Mangochi, tilling the soil of his father's plot before the season's maize planting. Back when he found pleasure in work. Before the generous societies of the West brought his people hybrid seeds. The first year's maze yield had been beyond all expectation. The tribal chiefs had thrown celebrations, the Guli-wan-kulu had danced in their rags and frightful masks. Entire villages erupted with festivities.

Till the donations stopped.

That was when his parents and all of their neighbors found out that the fancy gifted maze embryos were designed to prevent unauthorized seed saving by anyone who farmed them. Their birthright of collecting and replanting saved seeds harvest upon harvest had been stripped. Ten thousand years was taken in one

day; the self-serving gift of a million tiny sterile wonders. His family knew nothing of patent technologies, of genetic modification. All they knew was they no longer controlled the growth of their primary food source. He wondered if his parents would ever have planted something named 'Terminator Seeds,' into their land, their family heritage, if their benevolent patrons had printed the product's true name on the woven plastic sacks.

And then there was the bold and powerful America itself, where hardly one citizen in ten thousand knew how to grow a single potato. He had heard so on the morning shows Stella watched in her struggle to command the English language. And on this great island city, nobody even touched a vegetable before it was out of the ground. His children would be no different. He had thought that he was taking his family to a place free of war, disease, genocide. Yet among the many things they had lost in the exchange was soil. Growing life from dirt. He knew he would never pass on the ripening nourishment of his father's red earth at the base of the lake in Mangochi. His first memories where of that dirt passing through his infant fingers. If he could just reclaim for his children something of the essence.

As the hours passed Ndusen began to reach the fowled concrete at the base of the giant hill of rubbish. He could feel the soft tissue between the lumbar disks beginning to cry out, but he pressed on. The last of the festering rats scurried for new hunting grounds on the other side of the fence.

No one had asked him to do this. To excavate these decades of rubbish. But in this task, he did have a choice.

Finally, Ndusen pushed open the back doors for the last time. He surveyed his new domain.

The concrete courtyard lay empty.

CHAPTER THIRTEEN
BOUGHT IN

N adja Gropius lorded over her assistants as they hung a new show in her ghetto-chic Chelsea gallery. A nasal dealer with an affectation of old world gentility, her gallery's latest show 'HARELIP,' featured portraits of children, severely deformed by cleft lips, but adorned with high-end accessories.

Distracted by her team, Nadja didn't bother to look at Dorian as she talked, let alone the samples he'd brought by.

"It's not that the work is poorly conceived or badly executed, Dorian. It's just not..." Nadja paused pensively, as much for effect as vocabuleric struggle, "...relevant."

The sterile gallery air repulsed Dorian.

"You know," Nadja continued, "it just isn't pertinent to what's happening in downtown New York *now*. This scene at this time. The cultural moving zeitgeist of our urbanity—"

"Yeah, but..."

"And the production. The production, Dorian. I'm talking about the wow factor here. Everything you do these days is so... well I'm not going to say naive."

Nadja shifted her attention back to her assistants.

"Renée, that one, left wall. Next to the *brown boy* with the Ray-Bans."

Brown boy?

"I've got new work, stuff you haven't seen."

He felt physically smaller each time his mouth opened.

"Dorian, really. We haven't made money off your art in three years. It's like throwing cash into an incinerator. If you want to show, you have to become relevant again."

"Well, what is relevant?"

He'd actually *asked* the question. That mercurial fairy who held the last sprinkle of Dorian's artistic credibility was hemorrhaging crimson acrylic. And they both knew it.

"Look around you, sweetie," Nadja said through her nostrils.

Dorian forced himself to take in the congenital deformity staring back at him. Mangled lips and teeth. Prada handbags and Cartier earrings. A pang of first-world remorse hit. He averted his gaze, flushed with annoyance. He'd be damned before being manipulated by this course artistic subterfuge.

Witness to Dorian's entire mental arc, Nadja smiled like a proud mother at a christening. This pissed him off all the more.

"These paintings conjure an immediate, palpable reaction, you see. Look at them. Desire mixed with repulsion."

"That's mostly the way I feel about my life."

Nadja's smile grew even larger, "Exactly."

Dorian found himself even more repulsed sitting at the long wooden table of Barrio Chino that night, surrounded by a little Tinder biscuit of a model and her posse of designers, finance racketeers, indie-rock-waiters, restaurateurs, and furniture-crafting-leather-working-steam-punkers-who-not-so-occasionally-worked-as-bar-backs. He dutifully posed as the phones flashed, cataloguing the non-event for all of digital eternity.

"You tried the tasting menu at Eat/Drink yet? Kumamoto oysters with Key-lime gelée. *Coooome on.* You have to trek to Boerum Hill, but trust me, *okay?*"

"I heard the Iranian caviar with gold leaf flakes is *to die for.*"

Dorian shoved down another taco al pastor into the angry hole above his chin.

Eventually everyone got blatto enough on habanero cocktails that Dorian could finally give up faking a smile.

Desire mixed with repulsion. Nadja had really jammed her stiletto right in the sphincter on that one.

Begging off an invite to the newly converted jack-shack parlor in China Town, that was now "the trendiest underground club in the city, *EV-ER*," Dorian found himself alone in his robe and boxers, crouched in his empty bathtub as the wee hours drew on.

He held his legs to his chest, a state of deepest concentration, the cool ancient porcelain numbing the bottoms of his feet.

Desire. Repulsion.

Desire. Repulsion.

Repulsion. Repulsion.

Just a few short years ago his entire focus, his very reason for being, was to exude art through his hands. Canvas after canvas effortlessly filled in marathon sessions. Marijuana, PBR and Oreos his only sustenance for the sleepless bacchanals. Since his first visit to a modern art museum, before he could even properly pull his dong, his life's ambition was to express himself in pigment particles suspended in drying oil. Before the industry pillaged his soul.

Publicity, promotion, marketing, exposure. Signing with his first primary dealer. His first five thousand dollar sale. Then a ten. Group shows turning to solo expositions. Sold out receptions. Inclusion in prestigious private collections. Gallerists, dealers, curators, all wanting a piece of the ascending artist who was more willing than ever to pull down his pants and bend.

The art star on the rise.

And then of course, the inevitable fall. From peak demand, with back-to-back solo shows and his first foray into the secondary market, with a canvas on Christie's block. When he'd heard the news from Nadja he was so thrilled to be in the game, he'd painted a week straight without sleep. But from the first to final bid, his moment on the block lasted just thirty eight seconds, and his lot didn't even meet the seller's minimum at $18,000. "Bought in" by the house—it was the kiss of death. His prices immediately dropped fifty percent, and within a month, no one was buying anything at all.

Paint. The word sounded strange now. It evoked the painful future he most likely faced, cracking Benjamin Moore in lavish Upper East Side apartments and filling walls with egg shell latex. That was unless he got his fucking act together and made something. Something meaningful. Something so prescient, so repulsively desired, the likes of Nadja Gropius and her snobling ilk would kill to hang.

But why would Dorian possibly want another go-round in that spirit crushing coral? What was it about his makeup that forced him to vomit up works of art in the name of self-expression?

His father had been perfectly content sowing leather onto steering wheels in an Ohio auto plant—sure his hands had eventually given out, but his union earnings had scored a twenty-three foot cuddy cab fishing boat for his troubles. Why did Dorian constantly have to jam the spin cycle on his own misery? It was an unanswerable question; a paradoxical Zen koan which literally stopped his mind in its tracks.

He was suddenly aware of the passage of air in through his nostrils, expanding his belly and blowing back out onto the stubble of his upper lip. His sea of anger began to evaporate. Dorian's faculties dilated outward. He was aware for the first time the stillness of the room.

Dorian abruptly jumped from the tub and sailed out his apartment door.

He flew down the stairs barefoot, his bathrobe trailing. He spun round corners, using the banister for leverage, descending as quickly as gravity would allow.

Catching his breath, his dirty feet back on the rough wood of his apartment, Dorian found himself standing before a colorful abstract canvas nailed to his wall. Overcoming hesitation, he pushed a sheet of sandpaper against the stretched cotton, leveling painstaking hours of carefully placed brushstrokes. Decimating subtle variations in shade and color. Dorian splattered rubbing alcohol, wiped away what was left of the work with paper towels. He coated the canvas with acrylic gesso. Examined the pilfered photo in his hand for reference. Then finally, Dorian began to paint. Red sky and clouds in the upper right hand corner. A photorealistic ornate railing in the left. The corrugated grey top of a tenement.

Then a dark figure emerged in the canvas center: staring skittishly through bloodshot eyes, a leering smile on his face, bare chested at the end of a long summer day in the Lower East Side.

Rube peered out at the living room.

Dorian took a step back, his own face filled with an unmistakable mix of desire and repulsion.

CHAPTER FOURTEEN
BOOBY PRIZE

Mioko entered the tenement foyer. Something was missing. She glanced at her note, but next to it only sticky remnants of tape remained stuck to the glass. Her guts did a somersault.

The picture of Rube was gone.

"Fuck me."

She unlocked the inner door and continued inside.

Mioko leaned over her darkroom sink, oscillating photo paper in developing liquid with a pair of tongs.

"The first time?" she'd told the young hispanic kid. "The first time, I was twenty,"

Rube's image slowly appeared in the chemical bath.

"Shit, twenty?" Rube had sat across from her, his hanging shirt tucked in his shorts beltline on the humid summer evening.

Standing on a stoop on Eldridge Street with her Mamiya RB67 balanced on her knee. The sun dissipating into a wash of thick red lentil soup above.

"It was everywhere back then."

Rube had studied her close.

"What'd you do? D'you slam that shit?"

"Not that first time. But eventually yeah."

"And?"

"It was fucking amazing," she'd admitted.

Rube had nodded his agreement, "A satanic rush like a sledge-hammer, am I right?"

Mioko remembered the pavement below his white sneakers. The feeling of his eyes on her.

"Till a few years later when I found myself pissing and shitting my pants and committing crimes to stop being constantly junk sick."

His eyes had penetrated her like a violation, a starry-eyed sexual assault. She should have known right then and there.

"OK." he had finally said. "You can take my picture."

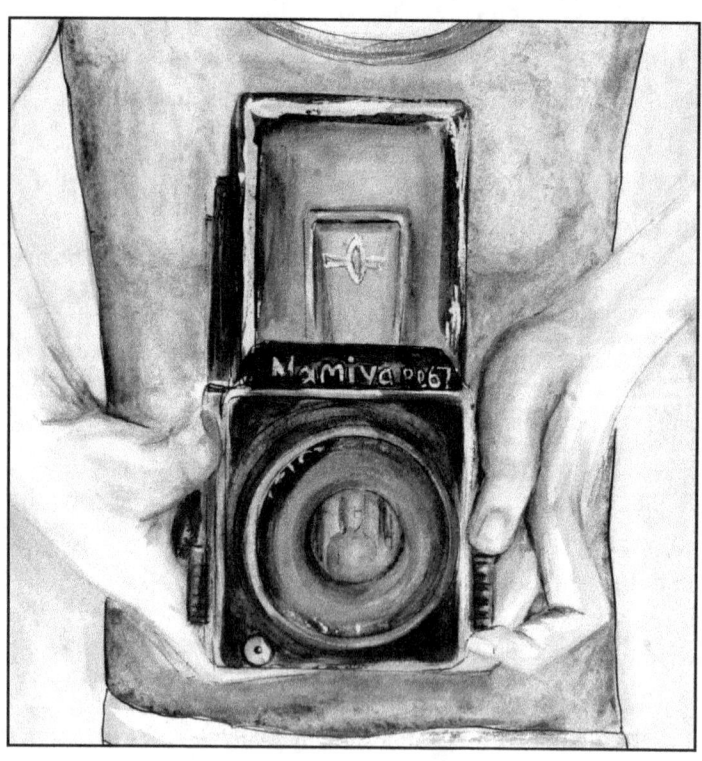

She had opened her metallic viewfinder and looked down at an upside-down Rube on the focusing screen. His chest grew as he stared down the barrel, the ground glass dividing his physique into to two dichotomous parts. She pulled the trigger.

Snap.

Staring at the print now. Rube looked to her like child. Handsome. Innocent. Weeks later he had reached out and grabbed her as she passed by the L.E.S. 1 projects, his true nature slamming into her body like a prison shiv. Sticking his hand up under her skirt, entering her between the legs with three fingers in a wedge. She'd screamed and shoved him away, but that was just a start. Over a year since she'd snapped the photo, he'd been trailing her ever since. Just as nobody was ever more than six feet away from a rat in Manhattan, Mioko felt the young stalker's presence on every city block now.

"Mioko. Hey. You home?"

The faint sound of knocking startled her back. Could he have entered the building?

Clipping the print to the drying line, she climbed over her inflatable mattress and pushed back the black curtains. Cracking the door, she found Dorian.

"Hi there."

Dorian looked a little startled, not expecting Mioko to defy the laws of answering doors by materializing directly behind him. Crossing the tiny hall, she unlocked her apartment door.

Dorian followed her inside clearly still trying to figure out the strange mirrored discrepancy in space-time.

"You have two apartments?" he finally asked.

Mioko ignored the question.

"How much you want?"

She climbed onto her bathtub, and noticed that Dorian couldn't help but stare at the tattoos wrapping around her inner thigh. She reached for the top shelf Tupperware and hopped back to Dorian's level.

"A quarter, or an eighth?"

She looked up at him from the Tupperware, which was filled with gleaming hydroponic. The inside soles of his All Stars lifted off her molten plastic floor, his nervous energy rippled like a dirty little puddle. He still had a youthful vitality, his dark hair as yet standing its ground amongst the growing shoots of grey that were beginning to swallow his scalp. She wondered how long it would take for Dorian to complete his metamorphosis to his final manifestation as just another tucked away troglodyte, winding away the days in a dingy apartment, with decades old newsprint covering the windows. She gave him five, maybe ten more years of jaded bohemian-hood before he was truly lost.

She popped the Tupperware, and pulled out a couple baggies.

"That's actually not why I'm here today."

"Oh yeah?"

She watched Dorian take in the charred edges of peeling paint, the crispy-fried floor.

"Isn't Axlerod gonna have this fixed?"

Mioko's head dipped, looking at Dorian through her eyebrows.

"Are you sleeping in here with it... like this?"

"What are you, social services?"

"Couldn't I just be being neighborly?"

"Is that what this is?"

"Look, I came down here to ask you a question..." he hesitated.

She didn't like where this was going.

"Would you sit for me?"

She shot a quizzical glance at a nearby chair.

"I want to paint you," he clarified. "Your portrait."

This was the last thing she needed.

"Look, no disrespect. I've already got one stalker."

Dorian laughed, pulling out a chair.

"Mind if I?"

"Sort of."

Dorian ignored her, taking a seat at her blackened table.

"Here's the thing. I've been thinking about this a lot. Back when this city had a soul, when kids were squatting all over downtown, making real art."

"That was a while ago, wasn't it?"

"Yeah, but the whole city was a found object then. The birth of graffiti, dances and plays on factory rooftops. Ephemeral, on site: there one day, gone the next."

Mioko interjected, "But now the whole scene is just glossy marketing? Elitist spoils for the uber-rich??"

"Yes!"

His motives were completely transparent, like a chunky kid chasing the Mister Softee truck.

"You want to get back to something real?"

"Exactly."

"And you think I'm real?"

"Yeah. I think you're amazing."

The earnestness of his compliment made Mioko laugh. Dorian visibly perked in the chair. She knew she'd better rip the band aid quickly.

"I don't think so."

Dorian's expression crumpled. A tiny part of her regretted the bubble bursting.

Mioko reached forward and fingered one of the baggies on the table in front of him.

"Do you still wanna buy some pot?"

He looked at the little green booby prize.

"Umm. Yeah, sure," he finally managed. "I'll take an eighth."

She hoped her deflection would stick, and yet she allowed herself a flavor of the unfamiliar sensation—the simple sweetness of being admired. After all, starting a collection of unwanted admirers was not a problem she'd ever imagined facing. As she took his money, she wondered for a split second what it would have been like to have his eyes darting over her body while he rubbed oils at his canvas.

Then she shut the door and threw the bolt.

CHAPTER FIFTEEN
FIGURE EIGHTS

"**R**ap is all Black. The Spanish guys don't get no love. Know
what I'm saying?"

Balmy sweat poured from Rube's pits. Late afternoon
wind pushed off the side of the bridge. Sweet relief as they hit the
corner of South 5th and Driggs Ave in Williamsburg. The gentle
twists of air coiling his skin was almost enough distraction to let
Deuce's comment slide. Almost.

"What you talking bout, son? Heresy. Cuban Link? Fat Joe?
Terror Squad? Pun? *Capital Punishment* murdered the game
ass-cheese. Platinum beeyatch. Nominated Best Rap Album,
1999 Grammy Awards—"

"Yeah, but it lost to Jay-Z, *ese.*" Deuce said, shielding a
pristine custom lowrider with his fat ass.

"Z got nothin' on the Pun," Rube spat.

"Jay-Z's put out a dozen studio albums, not to mention
collaborations, Pun drops one disk, flatlines from a heart attack."

"Stupid fuck. *Yeah Baby?* That shit went gold."

Rube whipped his "master key", a pair of colossus bolt cutters,
from his backpack. Deuce glanced over his shoulder, half-assed
lookout that he was.

"The studio released that record after Pun was a corpse."

"I oughtta split you in two for this shit. You got no pride? A
heart attack weaken the Pun's legacy? Who's this I'm talking to,
anyhow? You're well on your way to morbidly obese."

"I ain't no 700 pounds."

"Maybe you oughtta be. Might help out your MC skills."

"Suck it bitch."

"You'd like that wouldn't you? A man sucking off your *Bicho?*"

Deuce grimaced—checkmate chubs.

Rube shifted his stance to shield his activities, slicing through the chain securing the lowrider to a lamppost. Another day, another sucker.

"Wuss-ass white boy don't deserve such a nice ride anyhow."

Hopping the leather banana seat, he peddled from the scene with Deuce trailing on his clown BMX. Up the ramp, Manhattan bound.

Weaving through Hasids and posers crowding the Bridge footpath, Rube and Deuce tried to knock each other from their cycles as they wove figure eights. Their wheels traced the colorful squiggles of dripped paint, dropped long ago by a midnight street artist with serious surplus pigment.

As they shot down the chainlink tunnel into the city, Rube eased his roll and pulled a blunt. He baptized the dutchie, savoring the sweet tobacco pulp taste. Rube deftly lit up with one hand, his other pulling the handlebars to thread the needle between a pair of wig wearing brunettes, his pedals rotating inches from one of the tiny faces inside their double strollers.

"You coming out clocking for Angel with me tonight?" Deuce asked.

Rube offered the smoke, leaning left for counterweight.

"Got my own thing going at the pizzeria."

"The pizzeria my ass... Not for nothing, that slick land-owning motherfucker, Axlerod, gives the rest of these Heebs a bad name."

Rube nodded coldly at the unsolicited advice.

"That a fact?"

"Why you hanging with that fool anyhow?"

"I'm the talent. Motherfucker scouted my ass."

"What you talking bout?"

"Remember the night I sliced that emo cocksucker on Clinton. Axlerod peeped that shit."

Deuce took a hit, cupping the blunt in his palm—unlike Rube who brazenly hauled between index and thumb.

"The Rod's blackmailing your ass?"

"Nah. Ain't like that. Think he just liked what he saw. What we got's a mutually beneficial understanding. Mothafucka pays cash, son."

Deuce looked at him skeptically, "Then why you still slinging pies?"

"How else my clients gonna find me? Besides, *Rosarita's* be a front for how I pile my stash. Tax purposes, biatch."

Deuce shook his head, "Ain't no IRS looking into your stupid ass."

That was just because he hadn't racked a cold million yet. All Rube knew, he wasn't going down like his ma and pops, cleared from their home in the seventies under some Title I redevelopment bullshit, relocated to the L.E.S. 1 houses like yesterday's garbage. Or for that matter *Abuelo* and *Lita*, who ditched their island paradise off the Puerto Rican mainland after World War II, seeking out some "better life" crap in *América*, only to find *Los Estados Unidos* weren't hard pressed for a middle-aged conch diver who couldn't speak a lick of English. He wanted nothing to do with the losers that carried down the Carbia name. Who beat his ass senseless like it might fix the troubles they brought on themselves.

No, Rube saw himself as USA prime for organized crime. The gangsters and bankers, who'd taken New Jack City through an unending campaign of pillage and plunder. The Five Families of Sicilian mobsters. Infamous. John Gotti and Vincent "The Chin" Gigante. Bookmaking, loan-sharking, extorting their way to the top, all the while hedging more viable racketeering endeavors to invest and launder their so-called ill-gotten gains in "legitimate" industries. Even the drug-lords and pimps of his childhood—before Alphabet City got a clean sweep—held a special place in Rube's heart. But most of all, the modern moguls, the Bloombergs and Trumps, who gobbled wealth like anteaters sucking up entire insect colonies with their snouts, claws slashing anything and anyone in their way, dropping vast vertical empires on the landscape. Miraculous. Those were the motherfuckers to look up to, for real, and he'd be a motherfucking anteater too.

"Any pussy ass bitches standing in my way better look out."

"Wassat?" Deuce said, struggling to hear through horizontal air.

Rube took a hit off his blunt and gazed at the sweeping East Side, glowing orange as it slid sideways in the sun and smog. He had a good little mental smog of his own going now. He pedaled harder, wise to the fact they would have to hit the downward slope towards Delancey Street at speed, if they wanted to keep the piff burning and bypass the chump traffic cops at the intersection below.

CHAPTER SIXTEEN
DISCOVERY-RECOVERY

The voices were back at it, giving detailed instructions on how to electrocute himself. Pour water on the floor and pull the bulb from the light fixture. Fill the bath, an extension cord to bypass the safety outlet near the tub, and then lay back with the toaster for a cuddle. Morris could picture the lights flickering, blowing every fuse in the building as he flopped like a fish, nerves contracting, electricity pulsing through flesh. Ever since that night with the pigs at his door, the voices kept telling him to try.

Maybe when he got home, he would. Ludlow was mostly empty for a change as he turned the corner past Katz's deli. So the voices whispered, instead of having to scream over a crowd. That's when he spotted Moshe Axlerod, feigning slickness in a Hugo Boss suit, lounging on his antique shoeshine chair outside Bottle Store Bar. The last thing Morris needed was to talk to that fucker.

He shuffled past, trying to keep a low profile.

"Hey Hacking! You owe rent."

Morris took a deep breath. It didn't sound like the voices. As he crossed the street, he wondered what Axlerod would look like flopping like a toaster-fish in the bath.

"Listen, Moshe—"

Axlerod raised his palm, "Don't 'listen Moshe' me. This ain't my Pop's lending shop no more."

"Look, I lost my job. I called Avi—"

"Don't you be calling my father. My father is a sick man."

"He told me he'd get me some work round the building again for a little while."

"Excuse me?" Axlerod dropped his Italian loafers to the pavement.

Morris wished he could fuse his head back together.

"He said maybe you had some maintenance type stuff. Part-time work. For rent. For my mom's bills."

"Tell me you didn't, Morris."

Morris was puzzled. He was unsure how to respond.

"Tell me you didn't go above my head, Morris. I'm the one who decides who drinks in my bars, eats in my restaurants, lives in my friggin' buildings. And you know why that is Morris?"

He was starting to perceive a faint red glow around Axlerod. And his landlord's lips weren't in quite the right place.

"Why?"

"Because I own the whole fucking neighborhood!"

"I know that."

Axlerod leaned back in his chair, sizing Morris up.

"You been bothering the other tenants again, Morris?"

The red glow permeated outwards like a fog.

"No."

"Why not?"

Was this the real Axlerod talking, and if not what happened to the real Axlerod?

"Listen. You want work around the building? Anyone been there more than three, four years, you get unfriendly with them. Understood? Get right in their faces." He said with a wink. "But play nice with the new tenants. I'll call up Ndusen, see if he's got anything else for you, so you can make rent."

"OK."

"OK?"

Morris was confused.

"How about *thank you?*" Axlerod waved his benevolent palm "Get the fuck oùtta here."

Morris moved off, but kept a nervous eye on Axlerod. Would he have to have this same conversation tomorrow with another Axlerod?

Boy, he hoped not.

Across Ludlow, *Rosarita's* fluorescents gave the slick of curdled cheese-grease pooling around Dorian's disks of pepperoni a sickly sheen. Dorian couldn't help himself, he reached for the stack of paper napkins and patted down the slice. From the far side of the counter, Rube watched him closely with a look of disdain.

"Pizza's a little too greezy for you, huh?"

Dorian barely heard him as he sprinkled on the powdered garlic. *Rosarita's* slices weren't the best, but they were certainly the most proximate, and nine times out of ten with Dorian that won out over quality.

"I axe you a question Privilege."

"Sorry?" Dorian looked up from his first palate searing bite.

Even though he'd just ordered a slice from the kid, this was the first time he actually saw Rube. His white apron, Yankees cap, cherubic features, the golden tint of his skin. Dorian had an immediate wave of recognition.

The word "Weird" slipped out.

"What's that?" The way that bitch was ogling Rube, like he was admiring some bikini model with everything slipping out.

"I know you—"

"And what?"

Course that motherfucker knew him. Bitch practically lived off his slices. "I work here. You eat the pizza."

"I'm an artist. A painter."

"That's nice, Privilege." He didn't give a fuck if the guy was an astronaut, the way he was staring. Was this bitch rolling, his brain rushing on pink stars? He hadn't bought it from Rube. Either way, keep eyeballing, Holmes. Rube was about to grab little ho, smack him upside the head, knock the ecstasy right out with his prized mop.

"I painted you."

This fool was truly tripping, "Say what?"

"I painted this picture I found of you."

Was this some kind of a queer come on, or what?

"Do you want to see it?"

"What you mean you painted me?"

Homie did have paint caking every inch of his clothes. If what this locopuff said was true, maybe he should check it. If it was mad nice, maybe use that shit for his EP cover—or just rob the bitch blind.

"Where you live at?"

There was a loud thumping at Dorian's apartment door. He lifted himself from his stupor on the sofa to find Rube and Deuce standing in the hallway.

"Privilege." Rube nodded by way of introduction, "Deuce."

"Wassup." Deuce chimed in.

Dorian glanced at Deuce's navy hoodie, the words "NO BITCH ASS NESS" emblazoned in huge stacked letters.

He wasn't exactly sure what the appropriate greeting was so, he just grunted, "Yo."

They seemed to accept that.

"Dorian," he added.

He put out something between an awkward half wave and an anticipatory high-five. Deuce snickered as he and Rube pushed past.

Moving around the table, Rube was quickly sizing up the place, "Swish digs, player. How much you pay?"

In most other situations, Dorian would have spit sarcastic bile in response, but he was keenly aware of not wanting to make these guys feel unwelcome.

"Twelve-hundred."

Rube nodded, doing a little mental calculus, "That put you here, what, six years?"

"How'd you guess?" Dorian said, "You sell real estate when you're not slinging pies?" It was meant as a friendly quip, but Dorian worried he'd accidentally derided his guest.

"Mothafucker's clairvoyant, dog." Deuce replied for his friend.

Rube smiled coyly, continuing to look around. "What you got to drink up in this shit?" he said, finished with the pleasantries.

Rube and Deuce pulled chairs from the kitchen table, making themselves at home.

Dorian inventoried the meager contents of his fridge. "Beer. A coke?"

Rube shook his head.

"A coke? Break out the liquor man. You know gin, whiskey?"

Dorian reached through the glassless cabinet pane above his bathtub and pulled down a bourbon bottle. He kept an eye on Deuce, as his visitor began emptying tobacco from a blunt.

"Ice?"

"Nah."

Deuce didn't even look up.

Dorian poured. Deuce refilled the cigar with marijuana.

"Why you wanna go and paint my ass anyway, Privilege?" Rube asked.

Dorian wasn't exactly prepared for the question, "Why'd I paint you?"

"That's what you said, right?"

"Ahh... because you're real. The original element of this neighborhood. The real New York. Before these fucking rich Wall-Street-bridge-n-tunnel-fuckers took over."

This cracked Deuce up.

"Hear that, Rube? You're the real New York."

Deuce pulled a baggy and sprinkled yellow powder into the blunt, sealing it with his lips. Dorian's eyes grew wider.

"What's that?"

"Fairy dust, bitch." Deuce said, sparking the blunt with a huge smoke plume, then handing it off.

How cool was this? It couldn't have been easier. Dorian felt the rush of having actually followed through on a genuine inspiration. Taking the initiative to extend himself past his own comfort zone for the second time in two days and opening up to a potential subject—no, not just a subject, another human being—from such a distinctly different world than his own. And it was already paying off dividends. Getting high with his new homies in the mid-afternoon. If he could get their comfort level up, maybe the other one would even sit for him. At the very least they'd surely let him take some reference stills. Mime some real gangster shit right in his living room.

Check yourself before you wreck yourself, Dorian.

He accepted the blunt and took a huge hit.

"Thatta boy," Deuce said, clearly liking his style.

Was it weird that he almost felt like he was making a sexual conquest? Dorian exhaled a cloud of grey, a smile wrapping from ear to ear.

Out the window a satellite dish was the only thing still lit by the sun, the rest of the buildings were pastels of gray and tan. Soft rock played on the stereo. Dorian sat propped up by pillows on the couch, semi-conscious. Rube still sat at the table. Deuce browsed Dorian's CDs, lazy eyed.

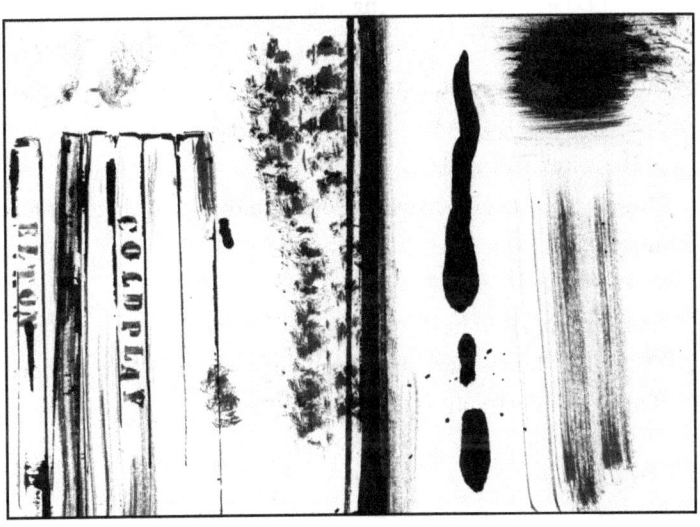

"This music is terrible, man. What is this Coldplay?" Deuce said.

"Elton John. Captain Fantastic and the Brown Dirt Cowboy..."

"Well it fucking sucks."

Rube didn't disagree, motioning to the stack of CDs in Deuce's hand, "Yeah, put on Honky Chateau... you got that one?" Rube garbled, "...It's a way better album..."

Deuce let out a cackle.

"Honky what?"

Dorian was surprised by Rube's familiarity. He dug deep for a thought, but all that came were lyrics, *"Every pose you strike, every frame they shoot, shows you dressed to kill in your monkey suit."*

Deuce scratched his head as if a spider was burrowing in the braids. "That cracker just call us monkeys?"

Clearly there had to have been some miscommunication.

"No, no, it's a newer track."

Rube stood up, he was starting to get restless.

"Aight. Let's see this fucking painting."

Dorian pointed across the room at his covered easel, "I wonder what's under that sheet, man?"

Deuce rolled his eyes.

"This bitch is stupid."

"...hey, yo, I can hear you..." Dorian said, "I'm sitting four feet from you..."

Rube peeled the sheet.

The fuck? Some kind of mirror image scam, he had to touch that shit to understand he was staring down a proper painting.

"Careful, the grease on your fingers..."

"Who dis?"

"Well, who do you think?"

"Nahh."

Recognition through the angel haze. It was that fucking bullshit Mioko had taped up. He hadn't appreciated finding her pic in the first place, much less the note accompanying. But splashed across a canvas. Vivid. A pretty dope likeness even.

"Motherfucker."

"It's just a study. I'm thinking much bigger."

Rube spun round and backhanded that little bitch, nice and hard.

"Hey! what the fuck?" Dorian said.

"What you show me this shit for, cocksucker? This ain't me! Got your ass confused. Hear me candy ass bitch?"

Rube ripped that little *huele bicho* up off the couch—hair clump in hand. Too bad he was chalkless. Should've had 16 in the clip and one in the hole.

"You do what you gotta do here." Deuce said, standing up. "I got your back, bro."

The room was electric. Rube could feel sheets of metallic rage ripping up his back. But what hadn't he touched up in this crib? A fistful of DNA ripping the man's scalp that very moment.

"Via con dios this bitch if you feel it," Deuce whispered in his ear.

"Shut the fuck up, ese."

This shit was all wrong. He had to turn the cards on this. The dirty could wait, till the work was clean. Besides, this deadbeat artist was undoubtedly on Axlerod's list.

Rube leaned till their noses were almost touching.

"Who'd you paint that picture of, Privilege?"

The artist's heart was clearly beating out of his ribcage.

"I don't know..."

"You don't know? "

"Not you..."

"Uh-huh."

"Someone else."

"Damn right," Rube said, "You wanted the real New York, motherfucker?"

Winding back, Rube plowed his fist into Dorian's face. His head snapped back as he crumpled.

"You got it."

CHAPTER SEVENTEEN
NOBODY COMES IN MY CRIB

"Jesus Christ. What happened to you?"

Dorian sidled up to the shop counter, looking sheepish with a monstrous welt below his eye.

"Got punched in the face."

"I knew that mouth'd catch up with you sooner or later." Althea said.

"How about a little sympathy?"

"For you or the other guy?"

Dorian shot her a sideways grin.

"Very funny."

Althea was the kind of girl who didn't mind if you monopolized dinner conversation with every detail of the Heaven Spa rub n' tug you'd had that afternoon, but she wasn't much for warmhearted sensitivity. Come to think of it, maybe the one quality precluded the other. But at least he didn't have to constantly worry about stepping on her delicate petals.

"You know that Polish Meathead you let sit back there and spin records for you girls, while really he's just ogling your tits?"

"Why'nt you go ice your face?"

"You got his number?"

"You're not still hung up on my going dancing with Emil that night at The Living Room?" She said.

"Sort of, but that's not why I want to talk to him. The guy's a cop right?"

"He's a detective," she said. "Why you got some investigating you need done?"

"This kid from *Rosarita's* who sucker punched me—"

"The pizza guy did that to you?"

Dorian's lips pursed.

"No?"

"Look, will you just set me up with your boy toy?"

"All we did was dance, which is..." she said, holding something back. "What's in it for me?"

"My undying gratitude."

"Thought I already had that."

Althea picked her phone off the jewelry display.

"You wanna press charges, why not just go to the precinct?"

"I'm not sure I do yet. The kid's kind of important to this thing I'm working on. He just needs a talking to."

Althea raised an eyebrow.

"Maybe I just want to put the fear in him a little."

"Oh, is that all?"

She started dialing the number.

"Well, Dorian always knows best, doesn't he?"

Dorian sat on a well-worn bench just inside the front doors of the 7th Precinct. He would have been bored senseless if it wasn't for a tall woman sporting such a distinctive wash of bling and boobs, that he didn't quite know where to rest his eyes. She had the etched plastic receiver of an old pay phone pressed to her burnt sienna lips.

"Mammy, those kids are all special ed. Retarded. All of them. Good for her. Good for her fucking ass. Goofoher," she was yelling.

"Nobody comes in my crib. She let all them bad mothafuckas in her house. Now she's up in this shit."

As he blinked in disbelief, Dorian wasn't sure what surprised him more; the sight of someone talking into the relic of a pay phone in this age of techno-fetish, or the incriminating scraps of bile the crazed girl was spewing mid-precinct into the oversized receiver.

"You don't let all those people come to your house. That house is for you. Mmmhhhmmm. You got to know how to have your shit and be humble. But have your shit."

He couldn't agree more.

"You should see how they talk to Millie. Cursing and shooting guns and shit in her house. No sir, I didn't do shit."

He could see himself hanging at the precinct more often.

"Those used to be free lunch bitches. Now they're section eight bitches. That's why Millie don't wash her hands when she goes to the bathroom. That nasty bitch. I would fuck all of them. They would have to jump me. I would throw that bitch on the couch, and POW."

The way she said the word pow was so violent, Dorian realized for the first time that he was staring. He averted his eyes, but it wasn't more than a second before he was creeping back up her camel colored UGGs to her ruffled tights again, resting for a moment where the metal phone cord brushed the chasm between her Rubenesque rack. He damned himself for not bringing along a sketchpad. He was getting good and stiff.

"Teasdale?"

The nubile figure was replaced by a tired looking steroid-case with neck tattoos, dark sunken eyes and a receding crew-cut spiking in clumps as if he'd just stepped out of a palm oil shower.

"You Teasdale?"

Dorian wasn't sure whether to nod or run. Neck tattoo reached out his hand and took a tight grip on Dorian's, squeezing his knuckles into a ball.

"Rozycki."

Dorian squinted, unsure if this was the same guy he'd seen sitting at the back of A&D flipping Benny Golson 45s on Althea's rickety turntable.

"Alright, let's go."

"I fuck her up! She looked like a hooker security guard!" his busty friend at the pay-phone was yelling now.

"Go where?" Dorian asked.

"For a ride." Rozycki said, as if it was the stupidest question he'd heard in a morning filled with stupid questions. "To find your guys."

Rather proactive for a cop. Even a cop doing his sexy bosom buddy a favor. Dorian had at best envisioned a half-hearted diagnosis at the desk and a quick prescription of the run-arounds.

A ride-along.

He had to admit that sounded rather promising.

Dorian took in a last eyeful of bulging cleavage wondering if he should try to get the crazy woman's number, if she even had a number, as he followed Rozycki out of the precinct.

Up in the front seat, Rozycki's partner, detective Jared Serilo, wasn't the talkative type. Swishing round each corner in a long slow stride, the detective's ride appeared as a regular yellow cab from the outside, but had all the inner riggings of NYPD Radio Motor Patrol on the inside. Rolling from the Williamsburg offshoot up Houston, Serilo leisurely spun the unmarked taxi cruiser, splitting his gaze between streets and rearview, sizing Dorian up for such long periods he was surprised they didn't pop a curb and plow a line of pedestrians.

Detective Emil "The Razor" Rozycki on the other hand, wouldn't shut up. He wanted to fill in any holes he'd somehow missed about the A&D Dress Co "gals".

"For sure, smart and cool is rare. Been pretty tight ever since they opened the shop."

"Lucky you."

"Yeah," Dorian said, more than ready to change subjects. "So are we undercover here?"

"Not exactly, Operations 6, plainclothes task force." Rozycki said. "You been in that building upstairs from them how long?"

"Going on twelve years."

"Twelve years. Twelve years's a long time, same building. You seen some changes in this neighborhood."

"Yeah. I've seen some changes. Not for the better."

"No shit," Serilo muttered underneath his breath, the closest he'd come to a sentence so far.

"Your landlord, that's Moshe Axlerod right?"

"Yeah, you know him?"

"Of him."

"You ever know Salvatore Agnelli?" Rozycki asked.

Serilo was really drilling into Dorian with his rearview stare now.

"He was a tenant."

"Salvatore Agnelli? I don't think so..." He thought it strange they knew someone in his building, then he realized who they were talking about. "Oh, Sal."

"Yeah, Sal. He lived in your building like forever, right?"

Of course Dorian remembered Old Sal. Sal with the raincoats, with the umbrellas on sunny days, Sal always out walking the block, always ready with a jowly smile when Dorian passed. Till his disappearance. "Sal. In 10. Yeah I never heard what happened to that guy. You know something about that?" Dorian asked.

"Never said goodbye, huh?" Serilo betrayed just the faintest touch of a sneer.

"No, not that I... recall."

"Your super, he put in a missing persons report." Rozycki asked.

"What? Really? No. I mean. It makes sense, I guess."

"Sal. He just disappeared. Poof. Didn't even notice, huh?"

"Well, I mean—"

How long had Sal been gone? Hadn't Dorian seen him just a few months back, or was that "Free Stuff," the hoarder on three who obsessively dumpster dived just to hang everyone else's first world disposables on the fences of abandoned lots around the neighborhood. The lifers all kind of ran together in Dorian's mind. Except of course for Morris. If that guy ever disappeared, the entire building would be thumping for days with the epic rager Dorian would throw.

"You guys figure out what happened to Sal?"

"We tried. For a little while. We was the assigned detectives. Had a nice line on him too or at least the guy who did him."

"Did him?"

"Couple steps away from a first-degree collar. Till the Feds took interest."

Serilo let out a little snort, "Smelled a bigger fish," barely audible, but there all the same.

"Those Alphabet Boys got involved, no further investigative response required from our end," Rozycki said, not bothering to hide his animosity in front of a lowly civilian.

"Like murder in the first degree?"

Serilo pressed his foot down on the brake pedal.

"This your boy's pizza place?"

Dorian looked out the window, the taxi cruiser sat catty corner from *Rosarita's.*

"Yeah, but I don't see him."

The three watched a plump woman plating slices through the glass for the sparse mid-afternoon patrons.

"You sure? Maybe he went and turn middle-aged Mexican broad overnight?"

"Pricey operation." Serilo jeered.

"Coulda been saving up," Rozycki turned to face his passenger. "It wasn't that lady gave you a black eye, when you didn't go down on her right, Sleazedale?"

"Pretty sure."

Was Dorian suffering from auditory hallucinations, or had this dimwitted pig just called him Sleazedale? What had Althea told this guy exactly? They always made a point of keeping their extracurricular entanglements on a need to know. Dorian now wondered if he'd somehow misjudged the arrangement.

The Razor lifted an eyebrow towards his partner, who gave a little one-sided lip twitch in response.

"Whatta-you-wanna-do-here?" Serilo mumbled.

"Hit L.E.S. 1?"

Serilo craned his neck sideways, releasing a pair of audible pops, "why the hell not." He shifted the cruiser back into gear, hanging a right. The Razor took his sweet ass time gazing in through the window of A&D as they sailed past. The Razor's face was obscured, but Dorian imagined the Polock licking his chops at this little misadventure. Enough date night chatter to fill an entire evening on Althea's wanker artist beau riding his backseat all afternoon like a pansy. Rozycki humoring the wet blanket to staunch any residual bad feeling she might harbor over poor little Sleazedale's getting a likely well-deserved fist in the face. Dorian could picture the Razor's neck tattoos pulsing as he went down on Althea just right.

"Rube and Deuce?" Rozycki checked to make sure he had the names right.

"That's what they told me," Dorian did his best not to sneer back.

"Pair of winning thoroughbreds," The Razor said as he stuck a Camel in his mouth and lit up. The sizzling tip filled the cruiser with delicious fumes. A surge shot up Dorian's body, his heart rate escalating, making him dizzy. He felt his right deltoid's twitch, his muscles instinctively pushing his arm forward to bum a smoke, or at the very least a drag.

It took the entirety of his self-restraint to tip his head back, open his jaw wide and satisfy his craving with a lung-full of second-hand smoke. He wasn't going to give this fucking swine the pleasure of doing him any more favors.

The Razor tapped Serilo on the shoulder and told him to hold up.

Down the block sat a purple Scion xB with a "Brooklyn Attitude" decal emblazoned on the front windshield in cursive. A pair of giant subs poked out the open trunk ready to rumble the block with gangster Reggaeton any hour of the day or night. A half dozen Hispanic kids lounged around the car. A couple of them noticed the discordant taxi and grabbed up rags, feigning to buff the side of the pimped out whip.

Dorian squinted. Three in from the right looked familiar. "That's him."

"Which one?" Rozecki asked.

"Cornrows."

"That's Rube?"

"No, Deuce."

"Alrighty then." The Razor threw open the passenger door and hit the street.

"Should I keep my head down?" Dorian asked his driver.

"You should shut the fuck up," Serilo said, as he popped the clip on his holster and flipped open his door.

The Razor moved on the Scion buffers, whipping a badge from beneath his shirt, "Fellas working for Angel?"

"Ain't working for shit," a scrawny kid with a cue ball 8 carved in his hair replied.

"I'm here to drop me a Deuce."

Deuce took two steps forward, fronting.

"Didn't I toss you less then a month ago?" the Razor asked. "And here you are with your dick up my ass again. You a glutton for punishment *Huelebicho?*" The Razor reached out and grabbed Deuce by the strap of his wife beater. "What's up player? Am I fucking with your flow here Deuce Bigalow the pussy ass wanna-be jigalo?"

Deuce recoiled, instinctively making a fist with his free hand, a perceptible smile shone on The Razor's lips.

"YOU GONNA FUCKING CHIN CHECK ME DAWG?"

The Razor grabbed Deuce's neck with both hands, cutting off his windpipe. "You're lucky I'm not a fucking rookie, you'd be a pool of blood on the concrete now."

"Yo, police brutality," one of the teens muttered.

"You fucking mopes can take a walk."

"Hey ease up man. We're just cleaning cars here."

The Razor pulled out his cuffs.

"Alright who wants my first collar of the day?"

Deuce's homies reluctantly started to back away. "That's right you little ball lickers, skedaddle."

The second the others were a few feet back, The Razor jammed his boot into the side of Deuce's knee, dropping him to the ground, ripping his arm from its socket, and tossing the kid's pockets.

"What's this?" The Razor asked as he produced three baggies of white powder.

"This on some bullshit. Ain't mine."

"Look Fuckface, this the way you wanna play, I'll cuff you right now and frog march you all the way to central. Where'd you get this shit? The dealer's name."

"On the corner."

The Razor grabbed a handful of cornrows and slammed Deuce's face into pavement.

As Deuce's grill hit the sidewalk, the feeling of inadequacy that Dorian had been experiencing all afternoon hit a deafening pitch. Dorian tried to remember the last time he'd thrown a punch himself, but he came up short. He'd never thought himself a pacifist, certainly wasn't shy when it came to verbal assault, but he couldn't help flinch from the violence he'd set in motion now.

"Don't give me that *mierda*," The Rozor yelled, his knee pressed into the small of Deuce's back. Between the detective's neck tattoos and his hood mannerisms, it was hard to tell the cop from the thugs.

Picking up one of the baggies, The Razor shoved it into Deuce's face. "What's this little funbag called? Foo-foo dust? Three strikes you're out? Ten-to-life?"

"It's called go fuck yourself."

The Razor smacked Deuce across the mouth.

Dorian pulled the door latch to put an end to this, but it was locked, like a stiff rubber band cutting the circulation to his balls. Serilo eyed his passenger with an "are we gonna have a problem here?" stare. Dorian unfurled his fingers from the handle, knowing better than to try for the window.

"Jesus you're a smart assed little cunt," The Razor continued outside. "You really want me to charge you with intent to sell? Violate your ass back upstate a couple decades?"

"No—"

The Razor's eyes lit up. He knew he'd won.

"Who you out here for? Crazy Vasquez? Daddy Daz?"

"Angel."

"Christ. Isn't that how we started this shit out? Always with the tough guy business. That's how you get your fucking nose broken." The Razor flicked Deuce's bleeding snout and snatched up the baggies, rising.

The Razor hopped back into the cruiser's passenger seat, throwing the bags of dope into the glove box.

"Well that was educational."

"What'd you find out?" Dorian asked.

"Nothing. I just did a little educating."

Both cops laughed.

"You're not gonna bring him in or anything?"

"Looking for a bullshit arrest, talk to a rookie. Cuff anything to boost their stats. I'm just doing Althea a favor here."

"But that wasn't even the guy who—"

"Listen, that skell who face pumped you, he'll get the message. Word travels the rat-vine quick."

But as Serilo and Rozycki dropped him in front of the tenement, Dorian couldn't help but feel he was in more danger than he'd been that morning.

"Hey yo, say hi to our girl for me."

And with that, the sham taxi drove off down Ludlow leaving a traumatized Dorian to contemplate just what words were travelling the rat vine now.

CHAPTER EIGHTEEN
THE LIST

W hat had been the back courtyard dump of the tenement had now taken a radically different disposition. Ndusen and his family were spread round the overhauled space, planting seeds and bulbs in dozens of plastic pots. The children worked alongside adults to transform the courtyard into a tiny urban farm, replete with fruit and vegetable saplings of a dozen varieties. Stella squatted, patting fertilizer as Ndusen shoveled.

Ndusen spoke softly in Chichewa as they worked, "Neighbors breathe each other's air, but will not even recognize one another's existence. We are all living above or below in this mammoth city. Each building like an organism. How can you ignore someone—hate someone, when you share their same breath?"

"Because you are afraid," said Stella.

A smile pierced Ndusen's melancholic expression.

"But, with every day passing, I feel myself becoming more and more like these people."

Across a sea of planters, Chisulo, kept his head down in his work as a melody grew from the small boy's lips, "Christmassy, Christmassy, Christmassy... Ooo-ou-ou..."

Stella got distracted as Dziko and Alile burst into song along with their little brother.

"Christmassy, Christmassy, Christmassy! Christmassy, Africa! Na Ya, Ma Ma! Na Ya Ma Ma! Ooo-ou-ou—"

Ndusen called out over the planters to his children, "When it is this humid summer, why must you sing of Christmas?"

The children ignored Ndusen, which made Stella smile. Perhaps they had it right. There was never exactly a chill in Malawi, and certainly not anything resembling frozen flakes falling from the sky. Either way, he felt his chest growing larger with each breath as he watched his children sing while working soil. Even if discarded asphalt buckets had to substitute a field of golden maize.

The children brought down the pitch for their finale, "Na Ya, Ma Ma! Na Ya Ma Ma! CHRISTMASSY AFRICA!"

Stella turned back to Ndusen, "Now we must start unwrapping the presents."

Ndusen snorted a laugh as he filled his shovel.

Kondwani's sulk permeated the evening meal as if they were seated at a memorial service. Ndusen had noticed this trend over the last months, and of course he knew full well the cause, but it was his right as head of the household, like his ancestors had done for thousands of years. Yet on this night, after such a refreshing afternoon, his wife's silent somberness was beginning to overtake his nerves.

"If you have something to say, then out with it woman."

Kondwani's lips parted, but she then shut her jaw and turned her head as if he'd said nothing at all. Perhaps it had come more harshly than he had meant. Well, feasibly all the better for it.

Kondwani diverted herself with the sight of Chisulo gobbling his food.

"Slow down, Chisulo," she barked in Chichewa.

Chisulo's spoon stopped mid-air. He looked to Stella, unsure how to proceed.

"What are you looking at her for?" Kondwani said.

Chisulo shrugged, hand edging back to mouth. Ndusen's cellphone rang and he stood, welcoming the distraction.

Once he reached the dim confines of the bedroom and saw the name on screen, he turned the ringer off. Letting Mr. Axlerod stew an extra ring or two had become a daily ritual.

"Hello?" Ndusen said at last into the phone, as if he did not know who it was.

"It's Axlerod. I need you to turn off the water to 9 and 10. I got Vasilli coming tomorrow. He'll flip the water back when he's done. And time's up for Irene Holt."

"Ok."

"Oh, and give Morris Hacking in 19 some part-time work."

Please, not that.

"I am not sure that is such a good idea."

"I'm not sure I asked you if it was a good idea."

The line went dead.

Ndusen experienced his highly unreasonable patron like a hemorrhagic fever, and he a patient in the death throws of Axlerod virus, bleeding from every membrane, his nervous system crushed under the viral juggernaut as his body disintegrated. Inhaling through the immense pressure on his ribcage, Ndusen shut the phone, and walked back to his lukewarm dinner.

With a last knock on the door, then a key in the lock, Ndusen poked his head inside number 9, Mioko Kimura's third floor apartment.

"Hello?" he spoke to the empty living room.

Pushing inside, Ndusen was immediately struck by the charred wood, scarred linoleum and half-finished wallpaper job Mioko had begun herself in earnest, after Axlerod put off paying for repairs, "until the insurance cleared," whatever that might mean. At least with Vasilli coming by tomorrow, perhaps things would begin to move, but Ndusen wasn't quite sure why the plumbing subcontractor was the first order of business, when clearly there were weeks of cosmetic repairs. Yet he had to choose his battles wisely, lest his affliction worsen. Setting his tools by the sink, he squatted to wrench the valve shut.

His next order of business wouldn't be nearly this easy.

Ndusen knocked on apartment 19, hoping for silence in return.

"WHAT?" A quaky voice bellowed from inside.

Ndusen tried to fill his constricted chest.

Morris peered out into the light.

"Mr. Axlerod called me." Ndusen said.

Morris opened the door, his hair a wild bird's nest, his shirt stained.

"OK," Morris said, standing an inch taller. "What do you need my help with?"

Ndusen just stared, he felt the virus coursing through his blood and wondered if it was outwardly apparent from the pallor of his skin that he was dying on the inside.

Ndusen grew even more nauseated as he and Morris dragged a faded love-seat across the living room of number 7. A uniformed City Marshal stood by as they cleared the soiled piles of rubbish.

"This is not how you treat human beings! I'm not an animal," the packrat declared as they angled the love-seat out her front door.

"Hey listen, lady," Morris yelled back, "you've been evicted, so SHUT UP."

Ndusen didn't have the energy to abate Morris's superiority.

The packrat hawked a gob of phlegm, spiting on the floor by Ndusen's sneaker as they carried out her couch. If one could compare the excruciation of tenant evictions, this one had now exceeded the norm.

In the stairwell, Chisulo watches his father and the smelly giant wrestle the cumbersome armoire down the stairs.

Morris turned from the small boy, to Ndusen with a thin smile, "Packing your entire sardine tin into a one-bedroom, just like this tenement was back in the day."

Ignoring him, Ndusen jostled for grip under the dresser.

"Y'all came a long way to live in squalor, huh?"

Ndusen yanked the armoire around the stairwell corner and down towards the foyer. If he just kept his mind on the lifting, he found he could keep the cellular toxicity of Axlerod virus momentarily at bay.

Outside the tenement, Ndusen and Morris lugged piles of magazines into the street.

"Mom told me back when she was a kid, you could smell this neighborhood from miles away." Morris said. "East Side used to have a giant black cloud above the streets from all the burning coal. Fourteen, fifteen living in one flophouse apartment. Folks renting out their beds. Sleeping in shifts. Opium dens, brothels, absinth bars. Come a long way, hasn't it?"

Morris stared at Ndusen, waiting for a response.

"Thank you for this historical recount," he said, hoping to put a close to story time.

"What do you think about America, Ndusen? You like it here, in this country? You like civilized living? Restaurants? Cable TV? Titty bars?"

"Yes," Ndusen said sarcastically, "Today is a wonderful day, with wonderful company. Thank you America. I am in my happy place."

"I think you're just sore, 'cause you miss your thatch-roofed hut. You know, your people, the Africans, you all got a long history here. Back in the day, 1 in 6 New Yorkers were owned by other New Yorkers. The wall that's now Wall Street, slaves built that."

Ndusen longed for the freedoms of his ancestral Massai forefathers, wishing with all of his heart he could run this fool through with the double-edged blade of his hunting spear. Instead he dropped his bundle of gossipy magazines, closing his eyes. The son of a warrior could do nothing but laugh in frustration.

"OK. That's enough for today. Thank you so much for your help."

"But we haven't finished the job yet. You gonna hump the rest yourself?"

Ndusen turned and walked back towards the building. Doubling his load was nothing compared to his day laborer's musings.

Inside his real estate office on Eldridge Street, Moshe Axlerod sat absentmindedly draining a glass of Macallan 18 as he typed projected numbers into a spreadsheet. Moving a hand through the slick thinning strands at the front of his scalp, he wondered if the topical regrowth foam was doing anything at all.

He looked up from his screen. His office had an old world simplicity, none of the flash of its modern counterparts; businesses which racked millions in commissions packaging upscale residences to ultra wealthy Manhattanites. Axlerod's office was a holdover from the days before corporate monopolies swallowed the realty market. Now, auto-withdrawals and building link apps created anonymity screens dividing tenants from property owners. Axlerod never felt quite at home in this old dustbox even though he'd crawled the floors before learning to walk. There were reminders of his father and his stale business practices in every ancient filing cabinet. Axlerod had designs on a slick street level space with endless offerings of newly available rentals digitally projected on the outside glass, enticing the pedestrian masses, with all of the pertinent property info magically suspended before their eyes. But he had other priorities for the time being.

Ndusen knocked on the ancient glass. Axlerod got up, walked past the empty secretary desk, and unlocked the door.

"It is done," Ndusen said. "Irene Holt no longer lives in the building."

Axlerod nodded slowly, "Well alright then. Nice work."

Turning back towards his desk at the back of the office, Axlerod sauntered toward his scotch glass. Lifting his libation, a devious smile on his face.

"To the old packrat. May she hang her discarded treasures from the scaffold of some other sucker's property."

Reaching into his desk drawer as he sat down, Axlerod retrieved a stack of files. He unclipped an old Xerox driver's license belonging to a much less haggard Irene Holt from a copy of her lease. He then ceremoniously dumped the Xerox in the garbage, setting aside the apartment paperwork. He continued to flip through other tenant's files.

Ndusen watched closely as Axlerod separated the tenants into two piles.

"How'd things go with Hacking?"

"Not well."

Axlerod smiled, anticipating the unfavorable review.

"Think that guy's crazy enough to get carted off to the puzzle factory?"

Ndusen looked at his employer in confusion.

"The loony bin."

"Oh, yes."

"Oh yes, as in, someone could have the guy committed?"

"I am not sure I follow."

"You follow just fine when you want to. Three hundred and thirty two miserable dollars that fruitcake pays for an eight hundred square foot hand-me-down. You know how much I could get for that place?"

Ndusen watched as the virus continued to sort his piles. He felt his guts squirming, bile and blood blending in the mix, his solar plexus crumbling inward.

"Stop giving me that look. Back when my father ran these buildings, there were junkies lining the block. You know that? Now we got lawyers, brokers, beautiful women walking the streets. Economic friggin growth. And what's wrong with that? Myself, I'd rather be surrounded by beautiful girls, than stray dogs and miscreants."

Ndusen kept watching as Axlerod returned to his work.

"You're still just standing there with that look."

Something lodged inside Ndusen's midriff, the beginnings of a deadly blockade.

"Is my apartment on your list?"

Axlerod let out a coy snicker.

"That a real question? You work for me, don't you?"

"I do. Yes."

"And how long have you known my family?"

Cyrus Axlerod had been one of the first kind men Ndusen had encountered while driving a friend's taxi on off nights. Back when he had little more knowledge of the city than the darkened grid of Manhattan streets and the apartment in Jamaica Queens he had shared with twenty other African immigrants.

"I've known your father for eight years."

A prize-winning smile spread across Axlerod's face.

"Then don't worry about the list."

Sorting through files for Dorian Teasdale, Morris Hacking, and a miscellany of other tenants, Axlerod stopped at a photo of Mioko. He spread out two sets of files: one for each of her apartments. His lower jaw shifted out of place as he studied them, a relentless finger tapping against the table.

CHAPTER NINETEEN
AIR GUITAR

Two teenage look-a-likes of Iggy Pop's Stooges smoked rollies outside the Ludlow dive bar. Mioko pushed past them into *Machine City* and its cavernous collection of automotive fetish. Darlene, a vampy goth bartender instantly recognizes her.

"He just stepped out, hon," Darlene said and smiled humanely like you would to a crippled dog.

Mioko glanced around all the same. "Alright. Well, can you tell him to drop in on me, I need a resupply."

"Sure. Hey, can I get you a club soda or something?"

"No, I'm cool. I gotta get going."

She would have liked nothing more than to pull a stool and purse her lips round a tiny black straw, but that was an easy slide towards the bathrooms and her old motley pals, the 100cc syringe, and his ne'er-do-well partner, the rubber tourniquet. Darlene must have caught Mioko's eyes wander back to the old shooting grounds, because empathy was creeping onto her face. It wasn't a look Mioko much liked.

"Mioko..." Darlene hesitated.

"Yeah?"

"Can I ask you a personal thing?"

"Shoot."

"You quit cold turkey, right? No AA. No methadone. Nothing?"

"It's the only way to do it."

Darlene looked off, lost for a moment.

"Right. Alright."

Mioko put her bag back on her shoulder.

"It's not like I'm, you know, I just dabble in a little blow here and there—" Mioko knew too well the anxiety, and eventual downright self-loathing of wanting to get clear.

"You call me if you wanna talk about anything, Darlene."

Darlene, winked at her, trying to brighten her own mood.

"Yeah. Alright. I will."

Darlene watches her go, sipping her pint of pilsner.

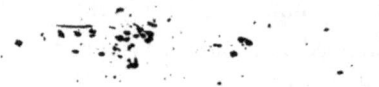

In the center of a pockmarked road filled with quarried Belgian blocks, below towering cast iron facades from the late eighteen-hundreds, a skeletal teen jumped a tiny trampoline with a Gibson Flying V strapped to her front. Jake sat on an apple box with a Hasselblad in hand in the middle of SoHo's Green Street, yelling at the top of his lungs, "One, two, three, AIR GUITAR! One, two, three, AIR GUITAR! Yeah, WORK IT!"

Surrounded by assistants, agency producers and stylists, Jake snapped away at the skeletal teen as she leapt into the air at his command.

"One, two, three, AIR GUITAR! Great, great, great, grey, grey, gre, gr, gr, GREAT! Check her out guys... HO!!"

Jake tapped his impeccable white tennis shoes at a rapid-fire pace as he continued to yell, frantically trying to amp the languid model. Mioko stood at the field monitor, scrutinizing the shots as they popped on-screen.

"One, two, three—"

The model wavered. Disoriented, she took a step in the air but didn't find the trampoline under foot. She collapses backwards hitting the side with a thud.

Jake was instantly enraged.

"Oh, that's it!"

Jake jerked his arm forward to throw the fifty-thousand dollar camera, but was intercepted by Mioko's palm. Jake stormed towards the model as the assistants and stylists leaned to help her.

"Would somebody please call her agency and tell them to force feed these daughters of Auschwitz before sending them over!"

Mioko pulled water from a cooler and headed for the trampoline. Jake grabbed Mioko's arm as she passes, completely disregarding that water might be some kind of urgent necessity.

"Fuck. This. Shit." Jake hissed, "I'm gonna slip out and do forty-five minutes of cardio. Text me when she's up and ready to shoot again."

The assistants did their best to lay the poor model out on the trampoline as Mioko leaned in and poured water down the pale girl's throat.

In the absence of their fearless leader, the photo crew broke for lunch at eleven-fifteen. Mioko was stuck between a pair of prop stylists discussing the injustices of a boyfriend's public urination ticket. A petite powerhouse of an art director was perched across the craft table from Mioko. Replacing the salad tongs, she reached down and picked up one of two identical black smartphones sitting between their plates. Turning the phone on, the screen saver was an arresting black and white image of three tattooed kids intertwined inside a dive bar toilet stall. The two girls kissed, while the boy shot up. The art director, looked at the image closely then realized Mioko's eyes were on her.

"Oh, I'm sorry," the art director quickly spat. "Is this yours? We have the same phone."

The art director reluctantly handed it back, but stopped before letting go of the device entirely, so that their index fingers lingered on the glass surface in cramped proximity. Mioko could feel her finger buzzing from the heat.

"Is that your photograph?" the art director asked.

Mioko nodded, embarrassed.

The art director finally let go.

"Are there more?"

Mioko reluctantly unlocked the phone and handed back a gallery. Flipping through, the art director pushed back her silver locks, squinting at Mioko conspiratorially.

"We have a concept on the table for 'Lamerica' that could launch from this style. Is that something you could replicate, commercially?"

Jake strutted back into the fray.

"I'm back!" He announced, "What the fuck are we waiting on now?"

Jake turned to Mioko as if she was the one who had hit the breaks.

"Mioko?"

Jake started clapping his hands like he was corralling kindergarteners.

"Let's do this!"

He headed towards the monitor. Knowing she only had seconds before the screeching started, Mioko leaned in to the art director.

"I think I could replicate it."

"Great. I'll get your from the call sheet and send you the boards. Let's talk tomorrow."

Mioko couldn't believe it, even though this was surely just an audition. She tried not to notice as the art director took her salad to finish lunch with the rest of her agency team. An audition she would undoubtedly fail.

CHAPTER TWENTY
TAKEOUT

R ube slung pie behind the glass cage of *Rosarita's*. Through the neon open sign he caught sight of that stained schizoid Morris, shuffling out of San Loco with a fat bag of tacos. Rube eyed the hefty oaf as he crossed Ludlow towards Axlerod's tenement. He pondered how a freak like that filled up a Thursday night. In hunter-gatherer days, dude like that would've found himself tossed out of the village. Hand him a burning stick, if he was lucky, before dropping a heel in that ass to fend on the fringes with the wolves. Rube figured modern days, that mental case probably squeezed some kind of companionship with the nastiest of internet porn sites—trannies and Japanese eel competition shit. Pitiful. Watching that sorry sack waddle in through the tenement doorway, Rube pondered if he ought to put him out his lonesome misery with a sick bag of piff. Maybe even some coke. Next couple days he'd be in for his usual triple chicken parm slice gorge fest—Rube decided he'd give cheebs a little sample bag. Why not? Who knows, maybe psycho-boy'd become a VIP customer.

Remembering the pie twirling on his finger, Rube grabbed up a pepperoni disc out of the troth and flipped it in his mouth. He got it nice and gummed with aural nasties, stuck it right in the center of the uncooked pie, launching it into the sizzle drawer.

"Bon appétit bitches."

With Demetrakas Funeral Home closed and nothing to fill the void but the increasingly persistent voices, Morris was relieved to be back in the comparatively safety of home. The TV on and his fifth meal of the day resting on the counter, trying to be a good boy, Morris was ready to wash down what he knew should be his final meal of the night with a healthy protein supplement. He pressed down on his milkshake mixer, then removed the plastic party mug, twisting a blue comfort lip ring onto the top—careful not to spill like he had last time. Satisfied the comfort ring was on tight enough, he took a big satisfying sip.

He then moved back to what was left of the tacos, wolfing them down, but paused mid-bite. His ceiling splintered like the creaking hull of a ship, followed by the loud thumping beat of what could only be Dorian's stereo. He looked up in anguish.

Morris climbed out onto the fire escape, salsa dribbling his fingers. His face tightened as he peered up the side of the building at Dorian's, the music thumping.

Trudging the fire escape, Morris reached the 6th floor. He peeked in through Dorian's window.

Dorian swayed naked by the blaring stereo with a huge black eye. Taking a toke off a joint, he moved towards one of Nadja's young gallery assistants, standing nude in his living room. Reaching out for her, they commenced a torpid dance. His eyes closed, Dorian moved his naked body against hers. As they spun, the girl's jaw dropped and she let out a deafening scream.

"What the fuck?" Dorian said in a panic. "What?"

The gallery assistant pointed to the window, now empty.

"There was a guy out there," she said wearily. "Eating a taco."

Dorian laughed, with a smirk. He grabbed the joint back.

"No more of this for you."

"I'm serious Dorian."

"I wanna show you something I'm working on."

"I'm not making this up," she said, crouching to minimize her body, the fear taking hold.

"I know. I know."

Dorian crossed the floor to a large hanging white sheet. She followed close, not wanting to be anywhere near the window solo.

"Easy baby. I'm here. You're safe."

She took his hand. He pulled back the sheet, revealing a large canvas painting of Rube.

"Oh, wow. That's really…" she said, regaining some measure of self-control. "It's way different from your abstract stuff."

A little weed, a little dancing…

"But do you like it?"

"Oh, man. Yeah. It's creepy and vibrant."

…hook line and sink-her.

"Think Nadja would show it?"

The mailroom theory: get the lowest on the totem on board, eventually your ambitions will make their way up to the CEO.

"For sure."

Dorian let his fingers trail slowly down her spine, lingering above her ass.

"Would you be willing to mention it?"

She looked up with her colossal blue eyes, her streaky blonde hair, perfect pink lips, crooked front teeth.

"Totally."

He knew she'd cinch it. These little sluts ran the entire industry. Nadja and her ilk of aging gallerists, wholly depended on these assistant's taste, their social talents for lubrication, their smooth rosy skin closing a hesitant sale.

"But tell her it's part of something bigger."

"Okay. Cool."

Dorian reached past her, cranking the stereo and guiding towards the bedroom.

As they began to get comfortable, a few feet below, Morris slammed the ceiling with the full force of his broom.

A Radiohead album that hit the charts the same year the gallery assistant graduated first grade blared from Dorian's giant stereo speakers.

"How long you think before Nadja gets shipped to the glue factory and you take over?"

"She's already losing her phone every couple of days."

Dorian massaged her shoulders with oil, then flipped her onto her front.

"I can't concentrate with all that banging."

"Just relax, baby."

"Dorian."

He knew he'd better do something about The Ogre before she got any whinier. Dorian leaned over her, reaching down inside his loft bed and produces a ten-pound barbell.

"What's that for?"

Dorian held the free-weight off the edge of the loft, then let loose. The barbell dropped 8 feet and slammed the hardwood. The banging instantly stopped. The gallery assistant licked her lips then moved them from Dorian's self-satisfied grin down to his stiffening prick.

A muffled yell emitted from the floorboards.

Swallowing the last of his tiny swimmers, the gallery assistant tried to nuzzle a post-coital embrace out of Dorian, who sat on the mattress edge lighting a roach. He'd already started to plan his opening. Who he'd invite. Who he'd conveniently omit. Wouldn't be long now till he could find a new studio. Maybe even finally ditch this roach infested shithole. A house in the Slope? Settle down with a nice girl. Maybe even Althea. He tried to remember how old she was. Was it her thirty-third he'd just been to, or her thirty-fifth? No trouble, he was sure her trust fund would cover in-vitro. How crazy would that be, walking Park Slope with a bundle... or two? Sid and Nancy. He could picture carving his little neonate's noggin into a mohawk.

"I think you're a super talent," the assistant was saying now. "I really mean that."

Dorian ignored her. She finally lifted her body and leaned sweetly to his ear.

"Do you want me to stay?"

"Will you go down and get me a slice of pizza?"

"Oh my god, that's such a dick thing to say."

"Is it? I take those stairs all the time, for you it's a novelty. Besides there's a guy at the pizza joint I'm kind of trying to—"

"You're serious?"

"Well, I don't know, I mean, I am hankering for a slice."

She sprung from the loft bed, and started gathering her clothes below.

"Where are my damn panties?"

"Being a little sensitive, aren't you?"

Giving up, she slipped her jeans on comando and opened the front door. Dorian's smile disintegrated as he realized she was serious.

"Hey look, wait. I was gonna buy you a slice too Babe. Hey, yo, don't forget to mention to Nadja what I'm working on—"

But the door was already slamming on her way out.

Dorian woke in the middle of the night wondering just exactly what he'd said to metamorphosize the little biscuit in his bed from an adoring fan into an apoplectic succubus. He hadn't remembered smoking more than a joint's worth, but Mioko's stuff was strong as hell, and for the life of him he couldn't recall much of anything that transpired between his cumming and her slamming the door. He'd wanted a slice. It was something to do with pizza, but what exactly?

He would have made a decision then and there to cut back on the smoke, but he knew he'd never get a solo show's worth of material together without turning off his innate proclivities for organized thought. But had he just gone and soured his best shot? He didn't like to think of having to buy the little she-devil a bouquet of groveling, so instead he switched the mental dial to Althea and reached for his cock to alleviate some stress. But no sooner had he conjured a picture of his girl writhing on top, he flashed on an image of detective goddamn "Razor" Rozicki underneath. He flicked his dick away and switched on a lamp.

And then it hit him. The Razor. The Ride along. Sal.

What the hell did happen to old Sal? Despite what half the women in the L.E.S. thought, Dorian wasn't a heartless bastard. He'd even go so far as to say he missed Sal. Not in any tangible way, but in the abstract. Like a childhood friends's family pet, Brewster the brown beagle who lived next door with the Madison's. Who was probably long dead now. Dorian hoped Sal wasn't, but he couldn't shake the possibility. As he squinted at the flickering lights of the financial district, the first rays of sunlight moving up over distant Brooklyn, he decided that he may not be able to get a gallery show, but he was going to get an answer to what happened to the old fart.

PART II
CAGED RATS

CHAPTER TWENTY-ONE
CROWDED F

J ake looked over Mioko's shoulder as she labored at a monitor in his self-aggrandizing—if nearly unaffordable—midtown corner office. Her hand rapidly manipulated color adjustments on a photo of two emaciated models in native African states of undress, their lips so close, their next move would involve swapping spittle. And for reasons beyond Mioko's comprehension, their Sapphic intimacy was supposed to evoke a mad consumer rush, propelling women to run to the mall and empty their purses for the overpriced cosmetics encrusting the models' faces.

It was a familiar refrain in the photographer's studio; Jake scrutinized as Mioko adjusted his work.

"My God, that props stylist was absolute fucking garbage, wasn't she? Look at that hut. Looks like a lean-to built by hobos after downing a case of Listerine. I could've built ten times that hut. Stupid cow."

Jake lifted onto the balls of his feet.

"Speaking of hobos."

He pulled a black and white photo of a junkie on the nod from the corkboard above Mioko's computer.

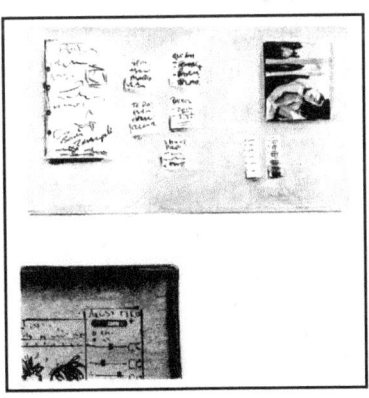

"Little Miss Old School," he said with the usual touch of a sneer. "You're the only person I know who keeps pouring chemicals. Still got that second rent-controlled pad for a darkroom?"

He glanced back at the monitor.

"More in the greens. No, not that much."

Jake's attention found the photo in his hand again.

"That your RB67?"

Mioko nodded, knowing better than to take her eyes off the screen.

"How'd you manage to keep that extra place anyway?"

"Trey's name is still on the lease," she said. "He shows up in court for me when I ask."

"Your ex? That happen a lot?"

She pushed the histogram, cooling the highlights.

"No. More magenta." He took a step back and studied the screen sideways. "Your landlord must absolutely L-O-V-E you. Yeah, boost the mids. Can't even imagine the market value on those two shoeboxes."

"A couple years ago, Axlerod, my landlord, actually offered me a ten thousand dollar buyout."

"What? Really. Don't do it." He said.

"Yeah?"

"There's only sixteen-hundred rent controlled apartments in the entire city left. I read it in the Times."

"No kidding?"

"This looks like shit. We gotta start over."

Mioko closed her eyes, not turning back to look at her torturer. Her phone began to ring.

"Do you mind?"

Jake rolled his eyes. Mioko hesitantly stepped out into the hallway.

"This is Mioko," She said quietly, the glass pressed to her face as she tried to move from a neighboring studio blaring death metal. "Hey, yeah. Sure, no, I think the high-contrast black and white thing is a strong choice." She listened to the agency art director with a smile, even as she blathered sycophantic about how Romen Gold—the arrogant and infamously temperamental Lamerica CEO—would be on set, and what amazing vision Romen had, and that they'd developed a lasting trust over two years of intimate collaboration, and that he'd seen exactly the same spark in Mioko's fantastic work that she had. "I'm really glad Romen's excited."

Mioko's suspicious mind immediately began to wander into conspiracy, was this fodder for some deeper manipulation—with Mioko lined up as some kind of pawn in the art director's agency power grab—only to be unceremoniously dumped as soon as the art director made her play. Mioko could barely handle the art director's phony effusiveness, but she was too adrenalized to do anything but grin and try to put one word in front of another.

"I love his stuff. He's a marketing genius," she heard herself saying. Selling out was so much easier than she'd imagined.

But as the art director got back to specifics, Mioko's panic rose. She was actually going to have to do this thing. Her own crew. Her lighting design. Calling all the shots. "Please. Sure. Of course. Sounds good. Yeah, just email me the headshots. Perfect. My guys are all lined up. Right."

She knew it was of the uttermost to remain judicious in her expectations, but despite herself she was trying on self-confidence for the first time in years.

"Wednesday. 10 o'clock. Fast Ashley's Studios. Perfect. We'll see you then."

As Mioko hung up and walked back, she lingered to take in a couple of bars of death metal. The thought of having to slave as Jake's magic hands for the rest of the afternoon was like an arthritic curse.

Jake. What had she done to deserve him?

Then she couldn't help but wonder if she'd stolen a client from her boss. But the notion was so unpleasant, she did a little shimmy with her hips to drive off the albatross, and remind herself of what a fantastic professional coup this was.

That evening as she rode a crowded F home, she found herself caught between either having to lean against the cool train doors, or letting her body press against a clean cut kid in a v-neck. It wasn't really much of a choice she decided as she relaxed towards his ample chest. As the fabric that separated their bare skin brushed, Mioko's eyelids fluttered, betraying the electric pulse that rushed her body.

CHAPTER TWENTY-TWO
THE GLUE AND THE RAT

Through layers of sewer and concrete two hundred feet above Mioko's speeding train, Morris sat in the Chapel of Rest, hunched over his mother's coffin, speaking in muted tones. He unconsciously pulled at the pocket of his blue blazer, the stitching long since come unraveled.

"I've been trying to watch less TV and I'm still taking my vitamins and drinking the protein shakes like you told me," he said. "I even ordered that Magic Bullet mixer set I told you about. They say it's a 'Personal, Versatile Counter-top Magician,' but it's not the easiest thing to clean."

Taking care of his own physical hygiene was bad enough, but scrubbing counters and dishes. Every time he picked up a sponge it opened a black pit of despair; he so desperately wished she could come home with him again.

"Everything's changing down here, Ma. It's like a cosmic joke. As if the gods decided to forbid anyone over thirty-five from living in the Lower East Side anymore."

He told what was left of Geraldine Hacking in great detail about his impossible upstairs neighbor, the prick artist, and about all the rich brats Axlerod was leasing apartments to.

"You'll barely recognize the place now, Ma. I can hardly afford to go get anything to eat around the building anymore. And the way these kids walk around, their stupid phones and pads and talking top volume into their headbuds, as if they're god's gift to the planet. It's despicable."

He knew she understood him, when no one else could. Always had. The hardest part was having to leave her here.

Come back home to Ludlow. Please.

His lip quivered. Then he heard the funeral director's voice from the other room and knew his time was short.

"I'll be by again in a couple days, Ma, I promise."

Seeing Morris walking through the front vestibule on his way out, the funeral director snapped into swift action.

"Mr. Hacking, we have to talk," the funeral director said loudly.

Morris ignored the pompous jerk, shaking his head as he shoved open the parlor door and walked quickly into the street.

But in his haste to leave, he'd forgotten to give her the most important update.

Axlerod had given him work, and it might just rid them of Dorian, that son of a bitch. Maybe then she could come home.

On the way back to the tenement, walking past CHP Hardware, Morris had a fantastic idea. He ducked inside.

Arriving home and dumping Super Glue from the paper bag, he smiled. The tiny cadaver in his freezer. What a brilliant idea. Just perfect. But he should have gone to a paper supply.

Goddamn it.

He moved to his workbench and started tossing aside newspapers and magazines. Until he found a little, soiled envelope.

It was just the right size.

Reaching the top step, Morris peeked over his shoulder as he approached Dorian's door. He knocked forcefully.

"Dorian? Hey asshole. You there?"

Morris waited, keeping an eye for anyone coming down the hall. All clear. He pulled the tube of Super Glue from his coat pocket. With a last peak over his shoulder, he twisted the cap, and emptied it into the keyhole. Turning quickly, Morris tried to contain his glee as he walked rapidly back downstairs.

But he stopped mid-step.

He was so fired up, he'd completely forgotten about the envelope. He raced back up, and was pleased to find the hallway still empty. He leaned over and placed the envelope below the front door, the penciled scribble "HELLO" clearly visible on the crumpled front. He stared down at it, picturing the prize inside. Maybe too long he realized as he pivoted back towards the stairs.

The last thing he needed was to get caught in the act.

That night Morris decided to celebrate his stroke of genius with a Jameson at Iggy's, but hard liquor was never really his friend, and after his third pour, everything got scribbled and names were backwards. He felt he was gonna piss himself every time he got a look from someone down the bar. He longed for nature. Pinecones. Trees. The deafening squeak of cicadas to drown out the voices. For time to stop being measured out in minute-by-minute increments of humanity. Humanity. What a horrible word. The scorning hordes crawling through the clammy streets, staring at Morris, outing him for the truth in what he was. "A loner," "a creep," "a waste of space." Their faces were colored with malice. He could tell. He could hear it in every look. How much they despised him. When it got this insistent, he wished he could be made of air so the sun would shine right through.

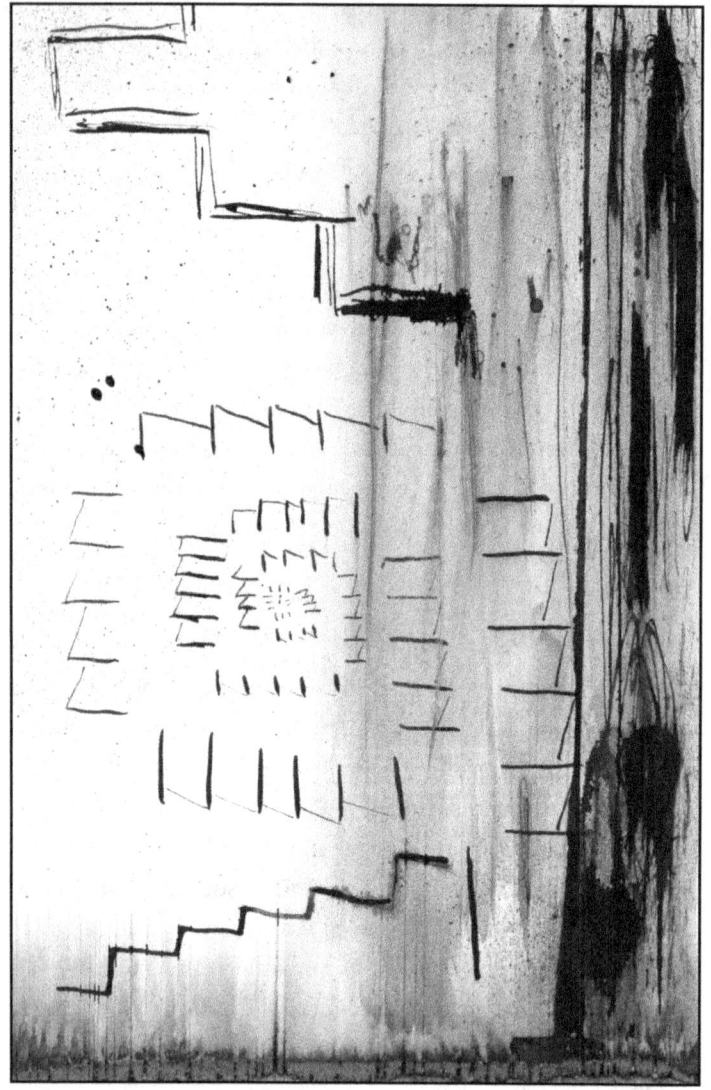

In their apartment, sitting with a pencil in his hand, scribbling another incoherent miniature stairway on the peeling paint across from his toilet, he wondered how long he'd had the hard wooden seat beneath him. Morris was unaware he'd walked home. He was past the point of pins and needles, so it had to have been longer than an hour. No more sound on the stairwell. Sometimes he'd get a lucky look at a big titter in a tight skirt through the peephole this time of night, but it was past that now, and the concentric stairwells in his drawing were starting to give him a headache. The blue blazer began to beckon from the closet. He wouldn't usually allow himself to put it on at night, because if she brought anyone with her he got scared and he didn't know how to make them go. So many souls in these splintered walls. He tried to mash the end of the pencil into a tiny knot in the wood, seeing if it would regain it's point, but only managing flaked graphite, descending to the floor in a rain of black dust. Try as he might, he couldn't push her off. Straightening, he fired his left then his right and he was up and off, lugging past his mattress, his toes doing their best to steady his hulking waver on the molding slats as he pushed on towards the far side of the bedroom and in towards her old Victorian dresser, he squeaked the top left drawer open first, digging in past the old photographs, the jottings from long decommissioned cruise ships, invite cards to the captain's table and a couple of love notes she kept bound with a postcard, Turkish stamps in the corner, naughty words he couldn't quite equate with her primness. Morris occasionally leafed through, but he was always terrified she was watching and would descend on him at any moment with the hairbrush.

He knew no matter how late it was, he'd better leave those alone, pulling back the dresser door, he noticed how neat her side looked next to his and he felt his chest constrict with his own pathetic inability to straighten his clothes and keep his shirts off the floor of their boudoir, he lifted out the navy cotton blazer, the stiff wooden hanger happy to greet his fingers, a creaking shudder welcomed him from the floor of the bedroom.

He could never mistake her footsteps.

Turning as the high pitched squeal started to hit his eardrums, he slid his hands into the sleeves and held them out to greet her, in the dim pixelation of blacks and browns beyond his bedroom doorway he could make out his mother's visage along with five more from the other side, his stomach started to tingle then turn.

Fear.

It was too late at night, he should have waited till morning, her face was peeling, she needed her makeup, and the other ones, what he could see of them inside the shadows, were shifting their heads side to side so rapidly the sockets of their eyes and mouths formed stacks of gyrating black gashes, as he continued to power his eyelids and point his face into the darkness he felt her slipping to where the shadows started to blur, they were everywhere now, all around, too many to count, a thousand ants emerged from his scalp and scuttled down his shoulders towards the floor, they were on him now and their faces were ghastly, even with the gyrations he could make out the dark slits of their eyes, the gaping blackened mouths, he felt his legs buckle under, slamming the floor boards, his breathing clenched as they started to drag him hungrily sideways across the floor.

He finally forced himself to snap his eyelids shut.

His only hope, as The Unwelcome filled his head with a thousand swirling stab wounds, if he could just hang on until the first light started to spill through the windows. Fear was compounded by mortification as his bowels let loose for the first time in days, he reached for his shins and pulled them in close so that as little as possible of his skin was exposed to the seething black clouds of hungry ghosts all around.

How could he have been so stupid? Had he really forgotten to turn on a single light, he knew she hated that. She couldn't stand traipsing around in the darkness, especially not when the others were about.

Morris recognized yet again he was not only a failure as a human being, but as a son as well.

Then it came back to him.

And The Unwelcome and their black cloud abated.

The glue and the rat.

Success.

CHAPTER TWENTY-THREE
THIS LITTLE TEARFUL PANTOMIME

D orian shoved a falafel into his mouth while walking down Stanton Street, distracted by a vibration in his pocket. He pulled out his phone to find a text from Althea:

CAN YOU PICK UP DINNER?

Looking down at his half eaten Turkish treat, Dorian rolled his eyes.

Slipping a box of rice noodles into his plastic basket in the Asian grocery down the block, Dorian's pocket vibrated again as he reached the Chinese ladies at the checkout isle. Another text from Althea:

MIDDLE EASTERN?

"Oh, give me a break," Dorian said out loud, as one of the ladies passed the noodle box under the barcode scanner.

As Dorian walked down the Essex Street sidewalk, a gorgeous young barista with a spiky Afro, hollered from her takeout window.

"Dorian!"

He turned to see her familiar cherubic face, and she reached out to gift him the iced espresso she'd just finished crushing for a customer.

Dorian smiled broadly.

His groceries hung on the back of his chair as Dorian and the barista laughed it up, snuggled in at a neighboring bar, sucking down enchiladas and sangria as she raved about the pair of cum goggles that the guitar player from the Deadly Condiments had given her a week before. Dorian didn't even know what cum goggles were, but he liked the sound of giving her a pair. An attractive male bartender-model leaned in towards their conversation, his eyes on Dorian.

"But it's really the bass player from the Deadly Condiments who makes me want to cream my panties," the barista was saying.

"Mine too," the hunky bartender articulated with a slight effeminate curl of the lips.

They all laughed. Dorian's phone vibrated on the bar as he ignored yet another communication from Althea. The screen lit up with the words:

I'M EATING.

In the barista's bedroom, four jugs of sangria later, Dorian found himself entwined between both the coffee maker and the bartender, underneath her combed cotton sheets.

Strewn on the floor, his cellphone was poking out from the pocket of his pants. He couldn't see the screen, but he was faintly aware of it vibrating through the denim, shifting a couple of millimeters across the barista's floorboards for a second nagging time. Nor for that matter could he see who's mouth was on his cock now, but in that moment, he was completely unconcerned with either unknowable variable. And in fact, the mystery made the sensation encircling the head of his prick that much more exciting.

If he had been able to read the text, it may have succeeded in communicating to him the depths of Althea's abandonment:

SUGAR? I SAVED YOU SOME FOOD.

Instead, he found himself wedged underneath the barista staring into her gorgeous green eyes, her body lilting up and down from the force of the brawny gentleman purifying the tail end of her bowels with his considerable girth, the lower extremities of which were slapping against Dorian's own nutsack with a force that almost hurt. He was faintly aware of the opening theme to Saturday Night Live seeping in from the living room as he came harder than he had in months.

Dorian woke at dawn wishing he could have slept longer. He pushed the Barista's arm off his chest and climbed over the bartender to reach for the floor. He picked up his phone to check the screen. Althea's last reach-out of the night had come in around three and now sat prominently on the screen:

YOU'RE A FUCKING ASSHOLE.

Dorian winced.

Brutally hungover back on Ludlow, Dorian climbed the sixth set of stairs in yesterday's clothes, feeling vaguely bashful as he tried to reconstruct the night and figure out just how gay he was. He wondered if he should add heteroflexible to his artist bio as he fumbled inside his pocket searching for his keys. His eyes closed into two tired slits as he shoved the key towards the lock.

But something was wrong. Hard as he pushed, the end of the key wouldn't enter. What the fuck?

He dipped his throbbing head. A small soiled envelope with the words 'HELLO' scrawled in pencil sat at his feet.

Was this a new key from the super? He wondered why on earth Ndusen would have changed his lock without any warning. Had Dorian gotten some notice he'd either ignored? And what was Ndusen doing, changing tenants locks in the middle of the night?

The questions were hurting his head. All he wanted was to lie down. So he bent and picked up the strange little mail dispatch.

"Hello," he replied back to it as he ripped open the envelope. At first he couldn't see anything, so he pressed the sides in. Dorian let out a yell. The envelope dropped to the floor.

A tiny decomposed face poked out from the torn sleeve. Dorian was dizzy, fighting the urge to puke all over his own front door as he kicked at the envelope and the minuscule skeleton of a dead rat slid out onto the welcome mat. A baby rat. No larger than a thumb.

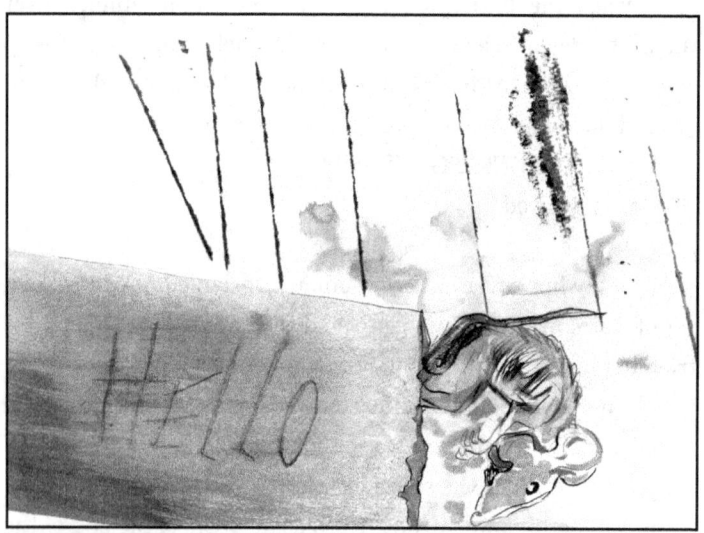

It was coming in waves now, but he had to stop the impending discharge at all costs. The idea of having to clean a pile of puke encircling dead baby rat seemed so much worse than what he faced now.

He put an arm out to stop the spins. The cold wall steadied him, and he took a deep inhalation. This wasn't really happening, he consoled himself. None of this was real. But the itty-bitty carcass was undeniably still there when he looked back at the floor.

Dorian spun round, suddenly feeling there must be eyes on him. That he was the butt of some macabre practical joke. Or perhaps this was a message. A death threat. But from who? Ivan the hoarder next door, watching from his closed-circuit camera? The kid from the pizza shop? Even Althea crossed his mind before he realized just how absurdly stupid he was being in his nauseated state.

He knew exactly who'd done it.

Looking like he'd just scraped himself off the sidewalk out front, Dorian ambled into A&D Dress Co. feeling rather out of place among the re-imagined vintage stylings in the candy-pink boutique. He walked towards Althea who sat behind her laptop at the counter. Helping a customer at the mirror, Dwyer gave Dorian a strange look; something between a friendly warning and a bitter spoonful of spite—he couldn't tell exactly which was winning out. Dorian did his best to ignore Dwyer and carry on towards the counter.

"There's something wrong with my front door. I can't seem to get my key in the damn lock. Can I go take a shower over at your place?"

"There's something wrong with your head." Althea said. She didn't even look up from her screen.

"Oh yeah, I'm sorry about dinner last night."

"Dinner? Oh, I'm over dinner. In fact, I'm over this entire charade."

Althea began to tear up.

"What are you talking about?"

"You and I both know this just isn't working out anymore."

"It's working fine."

"I think I'll come back," the flustered customer said as she handed a flared gypsy skirt back to Dwyer.

"The way you act. The things you do," Althea said.

"What did I do? I didn't do anything."

"I don't ask much of you, Dorian. I know we're little more than friends with benefits, but—"

"That's not true."

"Who you trying to kid?"

She was so flustered her Tennessee drawl was peaking through. So damn cute. It made him want her—her *and* her shower—all the more.

"Are you asking for space?" Dorian said, the words sounding a tad more desperate than he'd hoped.

"No. I'm asking you to remove yourself from my life."

Althea looked away as the tears began to flow. Dorian was genuinely shocked.

"OK, then. I'm gonna give you some time to think about this."

Dorian looked at Dwyer for help, who attempted empathy, adding a little gritting of teeth for effect, providing zero relief.

"So that's it then?" he said to Althea. "You're breaking up with me because I didn't respond to a couple of your texts? Am I getting in the way of your dancing plans with Razor Rozycki, and this little tearful pantomime is just an inconvenient hurdle you feel you have to hop over first? Be my guest. I don't give a shit who you see. I'm a modern new-age guy. I get it."

Perhaps it was a defense mechanism, but his mind had already started to wonder elsewhere anyway. For some reason the sight of Althea's tears evoked that very first time he'd made a girl cry in his bed. Freshman year at college. Halloween. Her name started with an "L". She was all slutted up in a little devil's costume, with sparkly red horns poking out of a headband, and somehow they'd lost all the other Star Wars characters and goblins, and found themselves alone sharing a pitcher of cheap draft, talking about her painfully recent breakup. An hour later they'd ditched the off-campus pub for his tiny dorm-room bed. A couple of thrusts, and that's when the waterworks broke. The timing couldn't have been worse. Why couldn't she have cried it out at the bar? Her tears tarnishing a perfectly good sexy Halloween costume for the rest of Dorian's life. Tears that hadn't even been for him, but for the last jackass. Her high school sweetheart. Try as he might, Dorian couldn't remember the last time a girl had shed any genuine tears for him.

And that's when it hit: what he felt for Althea really could be called something genuine. Althea was the closest Dorian had ever come to the thought of popping out a litter of Dorian juniors. But, he knew he'd never be able to kick the tight-muscled hot-flesh machines that walked past his front door every night by the dozen. Who were all too happy to have a bonafide (if increasingly stale) art star helping them dodge the rats and macho rabble rousers that barely figure out how to fondle their own cock, let alone please a young woman approaching her sexual prime. No, it was just too easy down here, where a different stranger could be straddling you seven nights a week with just five simple words at the pool table: "wanna get out of here...?"

Yes he did.

The tears were really beginning to roll down Althea's puffy, and somehow strangely renewed cheeks now, making her look less like a woman on the cusp of middle age and more like a pubescent school girl, his reflection glinting in each tiny drop of brine. He likened the sensation he was having now to a bad hit of ecstasy. This breaking up crap was never part of the male/female experience he particularly relished, but with Althea it was nails on the chalkboard.

"Look..." he started.

But he knew when things got this broken, they rarely bounced back, beyond an ill advised "for old time's sake" fuck.

And now Althea just stared at him through her deep heartfelt sadness.

He couldn't take it. He pivoted and exited the store.

As he sat at his kitchen table watching Ndusen rip out his deadbolt, despite his best efforts, he couldn't seem to stop his memory banks from serving a smorgasbord of lost days with Althea—mostly of a sexual nature, like the dirty choose-your-own-adventure stories she used to tell him while he pulled on it, or the fact that she could come from anal sex. But cloying sappy things as well. Pizza and streaming in bed on Sunday mornings. A Bear Mountain road trip upstate to a friend's cabin. Heading to Red Hook for key lime pie, but staying for all-night drag queen karaoke at the Hope & Anchor. He had to do something to put an end to this agonizing tribute, get his mind somewhere else—anywhere else—before he crawled into a ball on the kitchen floor and died.

"Hey Ndusen."

Ndusen removed one of the deadbolt screws resting in his mouth.

"Yes?"

"I don't want to interrupt you."

Such a stupid thing to say, considering he already had.

"What is it?"

"Well, maybe it's none of my business—"

Ndusen looked up at him.

"But I wanted to know," Dorian said, "if you ever heard anything about what happened to Sal Agnelli?"

Ndusen fingered the unopened lock housing, still encased in plastic on the floor.

"I was never told anything by the police, if that is what you are asking?"

"Oh, yeah I guess. They didn't tell you anything?"

Dorian almost felt bad pressing the issue with Ndusen, as if he was in some way insinuating that Ndsuen had something to do with the disappearance. But it was either that or let the parade of sickeningly sweet reveries creep back down mental main street.

"You're the one who made the report right?"

"Yes."

"Why?"

"Because Mr. Agnelli went missing. His apartment was not touched. But also... he was not there. For many weeks."

"And you knew something was wrong? That maybe somebody'd done something to him?"

Ndusen cracked open the plastic, pulling out the new deadbolt. He began fitting it into the empty circle in the wood. He didn't say anything for a long time. Dorian wasn't sure if this was because he was concentrating on the work, or carefully measuring his response. Satisfied with the lock's position, Ndusen picked up his screwdriver to begin fastening it into place.

"Did somebody do something to old Sal, Ndusen?" Dorian asked again.

"I felt that might be. Yes." Ndusen finally said. "So I brought the matter to the police."

CHAPTER TWENTY-FOUR
LOOSEN THINGS UP A LITTLE

A small set stood in the center of the large white cyclorama of Studio D, Fast Ashley's largest at thirty two hundred square feet. Three breakaway walls created a faux bathroom stall littered with graffiti, a prop toilet planted in the center. Inside the set walls, two rail-thin teenage models shared the lap of their tattooed male counterpart.

Mioko snapped photographs with a pricey Hasselblad, surrounded by Jake's poached first and second assistants, in a surreal reconstruction of a candid true life moment that seemed now to belong to someone else's autobiography. A sterile facsimile of the bathroom at Mars Bar; the debauched booze-hole and junkie hideout that for years had anchored the island's numbered street grid at the corner of First and First. A neighborhood institution, the motto "babysitting for drunks," had been proudly painted beside the door till a young graffiti artist tried to tag his handle over the slogan and got both his ankles curbed for his efforts by a couple of lit up regulars. Where, beginning at 22, Mioko had come of age tending bar and shooting smack for five formative years.

Her youth evaporating at a dive equally venerated and abhorred, but which no longer even existed, having been long since bulldozed by the unstoppable force of Downtown Manhattan gentrification. Not to mention her original subjects. At least one of the authentic members of the commode tryst, they were now spending tens of thousands of dollars recreating, the only one whose whereabouts Mioko had any certainty of had OD'ed on her twenty third birthday on the second floor of a Clinton Street flop house, that was now a luxury flat above a gourmet brunch destination. It all seemed somehow sacrilegious to dig into the territory of her own artistic work, her dreamscapes, and in this particular case, her lingering nightmares, to sell overpriced jeans to the world's über-entitled youth.

Mioko tried her best to table the irony that her "big break" was now forcing her to desecrate her own past. Instead she pushed herself to just keep clicking away at the Hasselblad's shutter that in turn triggered the strobes—which thankfully from her close proximity emitted such a blinding burst that they more or less obliterated any room for deep introspection.

But despite her best efforts to just keep trudging forward and get through the day, she was becoming increasingly aware that the infamous and visionary Romen Gold was starting to look dissatisfied. Sneering at the monitor with his underlings, a black cloud was gathering above the art director and the rest of the agency conclave.

"This is too slick." Romen yelled from thirty feet away, "We want more raw, Mioko. That's why you're here. More energy! I wanna smell the sweat. Let's do this already."

Mioko put down the camera and looked over at the agency folks. No help there. So she turned to her client in earnest, "Romen, just tell me exactly what you want. And I'll do it."

Romen glided over to Mioko, grabbing her by the arm and yanking her away from the set.

"I'm sure I can give you what you're looking for—"

"Come with me a second," Romen interrupted.

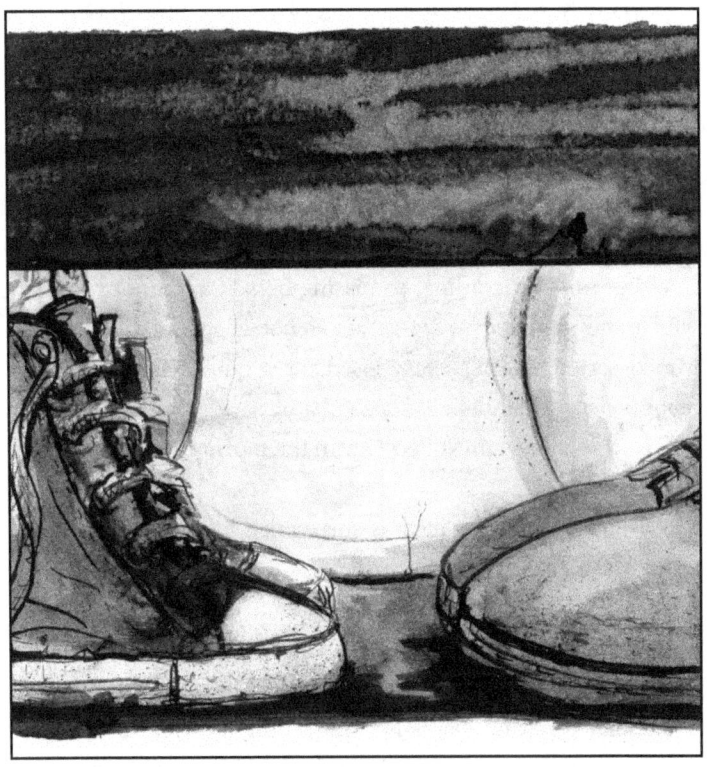

She quickly found herself in the studio's real commode pressed up against the wall to avoid contact with her client, who was now pouring out a long line of white powder from a vial onto the tank of the porcelain toilet.

"We just need to loosen things up a bit."

Romen started mincing up the powder with an AMEX Black Card and cutting it into fat lines. Mioko was visibly shaken, but Romen ignored her misgivings and snorted back a line, then smiled at her seductively, handing her a rolled bill.

"Pour vous," he said sweetly, but it was clear he was getting impatient. "Come on, Honey. I've seen your work. Don't play Suzy Strait-lace with me."

Coke had never been her drug of choice. She'd had a hard time telling the difference between a couple of lines and a double shot of espresso. Still, it had been such a long time since she'd ingested anything stronger than ibuprofen, her heart started throbbing out of rhythm. She could feel the palms of her hands getting sticky, and an unreasonably strong urge to urinate was starting to get the better of her. So it was quickly coming down to either nostriling a line, or pissing herself in front of Romen, which she assumed was a rather major client relations no-no. Mioko scrunched her eyes closed for a quick moment, before leaning over and inhaling a noseful.

"Nothing like a line of ecstacy in the morning to clear out the creative cobwebs."

"What?" Mioko croaked as she craned back towards him. "I thought it was coke."

"Coke? Blecch, no thanks."

Mioko's world was already starting to look muddled. With a huge smile, Romen grabbed Mioko's neck, she recoiled in disgust as he leaned in and kisses her full on the lips. Her lips tingled peculiarly, but the entire rest of her body shivered with repulsion.

"Let's get back in there and sell some fucking clothes, shall we?"

Mioko leaned into the stall, sweaty and euphoric, whispering seductively to the models as they kissed for her camera.

"...that's it... but open your mouths more..." she heard herself saying.

Romen, was now in a far brighter mood, standing a little too close to his team around the monitors. His hand was draped over a lowly student intern from the agency phalanx, her freckled face unsure how to reckon with the uninvited attention.

"Yes! Just like that."

Mioko turned back to her first assistant, her eyes hazy with narcotic.

"Give me a little more fill."

The assistant watched Mioko's strange demeanor closely as he reached for the light.

"Sure," he said as he started to adjust the strobe, but was startled when she pulled her trigger, popping the lamp right in his eyes.

Blinded, he looked back at Mioko who continued to click away, inches from the models' faces. The first assistant's vision was still burnt out in the middle, but he thought he saw the male model reaching out and touching Mioko's thigh. And when his vision finally did clear, he was astonished to find that it wasn't just a hallucination. Then he saw Mioko look down at the hand, nestled next to her crotch, but to his great surprise, for a girl who froze up when you tried to give her a platonic hug, she made no effort to move the hand away.

Mioko walked down the lively Rivington sidewalk.

A Fujianese teenager held a lighter to the fuse of an Outer Space Jet firework, while his two little friends, perhaps younger brothers, watched in nervous anticipation. The fuse started to sparkle and the teenager tossed the incendiary package underneath a nearby SUV. The firework slammed wildly between the pavement and the vehicle's undercarriage. The tourist family inside scurried like confused rats, shrieking in fright as their car exploded with a metallic cacophony. The teenagers laughed hysterically at their tourist prey. Mioko watched in baffled wonder.

Peeling her eyes away, she crosses towards *Machine City* Bar. On a night when it was this packed, Mioko would typically have avoided the bar like a plague, but in the lingering remains of her altered state, she couldn't think of a place she'd rather be. Pushing open the door, Nouvelle Vague's "Too Drunk to Fuck" blared from the bar's speakers. Mioko navigated through the packed crowd.

Making out with a ninety-five pound waif at the bar, Dorian immediately noticed Mioko. Pulling his lips away, the waif's head swirled downwards in free-fall.

"Hey! Mioko."

Mioko heard the voice, but looked confused.

"What's up?" Dorian said in a friendly tone.

Mioko stopped. The drunken waif was instantly jealous, giving her suitor an indignant look of "who's this and why do we care?"

Dorian quietly shushed the waif, the way you'd pacify a colicky child. His keen eyes were on Mioko.

"Did you think about my offer?"

Mioko looked at him groggily. What had he offered her? Money for drugs was all she could summon.

"Offer?" she said dreamily, but then the strange request came back to her, "Oh, right. To paint me?"

Played out, the waif put her head down on the table. The DJ cranked some obscure post-punk new wave at an unreasonably loud volume.

"It'll just take an afternoon," she thought she heard him say. He was slurring a little, and Mioko had to lean in to hear him over the booze-fueled dissonance. She made out the words: painless... some tunes... polite conversation... And finally a whole sentence: you just have to sit still for a little while. Mioko contemplated the idea. She didn't entirely trust Dorian, but then again, she didn't really trust anybody. It might be nice to see herself hanging on the wall of a gallery someday. She seemed to recall that he'd been kind of a big deal at some point, or at least on the verge. Not that she really gave a shit about any of that. Or did she just pretend not to?

"You know what?" she said. "Sure."

Perhaps because he was on his seventh Stoli and soda, or maybe just because he was always a little inelegant when things went his way, Dorian's face lit up in a strange grimace, which Mioko took to mean he was excited.

"Amazing. Fantastic. Wait, for real?"

"I think so."

The song was thankfully reaching its sputtering extro, and now the sound of the waif moaning softly on the surface of the bar became audible.

Mioko pointed to her, "Your friend."

But Dorian couldn't take his eyes off Mioko.

"She's fine."

Mioko was past caring, "Alright. I'll catch you later."

"Indeed."

Mioko made her way towards the bar, pleased to catch sight of a familiar face. Darlene looked pleased to see her too, "Hey ya! How you doing?"

"Good, actually."

And she was. For the first time in a while.

"That's great!" Darlene yelled over the thumping bass.

"I got a gig. A shoot of my own. For a big client."

"Holy shit. Who?"

"Lamerica."

Darlene curled her bottom lip, impressed.

"I know," Mioko said.

"I'd offer to buy you a drink, but—" Darlene smiled self-consciously. "You want a seltzer?"

Mioko looked at the tightly packed rows of bottles behind Darlene.

"You know what, fuck it. Pour me a Jameson's."

"Really?"

"Why not. I was a junkie, not an alcoholic. Besides," Mioko shouted, "it'll take the edge off the ecstasy!"

Darlene laughed, and Mioko knew it might be best to just let it be a joke. The last thing she needed was word getting back to Trey that she was rolling —who since they'd broken up had risen to a strict AA convert and petty weed kingpin/bar manager at the same time. Besides it wasn't the Nineties. The chances of more ecstasy hits finding their way into her stratosphere seemed slim at best.

"Umm... OK, then." Darlene said hesitantly as she reached behind her and doused a glass with a stiff brown pour. Mioko grabbed up the drink and took a hearty swig.

"Yeah, I kind of poached the client from my boss, Jake. But, the hell with it, right?"

Darlene nodded, awkward but trying to stay enthused. Other customers started to compete for Darlene's attention. Mioko got distracted by the gaze of a tall stranger jamming up to the bar beside her, but she was snapped back to reality by Darlene's words, "Trey said he'd be back in a bit, but I'm not sure when, or even if that's actually gonna happen tonight."

Mioko downed the rest of the whiskey and looked around at the semi-familiar faces, ready for another.

"I'll tell him to call you if you don't wanna stand round here with all these douches rubbing up against you."

Mioko wiped the booze from her lips.

"OK."

But Mioko didn't move. She just stood there mashed up against the bar stools, melting into the warm bodies all around her. Her mind was traveling elsewhere. And then she saw in the window, her stalker's beedy eyes filled with malice. Her chest stopped moving, but then Rube was gone.

CHAPTER TWENTY-FIVE
THE AVALANCHE

Dorian looked down the bar searching, but through a trick of prospective, he wasn't able to spot Mioko squeezed in among the crowd. His date snoozing on the table, Dorian made his way to the door.

He kicked a beer bottle out of his way as he moved past an inebriated young scenester holding up his girlfriend's hair as she wretched red wine into the gutter. There was something strangely intimate about their immodest display and Dorian was momentarily transfixed, but he kept walking.

Dorian climbed the stairs solo, hung in a melancholic trance. He'd gotten so sick of sitting at home wondering why he wasn't able to make himself cry over Althea, that a casual tinder had seemed like the best possible alternative. But the company had been so unbearably lame, he hadn't even managed to bring himself to rouse the girl and drag her home to his bed. At one time crying had been as easy for Dorian as laughing. In his twenties anything could be misconstrued as the deepest of heartbreaks. There had even been a strange bout of tears that had poured from his cheeks after he'd slumped down pathetically to the curb when he'd discovered an unexpected closing of a favorite Chinese restaurant. But somewhere along the line his tear ducts had turned to concrete.

Reaching his door, he pulled out a shiny key and inserted it into his new front door lock. The adjacent door of apartment 22 opened a crack. Ivan's timid face appeared in the exposed fissure, breaking the seal on his place perhaps for the first time in a week. The fresh air instantly equalized within his apartment, so that their shared hallway filled with a musty fetor.

"Dorian," Ivan whispered.

"Oh, hey Ivan."

Ivan pushed the door open another inch.

"Got a new lock, huh? That bastard downstairs really fucked the last one up good, didn't he?"

Dorian turned around to face his neighbor. "You saw him?"

"I see everything."

Dorian was unsettled by the fanciful statement.

Ivan motioned to the closed circuit camera above his door.

"Oh, right."

"You wanna see something?" Ivan asked.

Dorian hesitated. See something, as in go inside Ivan's apartment and see something?

Dorian had always been leery of his neighbor across the hall, unable to quite figure out Ivan's particular brand of damage. Until the morning last September when he'd been leaving his apartment, saying goodbye to Althea who'd been luxuriating in his bathtub, when he'd heard a discordant squeaky voice coming through Ivan's door; a mouse billowing through a loudspeaker a mile away. Trying to get a handle on the situation, Dorian had finally yelled back through the thick metal door, and had just barely been able make out the words "Help me. I'm stuck."

Stuck in crazy land.

"Call the police, I'm stuck."

Dorian had dialed 9-1-1, playing along with the crazy man next door. During the half hour wait for the fuzz, Dorian had done his best to keep his distant high-pitched neighbor talking. When the cops had finally shown up, a heavy-set Dominican who clearly had morning wood for Dorian's southern bedfellow, had spent thirty minutes trying to kick Ivan's door down while Dorian and Althea watched. Ivan's voice had been getting even fainter, and the words that were still exuding were sounding even less coherent.

Another half hour and a set of emergency services unit cops had shown up—the kind that cut people out of their cars, or dig victims out of rubble. They'd immediately gone to work with "the Rabbit", a pump action jaws of life that they clamped into the corner of Ivan's door, and with a series of pressurized pops, had managed to rip the metal from it's hinges. This too, had taken an unbearably long time, and with a dozen FDNY, NYPD, and ESU responders in the hallway, it had been next to impossible by this point to hear Ivan's squeaky far off voice anymore at all—leading the cops to speculate aloud if they were still trying to rescue a member of the living. Finally, the last hinge had blown, and suddenly the Hoover dam had broken. Ivan's door had surfed out on a massive wave of debris flowing through the open fissure, crossing the tiny hall into Dorian's apartment. After the avalanche, and the god-awful smell, they found a human arm sticking out from the bottom of a twelve-foot mountain of soiled miscellany: newspapers, videotapes, magazines, tools, cardboard boxes, plastic bags. *So many plastic bags.* The squeaky voice had been connected to that hand, and as the emergency services guys

had dug, they finally managed to uncover a face. Then a torso. And at long last a set of legs.

They'd pulled Ivan out from his mountain of hoarded crap and began to cart him off. In an adrenalized state of unfamiliar goodwill, Dorian had asked his ailing neighbor if there was anything he needed, anyone Dorian should get in touch with to come and see him at the hospital. Ivan had whispered breathlessly into Dorian's ear, words he could still perfectly remember: "Just make sure nobody touches any of my stuff."

Ivan pulled his ill-fitting year-old door open another inch, "Come on in, I won't bite."

"Um, sure," Dorian said, relenting.

Ivan closed the door and Dorian contemplated making a run for it while his neighbor undid the chain inside. Ivan finally opened his door wide enough for Dorian to see the dank inner chamber of his abode.

Dorian awkwardly walked inside and peered around at the house-broken towers of magazines, the blocked rear windows, the shabby old furniture buried under ancient piles of flotsam and jetsam; the newspapers, the VHS tapes, and the tamed, but still seemingly infinite assortment of plastic bags. Six months of lifting his unhinged door in and out of place, of sleeping in the tiny trench by the entryway that he'd almost died in, of scampering up to the top of his mountain and dragging thirty pound bundles of yellowed newsprint down the stairs at all hours of the day and night, and Ivan had eventually made some progress.

"Tea?"

The thought of consuming anything bourn of that place made Dorian queazy.

"No thanks."

Ivan sat down at his computer, flipping on the ancient PC. On the screen was a staticky black and white overhead video image of the hallway. Dorian momentarily considered working Ivan into his new project somehow, the old hoarder and his screwy habitation was nothing if not interesting, and certainly a fixture of the expiring neighborhood, but Dorian quickly pushed the notion away. He was too disgusted with the thought of standing there for more than a couple minutes, let alone bringing in an easel and trying to paint the guy.

"Evidence as a deterrent," Ivan said. "Ever since that nutcase Morris slashed my bike tires and threatened me with a box cutter few years ago. He knows that if he ever tries anything, even comes to my door and thinks about it—I've got evidence."

Ivan shuffled through footage, multiple instances of Morris slamming his fists on Dorian's front door. Wandering the hallway. Staring menacingly at the camera.

"It's a closed circuit," he continued. "Motion sensitive. Been recording this hallway half a decade..."

Dorian nodded, but he wasn't listening anymore. He'd had enough of Ivan's extraneous narration and he was starting to feel boxed in. Living in the tenement had its charms. Not just the proximity to the fresh faced talent cramming the sidewalks downstairs, but also the isolation tank that his apartment provided, high enough above the streets to block out the incessant honking, yelling and cat calls at all hours of the day and night. It was the perfect combination of exposure and withdrawal. Yet key to that cocktail was keeping his distance from the cyclically twisted inner narratives of the property's Ivan Hershbers.

"You said you caught Morris destroying my lock?" Dorian interrupted.

Ivan turned back to him, keenly aware of Dorian's agitation. Pivoting to the computer, he clicked a file on the desktop labeled Dorian. Erik Satie's "Gnossiennes Number 1" began to play. The empty hallway appeared again. Slowly two figures emerge down the hall. Dorian and a young woman. They entered Dorian's apartment, a dissolve showed them leaving. Another woman, another night. And then another. An endless stream of female strangers walking the halls, some escorted by Dorian. Most leaving his apartment alone.

Dorian watched, his face slowly melting.

"Every choice we make," Ivan said, as the blown-out black and white night visits continued, "leads us to become the person we may or may not want to be."

The haunting music slowed.

"You cut this together? Dude, fuck you! This is a complete invasion of my goddamn privacy."

Ivan looked back at him, surprised.

"I thought this might be of interest to you."

"Super creepy, Ivan," he said grimacing. "Fuck man," he added, at a loss.

Dorian turned to leave.

"I see that damn camera moving with me again, I'm gonna snap it off."

Crossing the hall, Dorian slammed his own door behind him, leaning up against it.

His face started to crumple, but still no tears. He swallowed hard as the images continued to sink in.

Some payback. After he'd snatched Ivan from the crushing weight of his own demise. That was the last time Dorian was gonna save anybody's life.

CHAPTER TWENTY-SIX
WHAT WOULD THE POLICE DO?

own on Stanton, Ndusen carried two immense bags of garbage along the sidewalk, delirious with fatigue. He opened his eyes just wide enough to see what he took to be a pair of Hispanic street thugs, shoving and yelling in frustration at three black teenagers on the corner of Eldridge.

Ndusen knew better than to get himself involved in the heated argument, heaving the bags of garbage into a dumpster, he turned to make his way back home.

A gunshot, followed by two more flicked Ndusen's eyes wide open. He spun back in the direction of the sound, catching sight of the two Hispanic kids sprinting across the street, disappearing down Eldridge.

Ndusen lay in his bed, next to Kondwani. His eyes wide, rife with insomnia. He rubbed his stomach in a clockwise direction, hoping to dislodge the spasm that he could feel spreading through the mucous membranes in his gastrointestinal tract. He had witnessed another crime, and felt entirely powerless to do anything about it, knowing that any kind of action might endanger his family. He even felt he had seen one of those Hispanic kids before, but he was not sure where. Then it dawned on him. He pulled back the sheets and made his way out past his kin, and into the hall.

Pulling open the door to the inner vestibule, the resemblance was undeniable.

'WARNING. This is Rube Carbia and he is stalking me...'

But who could be sure? He had a hard time telling Hispanics apart, in the same way he did white people. He could easily find himself accusing an innocent young man of murder. And even if it was him, what would the police do? A paltry investigation, and then? For all he knew this Rube was working for a gang. A gang that would not think twice to snuff out an immigrant super and his family.

Besides, he had not seen anyone hit by the bullets, he reminded himself of this as he replaced his slippers by the side of the bed and lay back down. He would wait and see. Perhaps there might be something about the incident in the morning newspaper. Perhaps another witness had already come forward.

As the hours of the night dwindled, Ndusen wasn't the only tenant who was still awake. Mioko stood in her darkroom six floors above, sipping from a highball and working the enlarger. Ignoring the throbbing in her heels, she sucked on an ice cube as she watched the sultry shots from the Lamerica shoot appear in the stop bath.

Pouring herself another glass, she appraised the finished prints hanging on the line next to the spare shots of Rube. She wasn't exactly proud of her Lamerica work, but it was certainly magazine quality. And looking at the images now, they were undeniably evoking a familiar—yet somehow alien—feeling. An intangible emotion set apart from the lingering MDMA in her system; besides she'd adequately countered the remaining effects of the drugs with liquor.

No, there was something about the images themselves. Something primal.

They turned her on.

Mioko's phone alarm stung the air next to her face. The smell of rubber and chemicals filled her nostrils, her cheek pressed against the velour plastic coating of her inflatable mattress. She opened her eyes to find the red safety light still glowing on the ceiling above. It could have been any time of day or night. Her head felt like she'd gone days without hydration, emerging from the Sahara. She found her footing and leaned in to the slop sink. Under the tap she moved to gulp thirstily, but nothing flowed out.

As she opened her darkroom door and crossed to her apartment, her eyes went bleary from the sunlit hall. She couldn't wait to have her back up against the cold porcelain tub, to douse herself with her handheld shower-head, tip her head back to allow the scalding water to fill her parched mouth. But instead

Mioko stood next to the kitchen bathtub wrenching the spouts in all directions, the faucet sputtering and hissing, but not a drop fell.

"Motherfucker," she said aloud.

In the ground floor hallway, she stood in her pajamas outside Ndusen's apartment, knocking on the door.

Alile finally answered.

"Is your father home?" Mioko asked.

She could see him in the background looking absorbed as he flipped through the morning's copy of the New York Post. He certainly didn't look like he'd gone without a shower.

Back upstairs, Ndusen was on her floor, his hands busy inside the sink cabinet.

Mioko was pacing to try and calm herself.

"Four days it's been off," she said. "Across the hall too. I figured the whole building was out."

Ndusen looked up at her, "I am so sorry."

Finishing the job quicker than she could have imagined, Ndusen sat up.

"Were you guys fixing something? What?" she said.

"Yes, well... what ended up transpiring is not what I was initially told by Mr. Axlerod."

"This is ridiculous. I'm two hours late for work."

"I am truly sorry."

Mioko shook her head, thoroughly fed up.

"And what about this place?" she asked. "I'm doing what I can to fix it up myself in my off hours. But it still reeks of smoke."

"I have asked Mr. Axlerod..." he said.

Mioko's leg vibrated. She was on the verge of tears.

Ndusen looked at Mioko's scouring brush and bucket. The leftovers from her efforts to scrub the floor. Her abandoned attempts to paper the charred walls.

"Let us, for this one time, not wait for Mr. Axlerod. I have plenty of eggshell in the basement. Today I will strip and paint your living room."

He smiled at her warmly. Mioko breathed through her nose, her lips pulled tight. She nodded slowly at him, fighting back the tears.

"Thank you."

"Of course."

Something disgusting and wet swiped Mioko's face, as she lay crashed-out on the white leather couch of Jake's studio. Standing above her with his pug on a leash, Jake's hands were full of his own dry cleaning.

"This. Just. Will. Not. Do."

Mioko peered up at her boss.

"You were supposed to pick Strudel up from my loft an hour and a half ago. He pissed himself on the Eames chair. *Not to mention the dry cleaning.*"

"Sorry."

Jake rolled his eyes.

"Sorry? Keep your shit together, Mioko."

Jake dumped the dry cleaning on top of her on his way to his desk. She sat up and stretched her shoulders back, closing her eyes for another quick instant, as Strudel started to soak her socks in canine saliva.

No matter what horribleness Jake threw at her today, it wouldn't mean a thing, because tonight she would be sleeping in her own bed.

CHAPTER TWENTY-SEVEN
FLATLINED

Dorian lay on his back, his head hanging off the side of the loft frame. He stared across at an untouched canvas looming large in the center of his living room. Upside down the workspace looked even more depressing; a pathetic maelstrom of crap strewn just about everywhere. He could picture each step down from the loft, every muscle that would have to come into play in order for him to get to work. Instead, he shut his eyes and hoped that the solace of another snooze might save him.

Still in his bathrobe by late afternoon, Dorian sat alone at his table pouring Rice Krispies into an archaic carton of chocolate ice cream. As he crunched down on the brown ice crystals and cereal, a shooting pain shot from his molar.

Just what he needed, a dental bill to add to his stack of unpaid debts.

Finally ready to face the virgin canvas, he squeezed out multiple daubs of oil, but then got distracted by a picture on a nearby shelf of him and Althea at one of his early gallery shows. He leaned and pressed his palette knife against the glass front of the frame, covering her face with yellow pigment.

Dorian stood before a large blank canvas, staring blankly, palette knife in hand. Who was he kidding? He didn't even have a show. And everything he'd ever made, everything he'd struggled so hard to create was long since forgotten. Inconsequential. He was washed up before he'd barely even made it out of the gate. The Dorian Teasdale market had flatlined. He'd signed his own Do Not Resuscitate order with a stream of pathetic efforts that amounted solely to thousands of dollars in wasted pigment. He slumped back on the couch, tossing his palette knife onto the paint-splattered coffee table. The evening light outside his window slowly faded as Dorian continued to wonder just exactly what the hell he thought he was doing with his life.

The apartment was gloomy now. At some point he'd slid off the couch and now sat cross-legged on the floor in silence, still in his bathrobe.

His droopy eyes were focused on something across the room.

The giant cockroach slowly made it's way across the floor towards Dorian.

Dorian quietly spoke to the insect.

"Just you and me, now, Frank."

Dorian picked a Rice Krispie off the floor and held it out between his fingers, trying to feed the little critter, but even the lowly insect kept its distance.

CHAPTER TWENTY-EIGHT
APPEAL TO REASON

Moshe Axlerod entered the foyer of his Ludlow tenement surprised to see a familiar face pasted to the inner door. "This is Rube Carbia and he is stalking me." It had the ring of a job well done. Axlerod smiled as he ripped the image and note off the glass.

Walking around back, Axlerod strolled into the rear courtyard of his building, shocked to find Ndusen and his family working a vibrant vegetable garden. Seeing his boss, Ndusen's solar plexus instantly seized up.

"Jesus Christ," Axlerod said. "This what you spend your time on? The Axlerod family paying your bills so you can fucking garden all day?"

Ndusen put down his shovel and walked towards Axlerod. This was not how he pictured sharing the news of his reimagined space. He had planned on inviting the elder Axlerod, Mr. Cyrus, over for a family dinner at his table and revealing the source of their rich nourishment with an after-supper tour of the garden. How could any earthly man resist his family's creative reversal of what was, after all, a useless garbage heap? Still, Ndusen knew there was an exception to every rule, and by the looks of it, the younger Axlerod was far from won over.

"My guy checked on 9 and 10 yesterday. I tell you I want the water shut off in an apartment, it stays off till my man gets there. I got enough to friggin' deal with here."

Ndusen decided that it was time to try and appeal to reason, "Four days she had no water—"

"Shit doesn't start getting done 'round here the way I'm asking, Ndusen, I'm gonna need to see a rent check. My father, the sentimentalist, he had a real thing for your situation. The Malawian in exile, and all that charming shit. Me, I don't give two turds about your exotic little history. I just want the job done."

"But this aggressive pushing out of tenants—"

"This ain't even up for discussion. What're you gonna do, move? Where you gonna put your frigging family? In refrigerator boxes with the rats?"

Ndusen stood as upright as he could. Axlerod peered around the garden.

"This all has to go. Who said you could do this?"

"Mr. Axlerod, this was a garbage deposit."

"No, no, no. Enough. This's the modern world, Ndusen. You gotta drop your little tribal mentality. Technology, my friend. Advancement. High finance. That's what drives this country. We're gonna clean this space up, but not like this. Next thing I know you're gonna have a market out here selling goat feet or what-have-you. Go to the friggen' grocery store, you need a zucchini."

Ndusen nodded, his lungs clamping in around his organs.

"I come back here, next time. I don't wanna see any of this crap."

"Yes, sir."

Axlerod took a last scan of the garden, with a little snicker.

"Some nerve," he said glancing at his watch. "Alright, let's do this."

Ndusen followed his employer out of the courtyard.

On the second floor, Axlerod walked through an empty apartment, followed by Ndusen, who scribbled notes into a small pad. The telephone was tolerable, but actually having to be in the same room as Axlerod was another story. Ndsuen remembered Mr. Cyrus telling him once of how he could see anger the first time he looked into his child, "his little Moshe's face," the day that he was born. At the time Ndusen did wonder if perhaps that had colored the way Mr. Cyrus had treated his son, always expecting anger before it had even materialized, which had in turn effected the person that Moshe eventually became. In any event, it wasn't so much anger, but an unswerving detachment that defined Moshe Axlerod now—and served to throw Ndusen entirely off balance.

"All these walls primed and repainted," Axlerod was saying about apartment #7. He pointed to the bathtub, sitting prominently next to the sink in the middle of the dining area. "Bathtub's gone. We're gonna put a glass shower stall and a sink in the ensuite." Pausing at the refrigerator, he opened the door. He turned to Ndusen, "This is relatively new, right?"

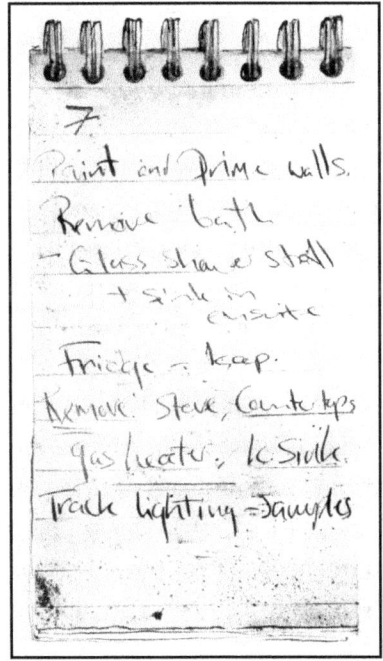

"Her old refrigerator stopped to function two years ago, I believe."

Satisfied, Axlerod shut the fridge.

"Keep it."

He looked from one end of the ancient room to the other.

"Everything else: stove, counter tops, gas heater, kitchen sink. That's all gotta go."

Ndusen scribbled quickly in his pad. Axlerod pointed to the ceiling.

"And we're gonna do track lighting throughout. You show me samples."

Ndusen scribbled and nodded.

Axlerod stopped pacing. He appraised Ndusen with his eyes.

"Think you can handle this, Ndusen?"

"Yes, Mr. Axlerod."

Hours Rube had spent deliberating over whether or not to surrender his piece to the East River, now that the pistol had the potential to link him to what he considered a highly justifiable homicide.

Not that he was complaining. He liked daydreaming about that shit. Just thinking about his chump-extinguisher finally being put to some good use testified to the fact that Rube was now one more notch towards a badass motherfucker. But at some point a decision had had to be made. He'd told Chubby D to keep his flabby lips sealed about the hostilities with the three black kids on Eldridge. But he couldn't be entirely sure that cocksucker wouldn't down a pair a forties and start blabbing to some ho to try and get some. So, late in the afternoon, Rube had finally taken out a slick insurance policy. Ingenious. He'd thoroughly wiped down his 9 mil wearing a fresh pair of sanitary gloves (his dago wop *Rosarita's* bosses would have been so proud to see him wearing them for once), then he'd paid Deucey a nice visit down at his ma's nasty-pad.

They'd smoked some vape. Then when Deuce had gone off to take his obligatory post smoke shit—that kid was beyond predictable—Rube had wiped the piece with a pair of Deuce's grubby boxer-briefs (for the nutsack DNA) then taped his Glock 19 'The All-Round Talent,' to the back of Deuce's headboard, behind that fool's stank-ass bed. That way, if 5 – 0 ever dropped Rube's door, he could tell NY's finest he hadn't even been at the scene that night, and if they started up on some "we heard otherwise" *mierda* whispered to them from a cornrow wearing chub chump, he could say, "Oh yeah? Well guess what Mr. Dumb Ass Police, cornrows be the one pulled the damn trigger, and I know exactly where he keeps his chalk."

Another plus, if he was ever really in a jam, he'd still have his burner stashed just down the lane for his own use. Keep the heat, beat the sheet. Genius.

Something bout the suave reversal reminded Rube of the time they were kids and D got himself a fresh pair of Taekwondo sparring gloves for Christmas, before Deuce's ma succumbed to the gin bottle full-force, pickling her liver day and night. Dropping by that afternoon, Rube had wanted to have himself a nice spar, see some of Deuce's Korean combat technique. He'd thrown on the left glove, giving chubs the advantage with the right-hander. But Deuce had kept yelling "you can't hit a friend, you can't hit a friend," while Rube just kept on poppety-pop-poping him in the face with his left hand. His nose was bleeding all over the carpet, hands barely able to block, let alone jab. Hey, what were cousins for? Poppety-pop-pop biaatch.

Rube's only regret now was wishing there'd been some more lamplight glowing up the block that night so he knew for sure he'd actually tagged that loudmouth midget. Or if that pussy fuck just dropped from piss soaked fear. Which wouldn't have surprised Rube one iota. And if he did ice the kid, a little illumination would have at least allowed Rube the pleasure of an indelibly burned commemorative facial expression as that *mayate's* heart beat out. Next time he'd keep his eyes peeled for a streetlamp before he popped off a shot on some dickrider.

But either way, Rube had other matters to attend to this evening as he now leaned casually across the street from 168 Ludlow, watching a young debutante unlock the front door of her building. The Blonde sashayed inside the modern glass facade, disappearing behind the door. Rube made his best efforts to look casual as he raced in her direction, slipping his foot in before the door latched shut, and he slid inside.

He took the stairs of the upscale domicile two at a time, breaking out onto the rooftop. Rube pushed towards the edge until his favorite tenement arose from below. Kneeling, he whipped a pair of tiny binoculars from his pocket and focused up a view through a third floor window. From his perch, the view was unobstructed into Mioko's apartment. There she stood in a black lace bra and a pair of shorts cooking dinner at the stove in the summertime heat. He could even see her lips pulling crimson from a glass of wine, his mind quickly conjuring what else those lips could do. First a bar, now drinking alone. She was coming undone. The edges of Rube's own lips curled towards the orange light pollution blocking the universe above.

His elbows resting on the facade wall, Rube squinted into the binoculars, inhaling through his nostrils—breathing her in.

Mioko walked down Stanton at a quick clip. She was unbelievably late for work, but there was always the off-chance Jake was having some kind of meltdown and hadn't gotten out of bed all day. Regardless, her legs slowed as she passed an unfamiliar site at the corner of Stanton and Eldridge. A large laminated photo hung on the brick wall above a collection of beer and liquor bottles, religious candles and flowers. The wall was covered with messages of mourning and a blown-up school photo of a scrawny Black kid, wearing his Sunday best. Dozens of smaller snapshots of the scrawny kid lined the wall.

A little girl of about 5 took a tiny roll of masking tape from her tearful young mother, then moved towards the wall. Mioko held up her Mamiya as unobtrusively as possible and snapped a photograph as the little girl reached to paste up her colorful sign.

Another printed sign already on the wall above the girl read, 'Cowards die many times before their deaths... but the brave only know death once.'

In the elevator heading up to Jake's studio, Mioko stood sweating, crammed in among the arty freelance designers, entrepreneurs, and filmmakers, a rolled up Village Voice under her arm.

Mioko entered the studio to find Jake seated at his desk, staring at the full page Lamerica ad on the back of the Voice.

"Can you believe this heat?" Mioko said hoping her nervousness wasn't apparent.

"It's seven in the evening, Mioko," he sneered. "Why do you even bother to show up?"

Mioko motioned to the paper on the desk in front of him.

"So you've seen it."

"Some bastard poached the Lamerica account."

"Yeah, I've been meaning to tell you about that."

Jake finally looked up at her.

"Tell me what? That you knew they'd moved with someone else?"

"No. Not exactly."

She eyed the floor.

"Excuse me? So you didn't know?"

"Well, I was meaning to tell you—"

Jake glanced down at the add. He squinted at the image. His expression changing.

"No. Not possible."

"Shit, Jake, how can you really expect loyalty, the way you treat people?"

And it was true. He would have done the exact same to her if the roles were reversed. But a hell of a lot sooner.

"You've got to be fucking kidding me."

"I guess they wanted a different style for this campaign. Something a little more raw. With feeling is what they said..."

Mioko suddenly had an incredible urge to twist the knife even further, for all the torturous years she'd spent babysitting such a repugnant excuse for a human being. A man who walked all over her, sprinkling the word mentor around like it was some kind of justification for the infliction of endless pain. An arrogant little man who hesitated at giving her a spare aspirin if she had a headache, let alone a shot at making some kind of name for herself on his watch.

"I pulled you out of the muck." He was saying now. "You could barely hold down a meal when I took you on."

"Jake."

He was starting to tear up.

"You little cunt."

"Jake, my world doesn't begin and end with you. I know I should have told you when it happened, but this is something I had to do. Maybe you should be proud of me—"

Suddenly the electricity snapped off. A patchwork of green and red grain filled their eyes. The office was black.

"What the fuck?" Jake said as he stood and shuffled towards the window, slamming into a desk chair on the way.

"Oh my god!"

He was starting to get even more worked up now.

"First you steal my client, now it's the bloody apocalypse."

"You're nuts."

"Look out the fucking window!"

Mioko stood up, approaching her disturbed boss. She peered out the window at a completely dark city.

Fifty blocks away, on the roof of the Ludlow tenement, the Lower East Side skyline was devoid of electricity. Having run up from his apartment, Dorian now stared out in nothing but his soiled bathrobe and a pair of boxers. He couldn't have been more invigorated at the sight of the blackened tableau.

A solitary word dropped from his lips...

"Blackout."

PART III
THE WORK

CHAPTER TWENTY-NINE
IN FRONT OF THE CHILDREN

Morris weaved through the crowded street. The scene on Ludlow was beginning to get tribal. Kids playing congas, dancing in the street. Fires in garbage cans. Morris shoved past them, his frustration building.

"Get out of my way."

A teenager on psychedelics blocked Morris's path.

"Isn't this great, Man?"

His enthusiasm was far from contagious.

"You're gonna regret standing there," Morris shot back.

But the teenager didn't move, so Morris pushed through him with a defensive lineman shove. It felt pretty good too.

A wimpy sound escaped the euphoric teen.

Morris snarled, knowing full well he freaked out these lesser adolescents by his very existence. The kid's expression melted. Morris was pleased with the idea his monster impression had succeeded in shifting the kid's euphoria into horrible trip territory as he continued to shove his way home.

Walking into the building foyer Morris found Stella, the young African who lived in the super's apartment, crouched down lighting votive candles in the hallway. She looked up, but Morris moved past without acknowledging her. The last thing he needed was another blind idealist trying to brighten his mood.

Inside Ndusen's apartment, his family lit more candles, unfazed by the power outage.

Kondwani looked up as Stella entered their flickering home. She turned to her husband, "I am sure that she spilled wax all over the entrance hallway." she said in Chichewa.

"Be kind," he said, switching to English, hoping to shift her off her fluent nasty footing. "Please."

"She is useless, Ndusen," Kondwani continued in Chewa.

Ndusen exhaled slowly as the children watched Stella disappear into the bedroom.

Up on three, Mioko sat in almost total darkness, rolling a joint at the table.

She'd given up trying to find anything in the dark, and she'd had enough with fires for a lifetime, feeling more comfortable in the pitch-blackness than surrounded by candles. The thought had crossed her mind she could assemble some kind of a simple dinner, but all she'd succeeded in locating was a stale bag of corn chips and her tupperware of contraband.

She licked the joint closed, telling herself it was a special occasion, that perhaps she would allow herself a toke the next time Manhattan had a blackout too. With that, she lit up, taking a lengthy toke but making sure to ash directly into the safety of a mug. The aromatic terpenoid began to release into her system and immediately started altering her perception, providing an intense overall feeling of well-being.

But it was short lived—she was startled by a knock on the door.

"It's me," said a gravelly male voice.

"Fuck," Mioko said to herself, stubbing out the joint, then going to the window to dump the evidence. She waved the air to clear the smoke.

Mioko opened the door. A mixed metaphor of an aging punk rocker, with a yoga t-shirt covering his tatted chest—but not the rest of the homespun ink sketches spilling out his sleeves—stood outside with a flashlight.

"Trey. Hi."

Mioko welcomed Trey Spencer in with a hug.

"Jesus, you oughta light some candles," he said. "Darlene said you came by *Machine City*."

"The craziest thing happened. I got my own commercial client. I'm shooting for Lamerica."

"No shit?"

"It's on the back of the Voice."

"I'll keep my eyes peeled for that," he said, but Trey was all business. Placing his lantern and backpack on the table, he unpacked two large ziplocks of marijuana. "Figured you were looking for a little refill."

"Yeah."

"Kids gotta get high. Especially in a blackout."

"Hey, have you eaten yet?"

Not that she had anything to offer. It just seemed like they hadn't seen each other forever.

"No," he said.

"I'm not even sure if restaurants are open or whatever, but—"

"It starts with dinner. It ends with the two of us skin popping and nodding out on the Bowery, babe."

Mioko bit her lip as it came boiling to the surface: their intimacy driven by mutual devotion to the needle. The ectopic pregnancy and subsequent abortion, the feelings of self-hatred as they worked their doses up to well past four hundred milligrams a day, until she ODed for the third time in five years and her parents finally cut them off.

"...I know."

Mioko took the flashlight and went to the bedroom. She pulled a wad of cash from a hollowed-out copy of Moby Dick, then returned and handed it to Trey.

"Trey—" She stopped herself.

"Yeah?"

Mioko shook her head, knowing better than to express any of it out loud. Sentiments better left unsaid. Besides, Trey understood.

He opened the door while the going was still good, but turned back, "Take care of yourself. It's getting a little scary out there."

Mioko stood alone at the table with her fresh bags of pot, a sad little smile on her face as he closed the door.

Ndusen lay asleep in the bedroom, his arm cupping Stella's midriff.

In the living room candles burned all around, Kondwani lay under a blanket, her eyes focused on her children sleeping nearby. Abruptly she sprang to her feet and marched towards the bedroom.

Throwing open the door, Kondwani ripped the covers off of Stella and Ndusen, revealing their nude bodies underneath.

"She is not your wife. I am your wife." Kondwani yelled in Chichewa "I am finished with her. No more sleeping in my bed. No more staying in this house!"

Ndusen jumped to his bare feet, the edges of his naked frame shimmering metallic in the candle flicker. "Have you gone mad, woman?" he shouted back in English.

"This little wife, we have no need for her here." Kondwani yelled as she stormed back towards the living room, followed closely by her nude husband.

"I want her out!"

"Be reasonable," Ndusen called after Kondwani.

The children sat up from their mattresses, watching in horror as Kondwani grabbed clothes from Stella's drawers in the communal chest and started tossing them at Stella's bed. They're naked father seemingly powerless to stop her. "This may work for you the way you want it to," she yelled in Chewa, "but it no longer works for me."

Stella walked to the bedroom doorway, wrapped in a sheet. Seeing her, Kondwani summoned her best English, enunciating every syllable, "You, out of this house!"

Chisulo began to cry.

"Stop this, Kondwani!" Ndusen roared as sternly as he could. "How can you act like this in front of our children?"

"I am the mother of these children," Kondwani said back to her husband in Chichewa, then turned towards Stella. "You have no place here. Get out."

"I will not leave this house, Kondwani," Stella said in Chewa, standing firm in the face of the much larger woman, "unless Ndusen says it is so." She had no hatred for Kondwani, but she would not bend to the elder woman's volatility.

"Kondwani, please," Ndusen said softly.

Turning back to her husband, Kondwani's whit-hot eyes pierced through the darkness, glistening incandescent.

"If you do not tell her to move off," Kondwani said in their native tongue, "then I will leave."

The children looked terrified.

"To go where?" Ndusen asked.

Kondwani began to tear up. After a moment she crumpled onto the floor. Ndusen sat down across from her, their bare feet touching, yet he had no idea how to reach her.

Crazed revelers with blazing flashlights brushed past Rube and Deuce. It took a hundred percent of his willpower not to cop each hot young ass Rube grinded past as they worked their way down Ludlow. Reaching the heeb's tenement, Deuce waited till the bulk of the carousers were clear, then smashed his cloth wrapped fist into the glass door of A&D Dress Co. Rube knew his involvement held a certain level of conflicting interest, bumping a shop owned by Axlerod without endorsement—commercial tenants and a half dozen fresh residents were off limits—but lawless was the name of the blackout game, and Rube couldn't help but capitalize.

Flipping on a torch, Deuce headed straight for the till. His plump digits fumbled to drain the register, flashlights bouncing outside. No planning. No getaway. Just a bright eyed tubby fuck peering fumbling in darkness. A classic halfwit robbing spree plotted by his recent three to five parolee cousin. But whatever, he was here, the least he could do was to make sure lardass didn't take all night—which of course he was.

"Hurry up, mothafucker."

Deuce ripped the register tray right out the drawer.

"Ain't shit here," Deuce hissed.

"Damn man, I told you they ain't gonna keep no float in the till."

In and out, wasting away in this shop was plain retarded.

"Oh shit, what was I thinking not trusting Mr. Service Industry himself?"

"Let's beat it the fuck outta here *maricon.*"

But chubs didn't listen. He slammed the entire register off the counter, bringing about a crack so loud they could've heard that shit down at the precinct. Still nothing. Thwarted like the chump he was.

Deuce scurried for the door. Disgraceful. He was about to shadow fatty, but then sheer disgust overpowered him and Rube ripped his hands into the racks, grabbed up as many of the flowery designer dresses he could fit in his arms.

Rube wasn't leaving a B&E job—even a half-assed one dreamed up by a plus-sized ignoramus—with empty mits.

CHAPTER THIRTY
BABYSITTING

ust outside the basketball cage at Roosevelt Park, an opportunistic huckster was planted on a cooler of water, holding up a sweaty plastic bottle.

"Ice is melting," the huckster hollered "Get your water while it's still cold. 20 dollars, folks!"

Staring down the icy refreshment, Rube sat on the stairs of the caretakers' shelter across from the courts in disbelief, a tiny baby girl, dressed all in pink, bouncing on his knee.

"Twenty motherfucking bones. Shit is usury," he said under his breath.

It was just too damn roasting hot, mixed with the jagged edge of post-blunt burnout, it was a real agro combination. He was ready to start drinking, throwing down hot beats, or at the very least loaf in front of the TV with some AC blasting. Damn blackout was played out.

"I ain't doing this no more Nastassia."

The child's mama, Nastassia Arias, pushed the short burgundy colored braids out her eyes. The ankle length A&D dress she was sporting did nothing to mitigate the toxic disapproval plastered on her face.

"Like shit you ain't," Nastassia said whipping back to face him on the step above her own.

"Na. Na," Rube said. "I'm not doing this no more. I'm not babysitting no more." His foot gyrated madly, turbo bouncing the tot so she wouldn't start wailing again.

Nastassia shook her head, making it clear shit was about to gets hostile, "It's not babysittin' *WHEN IT'S YOUR KID!*"

She had a point, but Rube didn't appreciate the way a couple of courtside sluts were sizing him up like he was some kind of *Mama bicho.*

"Na, this is babysitting. I ain't doing it. Shit is over."

It felt like every time Rube snatched the little *nena* up, her head rammed into a dresser, or she started balling cause Rube yelled across the avenue and her tiny eardrums were all stunned or some shit. Not to mention the titty-milk puke everywhichway, her stank ass nappies, the swimming pool o' drool on her clothes. Too much.

"Ruben you are so stupid. Besides, what the hell else you gonna do? Ain't no electricity in the entire city."

"I got plenty to do," Rube objected. "Gonna be running this neighborhood soon. My man Axlerod's got big plans."

"Ain't nothin' but a gang-banger fantasy. You keep this shit up, all you'll be runnin' is garbage detail at Riker's." Nastassia's voice was rising now. The sluts were laughing, playing like they weren't talking some shit about Rube on the other side the fence.

"Think you're a big man? Your baby girl's being raised by my mama. Food, clothing, education? We're eating your damn pizza every meal. Pretty dresses don't cut it. My moms sold her flatscreen; what are you good for, Ruben?"

"Yo, don't sweat it, I told you, I set you up Stass."

Nastassia rolled her blue eyes, her inch lashes fluttering, reaching a hand underneath the stroller.

"Just give her the damn bottle and shut your face."

Rube accepted the bottle, popping off the top as he looked back at the tiny gurgling inconvenience in his lap—wondering for the hundred millionth time why he couldn't have just used a damn poon balloon when he had the chance.

Chisulo and Alile played a heated game of tag outside the tenement, ducking and weaving through the overheated pedestrians, hiding behind parked cars, wheeling around signposts.

Laughing hysterically as he came within inches of his sister's outstretched arm, Chisulo peeled off and rammed through the glassless front door of A&D Dress Co.

Alile bust in after him, sweeping past Dwyer's broom as she did her best to gather glass from the broken window.

"Careful!" Dwyer yelled out, surprising herself with how much she sounded like her own mother.

Stella timidly followed the children into the shop, stepping carefully past Dwyer.

"Sorry."

Dwyer wasn't sure what to make of the invasion, "We're not really open."

Reaching Alile and Chisulo, Stella struggled to keep the kids wrangled, but Chisulo squirmed away. Alile ran her hands over all the dresses on the wall.

"Much too expensive, Alile. Do not touch that." Stella admonished the teen in Chichewa.

Alile disregarded Stella, grabbing each dress she fancied and holding it to her body to check herself out in the mirror.

Althea was perched on a stool behind the glass display case looking through the empty cash register, which she and Dwyer had wrestled back onto the counter. A half eaten takeout cheeseburger sat in styrofoam nearby. A young shop girl in her early twenties—a Xerox copy of her elder counterparts—lazed in a chair behind the counter, distracted by her phone. Althea took a sip from her soda watching her incongruous visitor.

Chisulo stared up at Althea with his huge eyes while keeping his distance. He smiled a toothy grin, but then quickly returned to a cautious stare.

"Give him a French fry," Dwyer said.

"I feel like I'm the animal in the zoo, here." Althea said. "He should be feedin' me a peanut."

Stella hesitantly approached the sales ladies and Chisulo, who inched ever closer to the checkout. Stella wrapped an arm in front of the boy's chest. Then spoke quietly in her broken English, "Come. We must go so that I can prepare your lunch."

"You speak some English?" Althea said, smiling but kindly, "Can I ask you a question? About your country. Malawi, right?"

Stella froze, she was suddenly feeling self-aware and therefore rather out of place in the designer boutique.

"A question. Yes. I am sorry."

"Is it real different over there?" Althea asked.

"In Malawi? My home place?"

"Is your life the same here?"

Stella wasn't sure where to begin. Of course it was different, but she didn't want to be rude or disparaging about the West. So much of the simple beauty of life was missing here. All of these people seeking and searching, but rarely finding, it seemed to her. The poverty she'd known as a child was certainly far from a blessing, but something as simple as sitting in the fields after the first rainy season downpour and watching termites hatch and fly to the sky. The perfect balance of nature visible to the naked eye. Uncomplicated, delightful and ever-present. This place of concrete and computers, big dreams and gruesome nightmares, was jam packed with humanity, but somehow felt so entirely lifeless to her.

"Yes. The Same. I am tending to the children. The laundry. I prepare the food for my Mr. Muluzi's and his big wife."

Dwyer turned her head sideways, trying to understand. "He brought you here, like as a babysitter?"

"But also Ndusen, he would miss the warmth of his beloved one," Stella tried to explain. "His bed at night. His little wife."

The sales ladies eyes grew wide, even the young shop girl set aside her phone.

Althea was almost afraid to ask, but she couldn't resist, "What's his little wife?"

"I am his little wife." Stella said.

They leaned forward in their seats.

"Y'all Mormons or something?" Althea quipped.

The other gals snickered.

Stella wasn't sure if the remark was at her expense or not, until Althea smiled reassuringly, then turned to the other ladies.

"I knew there had to be someone in this neighborhood with a more distorted approach to women than Dorian."

Above the shop, Mioko, drowned her conflicted feelings with a stiff shot from a newly purchased fifth of Jameson. She would be the latest judge of Dorian's distorted approach to the fairer sex, as she climbed the sweltering tenement stairs towards his apartment, unable to ignore her anticipation.

CHAPTER THIRTY-ONE
A LITTLE SPARK

The gate to the fire escape sat wide open, the blinds all the way up. Daylight spilled in through Dorian's living room windows.

"How long have you been painting?" Mioko asked.

"Forever."

Mioko sat cross-legged on a chair in the center of Dorian's makeshift studio. Deeply focused, Dorian sat ten feet away, his eyes either pressed an inch or two from the canvas or looking over to appraise the shadows and highlights around Mioko's form.

"I remember that show you had over at Gropius a few years ago."

"Oh yeah?"

"That was kind of a big thing, right?"

"Sort of, yeah," he said, hoping it didn't sound too much like false modesty.

But it HAD been kind of a big thing. The biggest thing in Dorian's life. He'd gotten more mileage out of that one show than the dozen others before it combined.

"This city, man. It's addictive." Mioko said. "A little spark, and then suddenly—"

Then suddenly a lengthy silent dud, Dorian remembered. An aching void of false promise that continued to fester and expand until it encompassed his entire being.

But he didn't want to let the darkness get the better of him now. Not today.

"Yeah, life down here's like a cheap novel." Dorian said.

"I moved downtown over twenty years ago." Mioko said. "This place was a disaster. You couldn't tell the droves of decaying Bowery boys from the genuine rotting corpses. Shit, now you can barely park a Mini Cooper on Chrystie Street."

Dorian squirted out another blob of red paint. He loved her salty edge. It was exactly the reason he'd asked her to sit. The more he looked, the more he felt she really did have a ramshackle beauty, unique to this time and place, but with a pleasingly repellant quality hidden underneath. She was a perfect set of contrary forces, striking yet somehow menacing. The more he looked, the stronger he felt it. She was perfect.

"It's unbelievable what people go through in a single day in this town." Mioko said. "This month I went from a dead end job, assisting an impossible prima donna of a photographer assassinate the final boundaries of fashion photography, to finally catching a break so I can try my own hand at it."

"Can you shift your chin up?"

Mioko looked up for him.

"We live in this city with so many people around us all the time, cramped sidewalks, stuffed in elevators. And we're so detached, you know?"

Dorian scraped the light around windows with a palette knife. Mioko took a sip of her mint tea, wishing he'd offered one of his dusty bottles.

"Although sometimes being crammed in a subway car's the best part of my day."

"How's that?"

Mioko looked down, she was suddenly feeling a little shy, wishing she could have taken it back.

"No reason."

"Come on."

Mioko bit her lip.

"Sometimes..."

Careful, she told herself, this man was not to be trusted. Everything she knew enforced that. But it was too late. Her lips were still moving independent of her control.

"...when I'm on the subway and... I don't know, well maybe someone lightly brushes up against me by accident or something. It feels nice."

Dorian began to work on her eyes. He knew better than to look directly at her. Let her take the lead. The more she felt in control, the more she'd want to reveal.

"Nice, how?" he asked, casually from behind the canvas.

"Just nice."

He liked the way she was getting embarrassed, but still somehow managed to retain her badass edge.

"I don't know. I can't describe it. That one little moment of human contact. You can't help it from happening, and yet rather than pull away, you let your leg stay where it is for a second."

"Sounds sexy."

Her beautiful, morose eyes began to take shape on the canvas.

"Yeah... I guess so."

He leaned out and smiled at her, hoping it didn't seem calculated.

They sat quietly for a moment looking at each other, both comfortable for the first time. Dorian relaxed his palette knife, he knew he could have her. But he worried that it would hurt the work. And he needed to succeed in this new direction more than anything. Or all would be lost. He'd have no other choice than to Bourdain himself with a bathrobe belt. He was surprised, he realized, that the painting took precedent over getting his willy waxed. Was this what finally growing up felt like? Dorian quickly distracted himself by picking up a nearby joint.

"Do you mind?"

Mioko, gave him a little half smile and a head shake.

"Right. Course you don't mind," he said. "You sold it to me."

Dorian lit up the joint with three quick puffs to get the cherry going. He savored the smoke for a minute then looked back at Mioko, her eyes locked on him.

"You want some?"

She shrugged. He knew she did.

"It's ok. You can move a little," Dorian smiled softly and handed her the joint. She concentrated on the spliff as she hauled, reassuring herself that it was fair game because the blackout was still on.

The severed synapsis and rapid-fire new connections brought on by the smoke reminded Dorian of the rest of the work. A Lower East Side web of endearment, strung through repulsion.

"Hey, you remember Old Sal, down the hall from you?"

"Sure. Of course." she said.

Of course she did, he thought, because she wasn't a heartless self-centered asshole. He couldn't say the same.

"You know anything about what happened to him?"

"No. Do you?"

He recounted the gist of his conversation with Detective Razor Rozycki and his chat with Ndusen, which he realized really didn't amount to much. He liked the way she listened, though. She was a good listener. And the way she looked at him as he started working his way down her neck, pushing the brush into her first-rate décolletage.

She was a real woman. Her dark eyes. Her life experience. She wouldn't blow over in the wind like some of the little waifs he'd become accustomed to picking up.

"What about asking Moshe?"

"Axlerod?"

The thought hadn't occurred to him. The landlord was someone Dorian avoided at all costs, not for any particularly good reason, just because he always felt like he was doing something wrong when he was around the guy.

"I'd imagine he would have known the Agnellis since before Sal's wife passed. Probably forever."

"Huh."

Dorian chewed on that for a second. Reaching out was likely the right thing to do, it was just pain in the ass. Unless if maybe Axlerod had a picture of the old guy he could paint from. Then it might be worth the trouble. If no one ever figured out how the guy vanished, in a way it was like he was timeless. Hell, maybe Axlerod himself fit into the work somehow? Part of the fabric of the neighborhood. There was something to that, but he wasn't quite sure how he could work it in. He forced himself to concentrate on what he was working on now instead. Mioko. And what drew him to her in the first place.

"Can I ask you something?"

Mioko smiled. She felt happy for the first time in a long while. She liked the way his eyes moved from one of her spots to the next. And he was a lot friendlier than she'd ever imagined. She could see why all the young ladies fell over. He was undeniably a charmer with his palette knife and easy smile.

And maybe it was just the weed, but she was starting to feel safe, and somehow a lot more open to the new experience than she would have imagined. She could almost see something more with this guy. But if so, it would have to be a casual friendship at first, instead of some crazy passion fueled fiasco, like hitching a ride home with a band and finding herself on a cross-country road-trip ten years later. This time she needed to have her hands on the wheel. She couldn't remember the last time she'd allowed herself a thought like that.

"Yes. You can ask."

"It's about the subway feeling," he said.

Mioko laughed self-consciously.

"You're still stuck on that, huh?"

Dorian laughed back.

"I guess so," he said. He looked at her with his intense brown eyes. "Was it like that with that guy?"

"What guy?"

"That Rube guy. The one in the picture downstairs."

She imaged the band van slamming against the guardrail, her alternate self flying through the windshield.

"Excuse me?"

"Did you lightly brush up against him in the subway, or something?"

Mioko's expression melted.

"Why would you ask me that?"

Dorian put down his palette knife. He knew the work had made him overstep. He'd let himself get too excited. He'd completely lost prospective on how important the attraction element was. The seduction. He was falling from the delicate ladder he had so carefully assembled to get inside this woman's head, which in and of itself was much more important for the work than any of his stupid questions about the circumstances of her and Rube's relationship. He moved towards her. Extending his hand, he touched her cheek, hoping he hadn't completely botched the seduction.

"No reason. I'm sorry. Just forget I said it."

Dorian leaned forward and their lips met for an instant. Just as quickly, Mioko pulled away.

"No. I can't."

She climbed down from the chair and walked out the door.

Dorian watched her leave. Picking up the palette knife, he flipped it in his hand, mulling over what had just transpired. Then with a tinge of sadness, he scooped more paint onto the knife and got back to work before the feel of her completely dissolved away.

CHAPTER THIRTY-TWO
THE HISTORY OF CIVILIZATION

Ndusen watched his boss from the other side of the glass sitting inside his dim realty office, counting out stacks of twenty-dollar bills by lamplight. It took all of Ndusen's willpower to push open the door and enter the dark office.

"There you are," Axlerod said, checking a handwritten list. "Listen, Ndusen. I got a little thing. I want you to pull the fuses for apartments 9, 10, 17 and 22."

"Pull them?" Ndusen asked.

"Yeah. When the power comes back, tell those tenants the blackout made problems with the breaker boxes. I'll let you know when they can have their power back. A week or two, tops."

Ndusen was bewildered.

"But, will they not notice that their neighbors have regained power."

A tiny glint of a smile appeared on Axlerod's lips. The sight of it made Ndusen's stomach seize.

"Might feel a little singled out, huh?"

By far the most brazen transgression yet. What started out as subtle manipulation, deceptive and mean spirited, was now adding up to what Ndusen deemed a complete betrayal of human decency.

"Your father, he would never approve of these tactics. I do not think I will be able to perform this task for you, Mr. Axlerod. You cannot ask this."

Axlerod set down his stack of bills and looked up at his employee with such disdain Ndusen could feel the plasma draining from his appendages.

"Get the fuck out of my office."

Ndusen stoked a small fire in the otherwise dark courtyard. Kondwani, Alile, and Dziko sat nearby chopping vegetables, freshly harvested from the now bountiful garden. Stella poured water from a hose into a large metal pot. Picking up the pot, Stella made her way towards the fire, but tripped, spilling water on the concrete between the buckets of earth.

"What is the good of this woman?" Kondwoni said in Chichewa.

"Mama, please." Alile said.

"Please, what? She is useless, can you not see that?"

Stella looked to Ndusen hoping he would stand for her. Ndusen poked at the fire. He shook his head, but kept his eyes averted.

Inside the building, all on his own, Chisulo climbed down the pitch-dark stairs with a flashlight. Dorian and a Wall Street bro (a prototypical douche the artist wouldn't have been caught dead with if it weren't for their adorable and unexpected guide) along with Wall Street's glossy skinned girlfriend, followed a few paces behind. They reached the third floor and Chisulo knocked on apartment 9. After a moment, Mioko opened the door.

"Oh, hi," she said, surprised by the tiny visitor.

"We are cooking in the courtyard, if you would like to join us." Chisulo said smiling at her warmly.

Mioko was a little taken aback at the sweet offer. She looked to Dorian, but he just shrugged and smiled. She wondered if this was somehow a scheme Dorian had concocted to win back her favor with what she imagined to be an impressive bag of tricks. But the young boy's face was filled with such innocent warmth, Mioko doubted Dorian could elicit such genuine good cheer from another human to service his bidding. Even so, her asocial tendencies made her lean back on her heels, but her apartment tomb was equally uninviting.

"Yeah... it does sound nice," Mioko said. "Should I bring anything?"

Chisulo shook his head.

"No. Just come."

Chisulo reached out his hand. Mioko accepted his small palm, and the boy smiled reassuringly.

"Do not be scared," he said "I have this flashlight."

Mioko couldn't help but smile back.

Chisulo lead them downward, carefully lighting each stair.

In the courtyard, the enormous pot of stew on the open fire was starting to boil over. Alile and Dziko watched in horror as Stella and Kondwani moved in a slow hostile arc, ready to rip each other's limbs.

"If I am so very stupid and you are so smart, why do you not try to insult me in English for a change?" Stella yelled.

"You are COW! Moooooo!" it was the worst insult Kondwani could conjure in the foreign tongue. Lashing forward, Kondwani struck Stella's shoulder with the frying pan in her hand. Stella recoiled; shocked the elder woman had actually stuck her.

"Stop! This instant." Ndusen wailed, slapping down the frying pan. "This is over. You cannot hit my wife!"

"She is not your wife!" Kondwani screamed. "I am your wife."

Chisulo lead Mioko by the hand, followed by Dorian and the others, out into the garden to find his family cleaving at each other in their native tongue.

"What does this stupid girl offer this family, Ndusen, tell me that?"

"You must calm down!" Ndusen said.

Chisulo was undaunted by the now familiar squabbling, "I have brought dinner guests."

The entire family turned their heads towards Chisulo and his uncomfortable guests.

The superintendent's embarrassment was palpable.

Morris stood alone in his underwear, pointing an industrial flashlight into his gloomy refrigerator. Offering nothing but the putrid stench of decay, he closed the fridge. Trying for the freezer instead, water gushed, soaking into the bottoms of his socks. Reaching inside, he pulled a package of half-frozen ground beef, and brought a freezer-burnt edge to his nostrils. Sour milk, Durian Fruit and Bubonic plague all mixed into one. There wasn't much that disgusted Morris, but the decaying hamburger meat traversed the bridge. He tossed the aging ground cow back into the pool of defrosted liquid where at least it would be contained.

Morris wondered if he should go downstairs and try to find an open take-out window, but the six-flight effort and potential for human interaction was just too much to face.

Then he saw it sitting on his kitchen table. *Hungry? Why wait. Snickers.* The wrapped brown bar just where he'd left it. Such incredible discipline. But he wouldn't eat it. Not now. Not ever.

Shutting the freezer door, a vague sense of nausea had taken over from hunger, so he lay on his mattress and tried not to think about anything edible. But as always happened when he tried not to think of a particular thing, faint wafts of stewed meat and firewood flowed up the fire escape, invading the greasy rear window screens of his apartment. These unfamiliar smells in and of themselves were rather disconcerting, but not nearly as troubling as the voices working their way up the back of the tenement. The voices seemed much closer than Morris was used to, and yet they didn't seem to be emitting from within his own prolific mental population.

Ndusen and his family sat in a circle around the fire sharing stew with their guests.

"This is delicious," Mioko said with a smile.

Stella smiled back, "Thank you. We made it together." Kondwani eyed Stella coolly.

Dorian surveyed his surroundings. His fire escape looked down onto this courtyard. He pondered how he could have possibly missed a miniature farm six stories below.

"You grew all these vegetables out here?" Dorian asked.

"Yes," Stella said, continuing as the goodwill ambassador for the family, for the first time enjoying the contempt in Kondwani's glaring, envious eyes. "It is our family project," she said enunciating flawlessly.

"When I was just a mwana, Chisulo's age," Ndusen said as he put his arm around his son affectionately. "When Malawi was still known by Nyasaland, the earth beneath our feet was a like-match to happiness. No phones, no screens. Simplicity. Complexity in my country, when it did arrive, only led to chaos and greed."

"Not so different here," Mioko remarked.

"My children, in America, they won't know these simple ways unless I teach them," Ndusen said.

Chisulo poked at the fire with a stick.

"These skills can be necessary, even here in this most modern society," Ndusen said. "We think other people making our possessions is progress. But we do not question what that progress really means. Since humans started to stand up straight, there has never been a society so strong, yet so entirely helpless."

The Wall Street trader smiled, "Civilization's need to destroy itself is the only consistent trend in the history of civilization."

"Now there's a cheery thought," Dorian said.

"Yes," Ndusen said. "We are like addicts of a drug. Financial disasters, natural disasters. We feel terrible, but we cannot help it, we just need more. More, has become the global economic model."

"You see a dark age on the horizon?" Dorian asked. "Waring tribes? The end of society as we know it?"

Ndusen pointed up to the pitch-black structure towering above them.

"I see a dark age here, now."

Dorian wasn't so sure he tracked a correlation between temporary power failure and the end of times. It wasn't like America had run out of coal, let alone natural gas or nuclear plants. Likely just some clusterfuck with the overtaxed grid, or human error. It wasn't like Dorian was a climate change denier— or whatever the environmental cause of the week was—he just didn't quite buy that the plane was going down and nobody had bothered to figure out how to build a parachute.

Mioko blew cooling air onto her spoon. "I guess impermanence is only frightening if you're clinging to the present." Her simple little smile made Dorian want her like no other he could remember.

Dorian took a bite of stew, his eyes glued to Mioko across the fire. He couldn't be sure if it was just a flicker, but he thought he perceived the faintest twinge of eye movement back in his direction.

Mioko climbed slowly back up the pitch-black stairs with the little yellow flashlight Chisulo had leant her. In over twenty years in the tenement, this was the first time she had ever experienced any kind of camaraderie with her neighbors. It was a foreign feeling, if not entirely unpleasant, and she wondered if this was what it was like in a village. To actually know the people who lived around you, their stories, their hardships, instead of just catching fleeting glimpses on the stairwell. The focal points of her neighbor's lives leaked through the walls: their music, their laughter, their tantrums, the invasive high notes of their orgasms—but those details really didn't add up to meaningful understanding.

As Mioko stepped onto the second floor a door opened momentarily, then shut again. It was one thing to see your neighbors and pretend to know them, but something else entirely to sense them in the darkness without their averted eyes, the feigning of a busy day. The lack of visual cues made her groundless. Mioko continued upwards, but she was beginning to feel uneasy now as she reached the third floor.

She shined her flashlight down the hallway before proceeding from the relative safety of the stairwell. Pulling her keys from her pocket, she unlocked her front door as quickly as she could.

A whisper punctuated the darkness, "Boo!"

Startled, Mioko swung round with the flashlight, hoping to illuminate Trey or Dorian or anyone other than the person she found inches from her face. Mioko screamed, dropping the lamp. She wrestled with the door, twisting the lock, but Rube slammed her door shut.

"YOU'RE NOT WANTED HERE!" Mioko yelled "Go away. I'm calling the fucking cops."

She fumbled with the handle, holding back tears.

"Don't you wanna be friends with me?" Rube hissed.

"GO AWAY."

"I seen you drinking, getting high. I get you smack, that's what you want?"

"Why are you doing this to me? What did I ever—"

Rube slammed his open palm against the doorframe. Mioko screamed.

"What are you still doing here?" he asked leaning in next to her. She could smell his acrid breath, feel the heat on her face, but she couldn't see a thing. "Haven't you had enough?" He slammed the wall beside her again, her instincts told her run, but paralysis shot down her spine. "That wallpaper don't cover the smell of smoke too good, does it?"

"Please..."

A receding whisper, "You'll fucking die here."

Mioko began to tear up.

"Leave me alone. Please."

She was completely helpless in the pitch-blackness.

"Just stop. OK? I don't know what I did to you, if I crossed or hurt you somehow, but whatever it is, I'm sorry."

Mioko listened closely.

She slowly tried the door handle, expecting another slam.
But he was gone.

CHAPTER THIRTY-THREE
DISTANT RELATIONS

The sun was just beginning to make its daily exit over the neighborhood roofs. Stella sat on the stoop watching Chisulo play quietly on the sidewalk. Hunched over, Chisulo's hands drove a pair of discarded coke can cars his father had helped bend into shape. Having already run the vehicles through a series of high stakes races, Chisulo's fist was now a prized pickup in the monster truck rally he'd seen advertised on Channel 4. The stands cheered as his cola monster grinded to the center of the dirt filled arena. He mouthed fire erupting from the nostrils of a gigantic metal dinosaur—the hydrant next to him—to mark the beginning of the show. Winding up, hitting the ramp and taking flight, his monster cleared a dozen stock cars, soaring through the air and crashing on the last few wrecks, decimating them on impact. A bulldozer dragged him off his victims, the cars erupting in giant balls of flames, the stands breaking out in cheers.

Axlerod sauntered up Ludlow, a most unwelcome addition to Chisulo's stadium. He stopped right in front of the dinosaur and smiled down at the boy.

"What you got there Chisulo?" Axlerod asked. "D'you make those cars?"

"My father made it for me," Chisulo said without looking up.

"Is that a fact?"

Axlerod's expression changed at the sight of Stella.

"I just came by to check, see how you guys are holding up without any power."

"That is kind of you," Stella said softly.

Axlerod took a perch on the stoop next to her. She kept her gaze averted. Chisulo didn't much like the look in his eyes. Axlerod leaned in close and hissed in her ear, but loud enough for Chisulo to catch.

"I don't know which one of you runs the household, but you—or the other one of you—better get control of your husband." Axlerod placed an uninvited hand lightly on Stella's stomach. Chisulo gripped his stock car till the aluminum notched his soft palm. "You remind him I keep your bellies full and a roof over your heads. Understand?" Axlerod leaned in even closer, "In exchange, your husband's job is to do the upkeep, follow every one of my goddamn instructions, and refrain from wagging his tongue about my business. You remind him of that."

Stella sat frozen. Axlerod abruptly stood.

Chisulo eyed the landlord as he strode back down the street, then looked down to find blood pooling in the tiny ridges of his hand.

Dorian turned onto Houston, walking past the massive new gelato flagship that had sprung at the base of his least favorite luxury monolith. 'Like a work of Art,' the building advertised all the amenities of postmodern convenience: spectacular views through floor to ceiling windows, white oak floors, stainless steel appliances, granite countertops, 24-hour doorman, valet, a pilates studio, rooftop sundeck, a media/billiards lounge, and of course hundreds of assholes willing to shell tens of thousands a month to let their dogs shit the common areas and gloat that they lived in an LES work of art. Dorian did his best not to puke in his mouth as he trudged past the sweet waffle cone scent polluting his world.

Across the street, at a quick clip past the holdover health food store, Axlerod made his way to his car. Dorian hesitantly blew a puff of warm air, then steeled and set off in his landlord's direction.

Beside the male members of his own family, there weren't many in this world that intimidated Dorian, but Moshe Axlerod had a way of making him feel so infinitesimally small, he wondered if they were somehow distantly related.

"Hey Moshe!"

Dorian cornered Axlerod as he unlocked his Dodge Viper, and immediately started spitting such a confused string of verbal diarrhea, he had a hard time listening to himself, "...you know... this new project... the authentic underbrush is the kind of thing I'm trying to get at... what was real then, when this place had an actual heartbeat, and now sort of sits below the surface..."

The landlord stared at him sideways.

"You want to know what happened to who?"

It wasn't just the tone of Axlerod's voice, it was the unmissable subtext; Dorian was an utter mornon for troubling a powerful real estate heir-apparent with these banal artistic trivialities. "Why are you wasting my time with this?" Axlerod flawlessly summoned the ghost of Dorian's father and grandfather before him. Dorian wondered if it was too late to cut and run.

"How the hell should I know? You're the one who lived upstairs from him."

"But I thought you guys went back? He and your father always chatting."

"No, why would I know that tenant from any other? You know how many residents I got in these buildings? You think I keep track of every fricken detail of each of your lives? Half the time, I gotta look you up in my phone I want to remember your names. What's your name again? Davis? Dickie? Doorknob?"

Dorian could feel the muscular fibers in his ass clenching. He hadn't expected a reaming, he was just trying to act like a human and extend himself outwards for once. Sure the work had a selfish component, but this went beyond his project. He was trying something new: showing concern for someone else's fate. It was a beginner's mistake, he now realized, to try his first hand at overarching compassion on what was more than likely a dead guy.

"Look, I happen to hear from Sal, I'll let him know you can't live without him, alright? That what you wanna hear? I'll tell him to send you a postcard."

He couldn't tell if Axlerod was purposefully obfuscating or if his landlord just plain didn't like him.

"Actually, I was wondering if you might have a picture of him?" Dorian managed to blurt out.

"A what? A picture?" Axlerod stared like Dorian was an utter freakshow. "Whatta you want a picture for?"

"It's um, for this show I'm working towards. Like I mentioned. Sal's disappearance could be some kind of a metaphor. I guess I thought maybe, like you knew him forever or something, so there was maybe a chance you might have some old photos or I don't know..." he was regressing into a sixteen year old, explaining to his father why he'd failed a physics test, when the truth was he'd written nothing on the page.

"Are you frigging retarded, coming to me with this?"

"No, I just—" Dorian stalled out. "Ok... Yeah, maybe."

Axlerod smiled. He reached out and slugged Dorian on the arm. Dorian grabbed his bicep. That shit hurt.

"I'm just kiddin' ya *Dorian*. If the old man has any kind of picture, I'll give it to you. I'll ask my pops about it when I see him this weekend."

"Oh. Cool. Thanks."

What had Dorian missed? There had been some trigger switch from the hostility to the creepy congenial thing going on now. Had Dorian won the guy over somehow? Was it possible that maybe he liked the sound of Dorian's new project?

"Hey look, you know, if you're interested, I'll let you know when I'm showing the work..." *When. If.*

"You do that," Axlerod said pleasantly. "Maybe I'll even buy a piece."

Dorian laughed. "That would be fantastic."

"Alright then."

Testiness was starting to return to Axlerod's demeanor and Dorian wasn't sure what to say next. He was almost tempted to invite the landlord up and show him something right away, maybe even work out some kind of juicy barter in exchange for rent. Then he realized his landlord's uneasiness might not be stemming from awkward silence, but from Dorian physically blocking Axlerod's car door. Dorian stepped back. Axlerod raised his eyebrows as he unlocked the car and climbed inside.

"Good to see you," was the best Dorian could come up with in parting, never his strongest suit.

"Yeah." Axlerod said, his excruciating stare glued to Dorian as he started the car. Dorian could still feel those burning eyes as the man who owned his floorboards, walls and the ground beneath rolled off down Ludlow.

CHAPTER THIRTY-FOUR
POWER

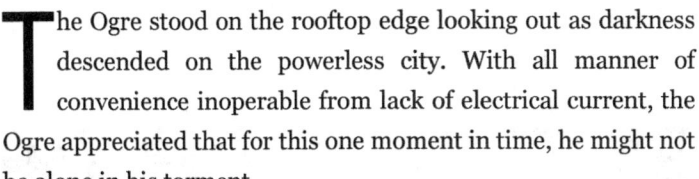

The Ogre stood on the rooftop edge looking out as darkness descended on the powerless city. With all manner of convenience inoperable from lack of electrical current, the Ogre appreciated that for this one moment in time, he might not be alone in his torment.

In a reversal of their usual spatial order, the Artist hunched sixteen feet below. Using a tiny metallic knife, the Artist applied the final touches to a massive stretched cloth, bringing out minuscule details in a woman's features. This was a rare instant where the Artist attained a state of mind uncluttered by distraction.

Three flights down, the Artist's Subject pulled a soft quilt filled with synthetic fiber up around her chin in perfect darkness, still overcome with the pleasures of having her own apartment back. A fleeting appreciation of comfort, the Subject's domicile at least somewhat restored.

And on the ground floor, the Superintendent leaned on one arm in the dim candlelight. His First Wife lay sleeping on the mattress next to him. His Second lay in the main room, her eyes locked with the Superintendent while the rest of their family slept. These tight quarters rarely felt so tranquil.

The tenement foyer sat in darkness.

The street outside was all but abandoned, except for the lone pizzeria Hustler—the decedent of a Caribbean archipelago loosely associated with the contiguous territories on which he now stood—making every effort to appear as if he were a law-abiding denizen on a midnight stroll. But the Hustler's eyes betrayed him, darting repeatedly towards a pane of melted sand lodged in slowly degrading bricks halfway up the residential edifice.

Inside the structure's entrance hall, the sound of an incandescent buzz not heard for days emitted from a ceiling bulb.

A spark of heat in the filament filled the bulb with luminous radiation.

The foyer lit up.

CHAPTER THIRTY-FIVE
FINISHING TOUCHES

S urrounded by candles, scratching away at his canvas, the light in apartment 21 suddenly flickered and Dorian's eyes were accosted by the glare. He was among untold millions who had left their overheads on when the five borough's electrical grid overloaded. His pupils slowly adjusted, he set down his palette knife, seeing his painting fully illuminated for the first time.

Standing, Dorian had to take a few steps back to take in the towering canvas.

He felt he was awaking from a long surreal dream. The painting somehow spoke for itself now. And for once, the end result had much to say. Leaning back on his heels, he knew it was finished.

Mioko lay asleep in her brightly lit bedroom.

A knock at the door. Then another.

She struggled to open her eyelids, raising a clammy bicep to shield the light.

Mioko opened the door a crack without removing the drawn chain.

"What time is it?" she said, finding Dorian in her luminous hallway.

"I finished the painting. You have to come look."

Mioko shielded her eyes as he stepped aside.

"What? Now?"

"Come on."

She tried to ascertain if Dorian's late night overture wasn't some new trick, but in the newfound brightness, everything seemed relatively free of danger. She pulled back her chain.

"Bring your camera. I want to take a picture of you next to it."

Mioko laughed at his boyish enthusiasm, but she grabbed her camera from the kitchen table all the same.

Standing behind Dorian outside 21, Mioko noticed the pile of discarded abstracts leaning against the wall. She wondered what was so wrong with them that he'd had to rip a hole through the painting that topped the stack.

"I can't thank you enough, Mioko," Dorian said, so effusive he struggled to slip his key in. He paused for a moment before opening his door.

"I was so stuck for so long. You unlocked something in my mind."

Mioko followed Dorian inside his apartment, the far wall slowly coming into view.

"I think I only just realized how frustrated I'd become," he said. "And then I started this work. You've lived below me all this time, you're like a portal into something I couldn't see before. Sounds corny. But there it is."

Two humongous canvases mounted side by side in a giant diptych ate up the inner wall.

The blood rushed from Mioko's face.

Surrounded by endless pencil studies and half-worked canvases were two massive, vibrant, photorealistic paintings. Mioko caught the intricate blots of light and color in glimpses:

an Eldridge Street stoop, a chair in Dorian's living room, Mioko's body completely nude, the tattoos on her legs moving up her inner thigh ending just below her navel. Then on the other massive canvas: Rube shirtless, glistening and dimensional, leaning out from the wall, his manic eyes staring back at her.

Gigantic.

Piercing.

Terrifying.

"Oh my god."

Her camera slipped from her hands.

The lens shattered on contact.

CHAPTER THIRTY-SIX
IT'S TIME WE HAVE A TALK

"Somewhere along the line, I don't know if something broke. I just stopped feeling like the people around me, these kids in the streets, have any good in them at all." Morris said, in The Chapel of Rest, before the open casket of his mother's corpse. "I wake up, I go downstairs. The streets are filled with puke. Used condoms. Broken bottles. Some days it's all I can do to not just roll over and go back to sleep."

The funeral director paused at the Chapel doorway, wondering if he could shrink back to his office.

"And then when I do venture down, I feel like such a leper. I walk into the grocery store and they stare at me. It's like they can smell the stench of... loneliness."

Emboldening himself, the director walked towards Morris and places a hand on his shoulder.

"Mr. Hacking," he said, "it's time we have a talk."

The director immediately regretted his own breach of protocol, seeing Morris's venom filled eyes.

Morris stewed in a plush chair in the squeeze of the funeral director's second floor office. The space hadn't changed in decades, except for a general paint fade from white to funereal-appropriate beige.

The director, rigid in his chair, also looked much the same as when Morris had first inked paper for mom's stay. Morris hated the man. The power he wielded over Morris's life, the snide way he talked, and stared down the end of his nose. Morris wanted to smash his drooping glasses into his face.

"It's not about the money, Mr. Hacking," the funeral director said in his most professorial tone.

"I'll get another goddamn job," Morris interjected.

He'd only missed two payments for fuck's sake. It wasn't as if he couldn't work if he needed to. The funeral director shook his head dismissively.

"This isn't a question of financing."

"Well what the hell is it then?"

"It's a matter beyond my control, I'm afraid."

Bullshit. Demetrakas's had finally just decided they didn't want to deal with an offspring as steadfast and devoted as Morris was. But Morris wouldn't just roll over for this pencil dick.

The director stood and moved to look out his tiny window. He couldn't even be bothered to look his client in the face while he pissed in it.

"Our property has already been sold, Mr. Hacking. This is not personal."

"Sold? To who? Under what authority?" Morris yelled.

"The new lease we were presented was astronomical, we simply could not meet the numbers."

"You can't do this."

"I don't have a choice."

Morris was losing his balance, and couldn't deny a sudden urge to defecate, which he did right there in the funeral director's plush chair.

Morris strained for the tenement handrail. He'd climbed these stairs without since he'd learned to walk, and now here it was, a lifeline. He started to cough. A few sharp phlegmy pants of air at first, but then another flight up, his esophagus seized and his breath became shallow. After all the nights of darkness the scuffed green stairs glared back at him. Each cough another razor in his throat. He attempted to shift his arm, but his brain was unable to process any data through his strangled neck. Air didn't pass, but memory reverberated, "We can't afford to do business in this neighborhood anymore." The funeral director had kept his face to the glass.

"Fuck your business," Morris wheezed between coughs.

His hands were moving again. Reaching for the landing. He pulled himself upwards, shifting his body a stair, then another.

That look in the funeral director's eyes when he turned his gaze from the bustling avenue to face Morris. He'd seen it before. The night it all happened. In the eyes of men with fancy instruments that didn't work. Blood on hospital tile. The night they took her away. Before he got her back.

His coughing filled the stairwell.

Patronizing superiority slathered on the hospital staff's pasty faces. "She's gone. I'm sorry."

"We're sorry."

"So sorry."

"Lovely woman."

"Call this number. They're good. Demetrakas. They can help you make arrangements."

Wheezing for air between fierce coughs, Morris began to hyperventilate.

"Yes, we'll take care of everything."

"You're bills are overdue."

"Perhaps it's time to discuss the possibility of cremation?"

"It's Wednesday the seventh, I'm sorry. That's final."

The blaring emerald green looked familiar, but he wasn't sure where he was anymore.

"You have no idea what you're doing."

His body thudded downward, inflamed with rapid-fire coughs. Tingling spread from his hands to his feet, his lips.

He could smell the black smoke billowing from under the junkie's doorway. Thick and cloying at his chest, his head throbbing. The carbon dioxide in his blood plummeting. His vessels constricting. His brain crying out for oxygen. Stranded halfway between the fourth and fifth floor, where time crawled backwards.

Dorian climbed the stairs with a bottle of Pierre Ferrand and a bag of Georgia's East Side BBQ—a little gift he'd splurged on in order to celebrate the completion of his latest piece. A nice fat joint, three quarters of a rack of spice-rubbed ribs, and a glass of cognac at four in the afternoon seemed appropriately decadent to fête a giant leap in his art career revamp.

Leaping the stairs two at a time, he was confused by the obstruction in his path; a shit-stained behemoth collapsed in the stairwell. Dorian pulled his keys in self-defense against the potential booby trap. The Ogre looked a tad worse for ware, doughy, pale and coughing his face off. But for all Dorian knew he was about to leap round and shove him down the stairs. Dorian cautiously approached the body, slowly leaning to get a better look. Spasmodic throat contractions seemed to limit The Ogre's air intake. His eyeballs rolled wildly in their sockets.

"Morris?"

No response.

"Jesus. Can you hear me?"

The lump continued to pulsate quick and shallow. Dorian stared for a long moment. He then climbed the obstruction, and headed up the stairs.

Fuck him.

Dorian stopped at the door to his apartment, the cognac clinking against his doorframe. Celebration. He closed his eyes. A deep breath. Weed, ribs, booze, good times. *Act like a human.* How had the insufferable thought ever lodged in his head? *Fuck.* Sure the work was about others. About not turning away. But perhaps it only needed the pair of paintings he'd already finished. Unless the project was a bellwether. The means of not carrying on as a complete and utter cock for good.

But The Ogre?

He reached into his pocket and pulled his cellphone.

Son of a fucking bitch.

"9-1-1: What's your emergency?"

Dorian burrowed into the hundreds of plastic bags crammed inside the cupboard below his dish-filled sink.

"How should I know? He's just laying there," Dorian spat into the phone. "Yeah hold on, I'm looking."

He finally found a small brown paper bag. He rushed the door, and down the stairs towards Morris's body.

Kneeling down, Dorian gingerly put his ear to Morris's mouth, listening to his fast-paced breaths just as the squeaky middle-aged 911 operator instructed. He placed the paper bag over Morris's mouth and nose. Then he waited.

"What's supposed to happen now?" Morris was continuing to gag on his own incessant coughs. Dorian's barbecued ribs sat congealing on the table upstairs, the fries and grilled okra were sweating beyond soggy repair, while he tried his best to save the guy he most wanted dead on the face of the planet.

"OK. It's not doing anything."

Middle-age squeak continued in her relaxed tone.

"Fuck's sake. Yeah, fine."

Dorian climbed the body. He awkwardly scooped his arm beneath the Ogre's sweaty pits. Sliding his body underneath, Dorian forced his neighbor's gelatinous mass up into a seated position, then pressed the bag onto his face.

The breathing slowed. Then his sluggish hand reached up and slapped the bag away.

"Look pal, you don't want help, I'm gone. Happily."

So happy, it hurt. The hulking beast in his arms, the thing of nightmares. The number of coital embraces he'd managed to impede with his slamming broomstick—in most cases seconds before climax. The shine of rotten teeth glaring from his cracked doorway. Who'd so freaked legions of impressionable young ladies, never again would they return to Dorian's bachelor paddock. For all Dorian could muster, any one of them could have been a stable contender. Perhaps without the Ogre upstairs Dorian would be properly satisfied in life and love. A demon who had somehow intuited the most upsetting day of Dorian's life to perpetrate his latest nefarious deed—injecting his locks with glue, placing a tiny enveloped rodent at the foot of his front door. And that was only in the last year or so.

A pitched growl squeaked from the Ogre's lips.

"What's that?" Dorian asked.

"Fire."

"Fire?"

"Lungs. Fire."

"What fire? What are you talking about?"

"Damaged from the fire."

Dorian squinted down at him, dubious.

"Mioko's fire downstairs? Really?"

A wave of fresh coughing followed a deep guttural throat clearing.

"Listen, the paramedics are coming, they're gonna help you."

"No hospitals!" Morris choked out.

"Look, whatever. You can take that up with them."

They sat in silence, the bag over Morris's mouth. His chest heaving as he worked to fill his diaphragm.

For the first time, Morris could feel the infinite finality of death. The echo chamber of last breath reverberating in perpetuity. How badly he suddenly wanted to look, and not just to look, but to really see another human face. He needed this like nothing else. Leaning back his head, he let Dorian cradle him. He stared into Dorian's perfect brown irises. It was the first time in his adult life that he had allowed himself to be this close to another person. And what he saw could only be described as beautiful.

"They're burning my mom." Morris said quietly.

Dorian was unsure how to deal with sudden emotional intimacy in conjunction with intense physical proximity.

"I'm sorry."

"When she's gone, I'll be completely alone."

Heavy-hearted, Dorian nodded.

Alone he understood.

"Yeah." Dorian said softly.

They lay there in the stairwell like that for what felt like a very long time, but was really just a fragment.

A team of paramedics filtered in around them. They took over, allowing Dorian to get out from underneath. The paramedics quickly applied oxygen and wrapped a blanket round The Ogre. His decade-plus neighbor. Morris.

They lifted Morris up, placing his body in an EMS chair with four handles for legs, cinching the blanket tightly around him, resting their oxygen tank on his lap.

Dorian watched as three grown men and a woman, strangers to both of them, lifted the chair and carried Morris's large constrained frame down the stairs and out of the building.

Long after the ambulance pulled away, as night mysteriously grew warmer than day, Dorian sat cross-legged on the tenement stoop, finally getting to enjoy his cognac the way it was meant to be, straight from the bottle, the brown lifesaving-bag pulling double duty.

Something had changed in Dorian. His breath was clear and steady as he looked out at the bustling droves, but he kept absolutely still, like an ancient Bodhisattva balanced in perfect equanimity. For once, he didn't feel the need to label every passerby. To categorize, fetishize or somehow denigrate each and every being in his field of view, coming up with something amusing, but almost always disparaging—sometimes a hundred times a minute—to pigeonhole a person by a haircut, the cost of a suit, piercing of an eyebrow, swing of a man purse, or the size of an ass.

Instead he experienced them as a frantic mass of bees, dancing in and out of the endless bars and buildings like so many flowers and honeycomb. He felt all of his senses moving outward with each new breath, until he could see, hear, smell, taste and touch in a three hundred and sixty degree field around him.

His body dissolved.

He became all space and time. Infinite.

And then in an instant, as quickly as this awakening had come—it was gone.

CHAPTER THIRTY-SEVEN
NASTY BUSINESS

A xlerod pulled up to the curb of *Rosarita's* in his Viper. Behind the counter, Rube watched him stall in his ride till a pair of sluts with Kardashian ass left the parlor, thinking the veggie slices they'd just ordered were gonna shave off the pounds. Watching them waddle a half block, Axlerod got out of his whip and into the parlor.

"I can't take it anymore," Axlerod said. "That's it. It's killing me. Makes no sense."

Axlerod dropped an envelope, fat as those girl's asses, on the glass.

"My father's lost nearly half a mil on that girl since the day she moved in."

No longer bashful, Rube fingered open the flap right in front of the landlord. Air mail was stacked. Fuck you money. Enough to quit *Rosarita's*. Move out of the PJs. Keep Nastasia's mouth shut by jamming her entire crib up with pampers. Rube tried to equate the cheese to ounces of hydro to break it up in his head. But he got up to pounds and he was still flipping hundreds. Now he was on to calculating if it was enough to buy an old Coupe De Ville and pimp it out with a brushed-steel grenade shift-stick. Just like Sticky Fingers, that Avenue C hustler extraordinaire had, may *ese* rest in peace. Back when the "C", Loisaida Avenue, was stills Alphabet City, instead of some high fashion East Village *mierda* (not that he was complaining, considering this upmarket realty was paying Rube's bills now). A slick ride and happy baby mama, was that really all he wanted?

No. All that shit was secondary.

Session time. In a real studio. Not some cockamamie basement pro tools-lite bullshit. Rube B Lethal a.k.a. Def Killah on the mic. The first full-length LP. With a sick producer, guest appearances, fucking catering, all that shit. Talking opulent. Twenty box chicken nuggets, rolled blunts, and blowcaine waiting on the coffee table at the start of every session. M&M's, with all the reds pulled. Huge titted 'rippers fellatiatin MCs in the vocal booth. And not crack hoes neither. High class Louis Vuitton bitches.

An uncompromised hip hop classic.

This envelope was the game changer he'd been waiting for. His ticket if he spent it right. A major step up the ladder of life. Rube wasn't about to pass this up.

"Yeah, a'ight," Rube said, because one thing was for sure, it was more than enough to bankroll the nasty business ahead.

CHAPTER THIRTY-EIGHT
DISTINGUISHING HERSELF

ioko sat at her table in the late afternoon carefully cutting her spread off the back of the Village Voice. She felt a little like a ten year old as she pasted the ad in her old scrapbook. Maybe the Lamerica experience hadn't been her life's pinnacle, but there was something undeniably affirming about pasting it in across from a Providence Journal clipping of her high school choir.

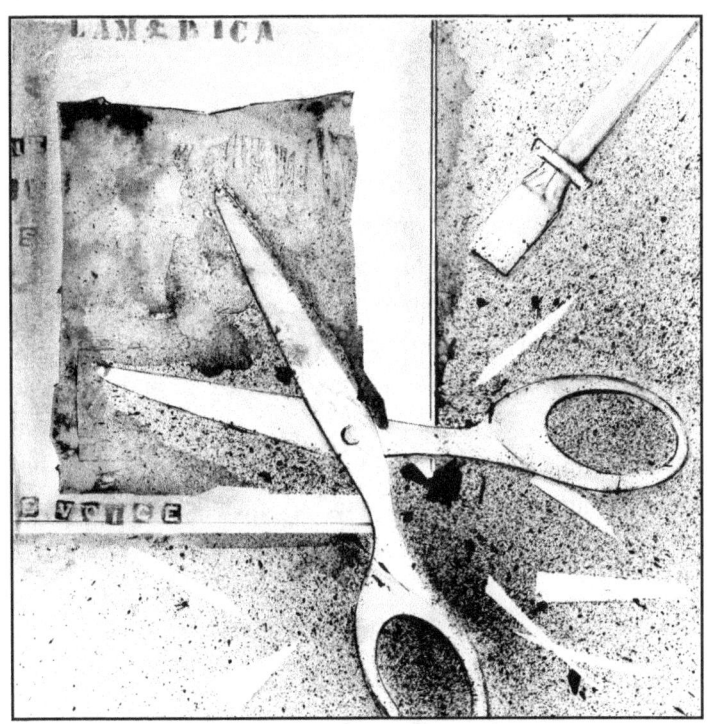

She could smell faint traces of smoke damage wafting off the pages as she flipped back through, smiling at the familiar mementos: state for forensics, her girl scout badges, winning the spelling bee, a spring photo competition. Such promising beginnings for a girl who went on to distinguish herself solely through an aptitude for epic screw ups. Mioko hadn't spoken to her parents in years, and she suddenly felt like sending them each a copy of the ad with a hand written update on the last half decade. She had a flash of one of her mother's expansive flower arrangements on the Tokanoma, the sound of her father's cello filling the halls of their home. But flipping back to the ad, it was so transparent as a glammed reflection of her darkest days, sending it off would doubtlessly widen the rift. If atonement was what she was after, better done with a postcard.

She closed the book, but one image fell out: her mother's hand holding her flower arranging clippers. One of Mioko's very first photographs. Now wasn't the time to get sucked back into the past. But she left the photo on the table.

She grabbed up the volume, and climbed her footstool, replacing it above the tall dresser, safe from prying eyes.

Climbing back down, Mioko was split in two. She wondered if she was now returning to the innocent little girl beginning her scrapbook, or just on a breather from the shadow world she'd magnetized in her adolescence. An existence so aptly depicted in Dorian's hateful pair of paintings. And, as if it could serve as some kind of a verdict, she grabbed a mug off the shelf and a box of peppermint tea, when all she really wanted was the rest of the Jameson, or a needle.

Sparks of sweet pain shot up her arm.

The needle buzzed away, jamming ink into skin.

The handle of her mother's clippers began to take shape on her wrist.

And then she woke. Panic in total darkness.

CHAPTER THIRTY-NINE
THE FUTURE

O n most evenings, at the end of his recycling haul, Ndusen couldn't wait for home and a shower before collapsing into bed, but tonight he was in no hurry. He ambled Stanton, weighed with his neighbors disposables and the knowledge that his family had somehow reached such a deadlock he could no longer imagine his way clear. He had hoped perhaps building the garden might be an opportunity to find their way, but had just exacerbated the tug-of-war.

When he had become engaged to Kondwani so many years before, he felt so young and inexperienced. He could still picture the ritual game of 'Guess Who' he had been forced to play at the engagement ceremony. A group of young maidens had entered, covered from head to toe in the traditional *zitenje* cloth. He had then been made to guess which one was his bride to be. Try as he might, he had not been able to tell which was his future. He had looked for her large childbearing hips, her gentle swagger, but under the *zitenje* her qualities had been difficult to decipher. He had accidentally chosen a young village girl, Buseje, about the same height, and of course all of the other girls had sung and teased him mercilessly. As he pushed open the recycling container, he wondered now if perhaps his inability to pick Kondwani from the others had been an omen.

Wandering slowly back towards the tenement Ndusen's mind summoned the much happier time years later—after Dziko and Alile were born and he had worked his job for Malawi Safaris for some time—that he had met Stella. After yet another tedious drive back from Luangwa National Park, he had been pleasantly surprised to find a new lovely girl working in the Zambian camp. After he had done his duty dining with the safari guests, he had made the young girl laugh by catching a giant beetle and threatening to release it next to her ear while she did the washing up. A few Carlsberg browns by the staff fire and they had quickly become friends. She was gorgeous, and so easy to talk to. From then on, the long washed out roads in and out of Luangwa were no longer a chore, for he could not wait to go on his Zambian trips. By the time he had decided to ask for Stella's hand, the traditional games of guess who, and such quaint rituals as the exchanging of chickens between families to mark a couple's engagement seemed childish. He had elected instead to give Stella an engagement ring.

The modern world had begun to seep in, and it was not so long before he was announcing to his little tribe that not only would they have a second mother, but he had decided they must save their *kwachas* for a move to the United States. He had managed to get Stella work as a secretary at the Malawi Safaris head office in Lilongwe. The second income had facilitated his decision, but unfortunately so had it offset the balance of power. It was not long before Kondwani had begun maneuvering for authority. At first Ndusen had decided he had better let Kondwai have her way, proclaiming her rightful position as first wife, but now that seemed a miscalculation.

Reaching the front door, the warm hearth of his family had always been there to welcome him home after each unyielding day. Even if he returned after they were asleep, just their slumbering presence reassured him and brought a sense of ease. But not this night. The slightest possibility that Kondwani was awake elicited a deep anxiety, not so dissimilar to what he felt in his Axlerod dealings.

His work, his family, the crimes he had witnessed and done nothing about—Ndusen felt paralyzed. Their first years in the Tenement ground floor, life in this city had suddenly felt like a liberation, a place were if he worked hard enough, he could eventually walk the concrete with pride, rise up the towers, carve out whatever was left of the dream. Looking at the crumbling columns and impenetrable glass all around, restaurant food he'd never tasted; bars, stores, pop-up shops. He'd walked past so many, but entered so few. He felt less at ground floor level, than he did trenched in by a world he had no means to ascend.

Ndusen flashed on his father, who despite his lack of formal education was invaluable to the village; a counselor, solicitor, barrister and judge, regardless of his inability to read a written word. He wondered if such a man had ever experienced crippling uncertainty. "If the future doesn't come toward you, you have to go and fetch it." His father's favorite Zulu proverb returned its cryptic answer. As Ndusen looked past the concrete, brick and glass—at the night sky reflecting Manhattan's citrus glow back towards him—he felt powerless to summon what lay ahead.

What was taking this clown so long? Rube had more important business than watch this punk-ass African statue staring at the sky.

He mulled heading home and chilling, maybe pickup a forty, play some Grand Theft Auto, but adrenaline was keeping him pinned in his choice hunting blind alcove across from Axlerod's tenement. He could feel that hot tingle coursing his veins, kicking something fierce.

Rube did his best to ignore the star gazing bitch and kill time going back through his baller list of envelope spending: after the album was mastered, the next big ticket item was a pair of tournament grade paintball guns, an entire new closet with ill tailored suits and custom shirts, then obviously 'rippers and crystal. And not just punk ass lap dances neither, some roped off VIP shit. He'd just about triple spent his loot, but fuck it, more where that came from. Spend money to make money. If he was driving that slick ass Cadillac, cash would be magnetically pulsating. That was laws of attraction shit.

Ndusen dropped and spun his starry-eyed stare, eyes almost grazing Rube. But he was pretty sure the Super missed the hunting blind. Either way, Rube didn't sweat it, this town, some Hispanic loitering the street didn't mean nothing.

Go inside to bed *traga leche*. Rube wasn't thrilled with the super hesitating at the door, like he was about something. What was he waiting on, the midnight ice cream man?

Finally that biatch cleared out. Rube waited till the door was good and closed, the Super disappearing down the first floor hallway.

Stepping out, Rube moved slyly across the street till his face was staring through the glass in the front door. Flaking green paint a century deep. Rube waited there perched a half-step. Feeling skittish. Ready to swivel. Ill at ease with the night around him. But he could feel her upstairs, laying in her bed. Black garters. Japonica tattoo crawling up like waves of a snake, treacherous. Divine. Red and black dyes wrapping, Rube's mind wandered all the way up.

He pulled a front door key from his pocket, slipped it up in the lock, nice n' easy. But then he turned and shit didn't move. He had to wrestle the unfamiliar lock, fighting panic. Finally it gave in and he moved into the foyer a few feet. The tiny mail area. The second lock to wrestle with. Cock smoking Super, staring up the damn night sky instead of fixing doors. Useless.

Finally in the hall, he could hear some bitch walking in behind him. Peering round, Rube spotted the damn artist in the lamplight, fumbling. About to enter the foyer if he ever worked out the lock—and that worthless *pendejo* lived here.

Rube ducked down the hall, the back door. The courtyard.

Stunned, he froze there, his face turning childlike, dazzled by strings of colorful Christmas lights illuminating the garden. It didn't fit right in his head. A place like this out back of this run-down apartment block. It reminded him of his *abuela's* back yard in Hoboken, his grandpa cooking up dogs on the Weber while he helped his *Lita* pick tomatoes straight from the vine.

He walked along the rows of buckets, the familiar smells of plant life all around him. He reached out and touched some fresh mint, the smell intoxicating. But Rube caught the glint of his watch.

Time to get on with this shit.

Rube bounded the stairs quick, but tried to keep his footsteps light. As he passed the sixth, Ivan's closed circuit camera came to life, following Rube, the red lens light blinking.

Reaching the top, Rube pushed the rooftop door, trying to minimize the rusty squeak.

Planting his kicks on tar, he hadn't been up here since the night he'd taken that old fucker Sal Agnelli, priming himself with a nice fat blunt before the deed. But he weren't gonna be smoking no blunt tonight. Decrepit old guy went easy. Sixty seconds muscling a pillow to the face. Probably should have just left his ass there cold in his bed. Natural causes and shit. But that heeb was some paranoid motherfucker. No corpse, no forensics. His dime. His MO. Slicing the carcass to 6 pieces was easier than he'd imagined—like boning a man-size chicken—but then he'd had to call up Tubby-D to drive him all the way out to some shit Delaware, before they finally found a spot to bury the stankass hunks, slamming at the frozen ground for hours with a rusted shovel.

This time Rube had a little something cleaner in mind.

Kneeling down on the sticky blackness he whipped out a leather case from inside his jacket. Unzipping, Rube extracted the bag of tan powder, pure china white, and the soup spoon he'd nabbed from his ma's kitchen that afternoon. He bent it back. He figured she'd never notice one spoon gone AWOL as he loaded up her vanished flatware with a humongous hit of powder. But she'd have a tolerance for that shit, so then he tapped out the real deal, careful not to get any on his skin or atomize it up his nostrils. Fentanyl. Murder 8. Enough to drop a horse.

Rube hesitated.

Fuck it. Pulling a butane from his pocket, he started cooking.

Morris stood in his bathroom, cramped up into the corner, staring out his peephole. He wasn't sure what he'd heard, something like a jaguar. He'd shot across the apartment determined to get a look, but been too slow. Restless from the hospital meds after "the suffocation" on the stairs, though his thoughts were becoming a little clearer, he couldn't sleep. Whatever wild animal it was, it wasn't materializing again. Morris thought he should give his mattress another shot.

Then he caught site of a young man with a capped syringe between his teeth sneaking down the fifth floor staircase, tilting his hoodie-covered head to see around corners. Morris stepped back from his peephole. His heart belting. Had the hospital sent him here? They'd said he was discharged, but maybe it was some kind of test.

He peered out again as the man with the syringe disappeared downstairs. Reasoning it through, this figure seemed even more fantastical than a large spotted cat. Sitting back on his mattress, Morris consoled himself, it must have just been another of his "fictional ideations".

Down on three, Rube pulled a set of disposable medical shoe covers out of his pocket, stretching them over his red high-tops. Back when he was sixteen, he'd swiped a whole box of surgical overshoes on a midnight hospital wander-through, along with a box of drug samples, and a stray wheelchair. He'd dared Deuce to ride the chair an entire week as an entertainment exchange for some samples. Back when tubby could still squeeze that gargantuan ass in a chair. He'd need a double wide now. That chump hadn't lasted in the chair three hours. More for himself. But the drug samples just gave Rube migraines. The shoe covers on the other hand, over the years they'd come in real handy.

Rube knew he better center his shit. Even without the weed, he was drifting. His dome working overtime as his veins continued to pulse. Euphorical. He pulled the syringe from his mouth, his eyes lost for a moment in the dark-brown liquid.

Rube licked his dry lips, then put the needle back between teeth. He slipped on a pair of *Rosarita's* sanitary gloves, then pulling out a key, guiding it silently into the lock. His skills beyond masterful.

Showtime.

He closed the door to apartment 9, delicate. Rube moved across the kitchen floor with huge slow arcs and soft steps. Silence. Complete domination.

Her bedroom, the inner sanctum. Mioko's sleeping body. He took his sweet time looking her up and down. He could feel his prick tick up. Then Rube closed in on her. He took the syringe from his mouth, delicate as ever. Then without warning he lunged out, his plastic-covered palm crushing her lips.

Shocked from slumber, some primordial shit filled her baby blues. She knew it was on. Staring down the reaper. The Def Killah. For Rube B Lethal.

He stabbed at her arm with the syringe.

Blood splatter. He wasn't looking for no skin pop. He needed a vein. He had to keep stabbing till he was good and sure. His hand pushing down that pretty face.

Thrashing now, Mioko chomped the soft flesh of Rube's palm. He jolted back, his glove filling with blood.

"Ahh FUCK!"

She grabbed at the bedside lamp something desperate; she managed to swing his way. Rube dodged the lamp, easy. But she swung a second and clocked him upside the head, the bulb exploding in his face.

She leaped off the bed past Rube.

Snatching the needle off the mattress he chased her into the kitchen, slamming her into the table.

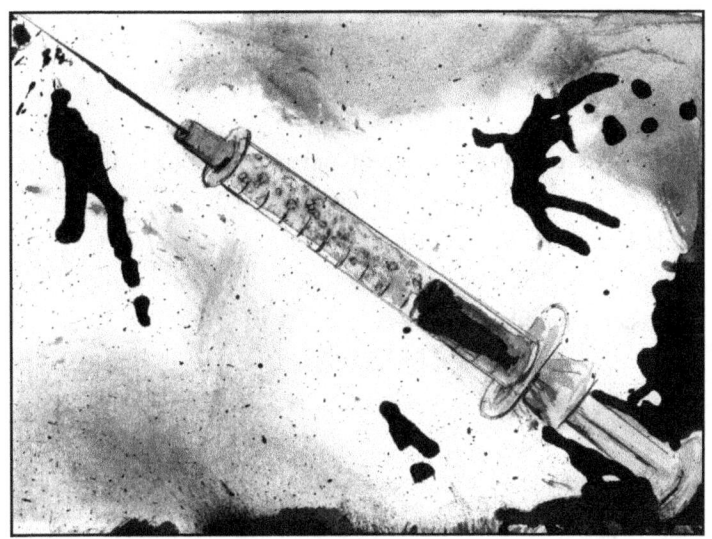

The devil's dance to the floor. Looking down into those soulful orbs.

Desire. Lust. Yearning.

Love even.

Shelve that *coño* where it belonged. Rube shoved his forearm against her neck, pinning a tiny wrist with his knee—same way his *carajo* of an uncle, Gervaso the Perv-asshole, always did him when family visited.

He tried to pin the other wrist, that *puta* slammed against his lightbulb head gash with her free hand. Some truly last-ditch struggling to liberate herself shit. He had to admit this was getting out a hand, but the surge in his boxers was driving him now.

Shoving the needle in below her bicep, Rube slammed down the plunger.

Enough foreplay, time for climax.

Mioko heaved in a contorted arch as the opiate cocktail flooded her system. Rube watches her body spasm and heave as she gasped for air.

He backed out of the apartment, one last look at her. Then sprinted down the stairs.

Life still clinging to her pinpoint pupils, Mioko nudged her torso on its side, then dropped down with a thud.

Using what strength she had left, she crawled down the stairs—the world pulsating before her, the tunnel compressing with each dwindling heartbeat.

On the verge of losing consciousness, she dropped to the ground at the bottom of the stairs, kicking out with the last of her strength.

As her brain function began to slow, Mioko's thought process struggled to increase by exponential proportions, laying there at the bottom of the stairwell. Not life flashing, but instead cosmic busts of all the things she'd left undone. All the people she had loved, whom she had lost. All her hopes and desires which she had put off. The places she would never see. Experiences she would never have. Feelings she would never feel. Children she would never birth. Generations she would never meet.

Stella climbed past Chisulo, making her best effort not to wake him, but the ignorant fool slamming at their door had already started the children down the road of moving limbs and fluttering eyelids.

The keyhole was empty. Could this be some practical trick?

Pushing open the door, Stella peered out.

At first nothing. Then she looked downwards.

The sight of the tattooed woman sprawled on her back at the bottom of the stairwell filled Stella with alarmed wonder.

As Mioko's heart slowed, then finally ceased, there in the first floor hallway, she could feel moonlight on her skin and could see the barren winter trees outside her parent's house lulling softy from side to side above her.

And then, she was home.

CHAPTER FORTY
CREMATION

A wooden casket sat inside the crematorium chamber engulfed with flames spitting from the industrial furnace.

The Demetrakas funeral director monitored his only guest. Morris stood in the large viewing room, his suit more tattered than ever, his eyes teared up, but otherwise remarkably composed.

It had been three weeks since his visit to Bellevue's psychiatric emergency. The meds had more or less shifted his mental chemistry. Now he felt as if he had to learn everything over again. Like a newborn: hungry, intimidated, but seeing everything with fresh open eyes.

Eyes that watched now as the door of the chamber slowly closed on his mother's timeworn corpse. His pain was centered below his chin, spreading down through his neck, making it hard to swallow. She had been his everything. Without her he had no identity. It was terrifying to even contemplate what tomorrow would look like. And yet, as his gaze came to rest on the stone slab chamber door, he had some notion that the key to keeping on was in the newness of it all. If he could just stay with the feeling of beginning and not get lost in filling in all the pieces, he might just be all right.

Standing on the tenement rooftop, still in his suit, Morris's eyes were glassy as he looked out at a storm brewing over downtown. He had never thought of storm clouds as anything but a reason to go inside. But with these clouds, he could feel their force. Their authority over the heavens. Yet another new emotion he had neither anticipated, nor could figure out what to do with.

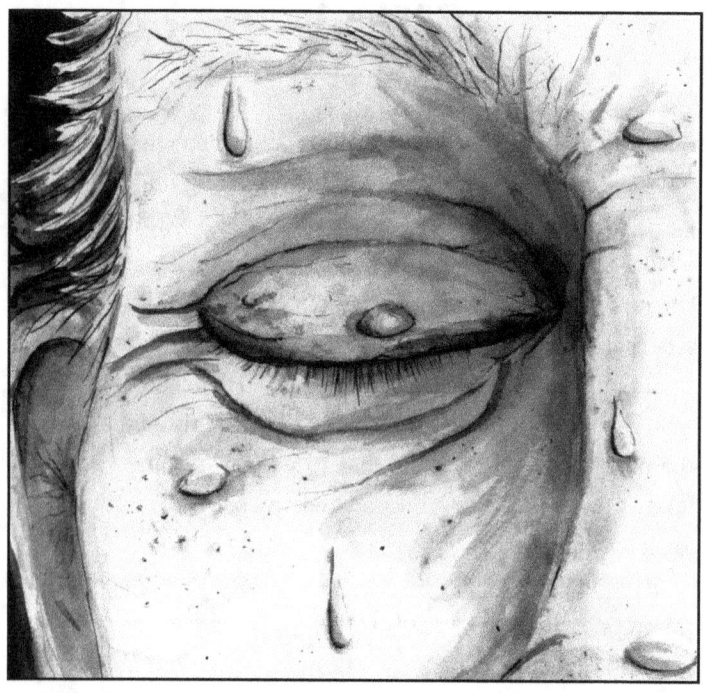

With the first drops of rain, Morris closed his eyes and drifted as if he were affixed to one of those majestic atmospheric beauties. The cool rain felt surprising on his skin. The raindrops washed away the dried saline on his cheeks from the cremation. The drops turned to a downpour. Morris spread out his arms to take it in. A timpani of sound engulfed him, each drop an intonation in an orchestra of kettledrums. His mouth filled with rain, the drops soothed his scalp. His fingers tingled with sensation. Then the sound of thunder came, impressive resonance suddenly all encompassing, and he realized it was time to head back in.

Walking down the stairs Morris halted mid-step when he spotted a trio of discarded paintings resting next to Dorian's doorway. He picked up the canvases to take a closer look.

One of the paintings had a hole through the center. Morris touched the ripped abstraction, pushing the hole back together with his finger making the image complete again. They were so engaging, so expertly crafted; he couldn't understand why his neighbor would ever want to part with them.

CHAPTER FORTY-ONE
SUSPENDED ANIMATION

D orian stood in a starched white shirt, staring at the towering back wall of Gropius Gallery. The exhibition space behind him evolved and changed shape as morning turned to afternoon. A team of gallery assistants painted a white wall red. They hammered and pinned. Hung a series of canvases. The assistants brought folding tables, then were replaced by serving staff in evening jackets, who lined the tables with white cloth and rows of wine bottles.

The room filled with art patrons in eveningwear. They crowded, milling around Dorian with cheap wine, looking in the same direction as his empty stare. Some tried to engage. Others didn't. As the room reached capacity, Nadja Gropius expounded about the images that everyone was looking at, lifting glasses in toasts and generally beaming her wide fake smile. Patrons enthusiastically shook Dorian's hand, opening their wallets and purses. His coffers filled while beautiful women swooned. But Dorian ignored them all, continuing to stare at the red space between the two massive canvases before him.

Slowly the room began to empty out. Nadia's lipstick stained his cheeks along with a crude whisper. Dorian stood alone again. A few stragglers exited into the rain as the gallery lights shut off.

Dorian continued to stare.

In the darkness, he finally allowed his gaze to widen.

Rube and Mioko hung in suspended animation, two massive canvas paintings on the red gallery wall; a daunting mismatched pair of urbanites. Somewhere between photorealistic semi-nudes and impressionist twisted corpses. They looked so fragile. Such delicate beings.

Dorian couldn't begin to fit the pieces in his brain. He was so caught up in his own hunger; he hadn't seen the clues all around him, all the roads that could have made him whole. A true sympathetic soul. A person. One that others actually liked. Not just a peddler of intangible works they could paste value on. To buy, sell and talk about. Feed their own egos.

He'd grinded so hard, and had received everything he'd ever wished for. And yet he was completely numb.

The creation of suffering with a palette knife, his words, his prick. That was his Midas touch.

Dorian sat up in his loft bed for what was left of the night, knees pressed to his chest, staring out at the twinkling skyscrapers.

As the sun rose over the cubist skyline, he finally started to cry.

He hadn't cried in years.

When Althea had made her exit, he thought perhaps he'd forgotten how. And now the tears were streaming down in droves. His tears dripped to the floor, entering the thin boards that separated him from Morris. And below that, he cried for Old Sal, now lost for good. And on down to what was truly undeniable. As much as he wanted to pretend, he knew Mioko's overdose was entirely his fault.

And still he couldn't place exactly why.

Dorian held his legs tighter, the emptiness like a vacuum.

CHAPTER FORTY-TWO
WANNABE

T he nasty gash just starting to heal on his forehead, Rube slammed the front gate of *Rosarita's* and clicked the padlock. In the corner of his eye, he caught Axlerod's Viper cruising down Stanton. It was the only moving ride in sight, the street abandoned this early on a Monday.

From behind the wheel as the landlord pulled up, he slung a bulging envelope towards Rube.

"Nice work Kid."

Rube leaned down, peeled the envelope off the pavement.

"The second half."

Second what? Was he really such an amateur, he didn't realize the first envelope was a deposit? Last time there wasn't no second half.

Who cared, he was rolling in cheese now. He didn't even need to open this one, he could tell by the rubbery give, like an uncooked chicken. Least another ten G's.

"Just so there's no confusion," Axlerod said "there's a little something extra for you in there to stay clear of me and my affairs from now on."

Rube tilted his head, perplexed. Axlerod winked at him, "You feel me, playa?"

Rube nodded slowly. Much as he was ecstatic about this unexpected cash influx, the brush off from Axlerod was the last thing Rube expected. He was under the impression he and the lord-of-land had some mutually beneficial tastes for empire building. That this was just early days. There was plenty of money to be made with what Rube brought to the table. Especially now that he was a bonafide badass mothafucker, slaying bitches and geezers with a cold heart and a warm hand. Not to mention dropping that *bicho* teen on his own time.

No, Rube was on his way uptown. Blue Chip. And he reckoned Ruthless 'Rod was gonna play an integral part in his rise to Tony Montana-hood, tearing through cocksuckers with a grenade launcher strapped to his "Little Friend", the M16A1, as they snorted titanic mountains of blow together.

But the heeb was putting up the power window, like Rube didn't represent shit. Had he been worked like a virginal hoe, tossed to the street after catching the clap her second trick?

Rube was about to command Axlerod's ass to a halt. Tell the landlord all his grand plans. Show this half-dick he wasn't some dumbass pizza slinger, but a powerhouse baller who ripped shit up with razor street smarts and a magnetic personality.

Instead Rube looked down at his soiled apron and wondered why he'd even come to work that day. Why he hadn't quit *Rosarita's* yet. He had enough money to take a crack at the big time. Even before this second half envelope. Forget about childish toys, he could throw down a proper album if he wanted. Now hip-hop producers would take his skills seriously. What was he waiting on?

Rube Carbia was a fucking star in the making and who the fuck was Moshe Axlerod? Over-the-hill phony-ass Long Island-living *huele bicho*. At best, an insecure power-hungry douche, a self-hating Orthodox with daddy issues, a handful of real estate handed him on a kosher platter. In short. *Nada*. An insignificant little biatch.

But he was talking to taillights. Axlerod revved down Stanton. No matter. He was a fucking heavyweight now.

Tomorrow Rube would be buying and selling *bichos* like that by the dozen.

As he pushed his bike home, in no mood to ride, Rube mulled the turn he'd hoped would bring him some kind of juice. And he wondered what kind of fool would kill a person not even realizing he actually had some genuine love connection with. Maybe if he'd been wired different, they might've had some kind of chance together. He'd understood her. They were kindred in some way by their adversity, like a pair of parasitic twins.

But he wasn't wired another way. Just a shit disturbing PJ rat who dropped high school to sling pies after he'd baby daddied at seventeen. And it was some stupid delusional shit to ponder even a damaged loner like Mioko would've wanted anything to do with his forsaken ass.

But damn *ese*. This feeling sorry bullshit was getting depressing. Besides, at least now he had something to bust rhymes about. How many motherfuckers had killed their own true loves? That shit was certifiable.

Then he saw him. That *mama bicho* of an artist. They stared each other down across Norfolk, Dorian surprised at first. Then almost nodding his dome. As if Rube made perfect sense, the lost piece of some grimy puzzle.

Rube hopped his bike and started peddling fast, but as he hit the street, his eye caught a perception that made him freeze: a single stark white tree stood tall, springing out at the end of the sidewalk. He wasn't sure if it was the way the light was hitting it or just the tree itself that made his jaw hang open, but it seemed completely out of place. Petrified white perfection in a sea of red bricks and black steel. His feet slowly pushed down on the pedals, ready to make a move on his behalf, but he couldn't take his eyes off that tree as he wheeled away.

As it receded, he wondered if those branches contained some link to the paradox of her life. It seemed crazy, but he couldn't shake the thought that the surreal white tree had spontaneously materialized at the moment of Mioko's death.

CHAPTER FORTY-THREE
FRESH APPLIANCES

A rriving home, Dorian placed his keys on the kitchen table and looked up to find his apartment suddenly seemed a dilapidated shanty.

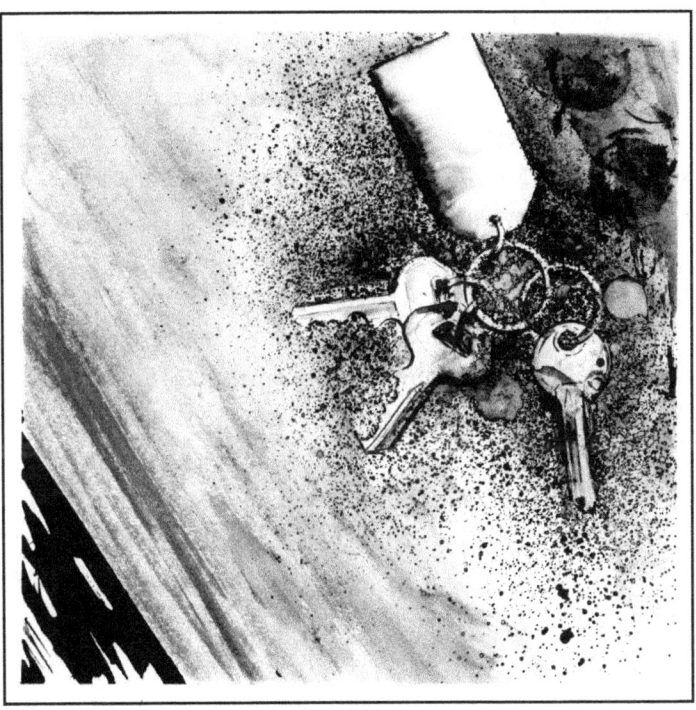

The fixtures and furniture all looked worn and encrusted with dust. He'd always considered himself at odds with his lifer neighbors, the creepy old shut-ins who still occupied hundreds of these Lower East Side tenements like a checkerboard of atrophied castoffs. But the more he thought about it, the more he'd progressed toward one of these urban hermits.

This tenement room had come to define him, just as Mioko's coveted pair of apartments had defined her, or Morris, Ivan, Sal or even Free Stuff for that matter.

Just allowing himself the comparison for an instant made his stomach turn. There was something fundamentally wrong with those people, whereas he was basically a pretty together guy who was maybe going through some kind of an extended rough patch.

He imagined what some of the newly renovated apartments in the building must look like with their fresh appliances and cabinetry, and what his place might have looked like completely empty—or better still, burned to the ground along with the rest of the building in Mioko's fire, a near miss if ever there was one. And to his great displeasure, Dorian suddenly couldn't help but envy the young debutants and trust funders with their clean hardwood floors and expanses of white walls to come home to. Shower stalls to stand in. Working door buzzers to let Chinese food into the building without having to run down six flights of stairs to greet the delivery guy, or toss a key in a rolled up sock off the roof for a girlfriend's visit.

He wondered if he could even bring himself to move to a new place, considering the jackassery quotient for giving up a rent controlled one-bedroom in one of the most desirable neighborhoods in the city.

Dorian started to do a little mental arithmetic on square footage. What the place would go for at current market value. Hell, maybe he could talk Axlerod into a buyout. Because of the rent stabilization, Dorian paid just over a grand a month for what could easily be rented between two and four, depending on how much of a sucker the new tenant's rich father was.

Then he started to factor in the half-dozen other buildings the Axlerods owned, and all of the eligible apartments they could flip, multiplied by the thousands in income they were losing off the Dorians and Miokos and Morrises and dozens of other long term tenants—he'd lost track of the numbers and variables somewhere in there, but Dorian realized that equaled a shit ton of money. A buyout of a few thousand bucks seemed more than reasonable.

He opened his cabinet to pull down a bottle of bourbon, thinking perhaps moving was just another escape. After his Gropius show, he could at the very least now afford a new studio space, which would undeniably cheer him up. But his mind quickly wandered to more murky territory. Just who's money was that anyway? His, or the dead subject whose life he'd had a hand in destroying? And what of her young stalker? Did he deserve a share of the pie? Certainly a share of the blame. He had to hand it to the kid, stalking his prey all the way to the grave, and then sticking around the neighborhood like it was nothing. Dorian lifted his glass to Rube.

"To sharing the blame."

The brown elixir immediately worked its magic, soothing Dorian's withered head and making him wonder who else he might offload some culpability on.

And then it hit him like a shotgun blast.

The lost rent income, the stalker, the fire, Old Sal, all of it. Sal hadn't just disappeared. His landlord had killed him. And now Mioko was gone too.

Moshe Axlerod was cleaning house.

CHAPTER FORTY-FOUR
LAST HARVEST

C hisulo watched as Stella harvested the last of the tomato plants into a cooking pot. Despite all the encouragement to the contrary, Chisulo still felt a singular allegiance to Stella, who was after all his own flesh and blood. Kondwani had been acting so erratically, he couldn't help but wonder if perhaps he and Stella faced the possibility of being cast out, not just to the courtyard garden, but from the family entirely. It was a terrible thought, but with the tone of the yelling between his father and Kondwani inside the apartment, he couldn't seem to shake it.

Stella looked from the tomatoes to her son's distraught face and smiled, she could tell he was agonizing over their troubles.

"Bring these inside," she said sweetly.

Chisulo accepted the tomato filled pot and walked into the building.

Entering the hallway, he walked towards their family apartment, but hearing the stormy voices inside Chisulo thought better, and continued through the hall, exiting the building.

The air had a slight chill and he wondered how long before he would see the first flakes of snow. Chisulo turned towards A&D Dress Company. Approaching the shop, he peered inside, seeing Althea helping a customer try on a dress towards the back of the boutique. Chisulo leaned down, placing the pot of tomatoes just outside the door. He stood tall for another peak, then quickly disappeared back inside the tenement.

Ndusen and Kondwani sat at the kitchen table. Kondwani's face filled with tears as they spoke in pained Chichewan.

"I know things did not go exactly as we had hoped in this country," Ndusen said. "I had imagined something quite different."

"What did you imagine?"

"That we would make a life here for our family."

"You want to go back, is that it?"

"I think we both know it is time for a change. That perhaps you would be better off returning home."

"Yes, I believe it would be better for us there."

"No Kondwani. We will not all be going back."

"Then what?"

His silence was answer enough.

"How can you do this, Ndusen?" Kondwani asked.

He held kindness on his face, but he had made up his mind, "I cannot see things will be changing for us."

Kondwani momentarily broke down. Then quickly filled with anger.

"What of the children?"

"When they are old enough, they can make their own decision."

It was the most difficult determination he had ever made in his life. He would never be able to forgive himself for bringing her to this place, only to separate her from her own children, but it was clear he had no other reasonable choice.

Ndusen slid a tin across the table.

"There's enough in here for a ticket home to Lilongwe," he said.

Kondwani reluctantly accepted the tin. Ndusen reaches to take her hand, but she pulled away.

The sound of knocking brought him back, and he wondered

if his children had become so timid that knocking on their own front door felt necessary.

"Hey, Ndusen, you home?" a tenant's voice called.

Ndusen stood up from the table, but far from feeling cured of his troubles, the pain in his solar plexus was stronger than ever.

From the doorway of the courtyard garden, Chisulo watched as his father opened their door to find Dorian the painter waiting for him.

As Ndusen stepped out into the hallway and the painter began to speak, the look on his father's face alarmed Chisulo, and he wondered what fresh trouble awaited his family now.

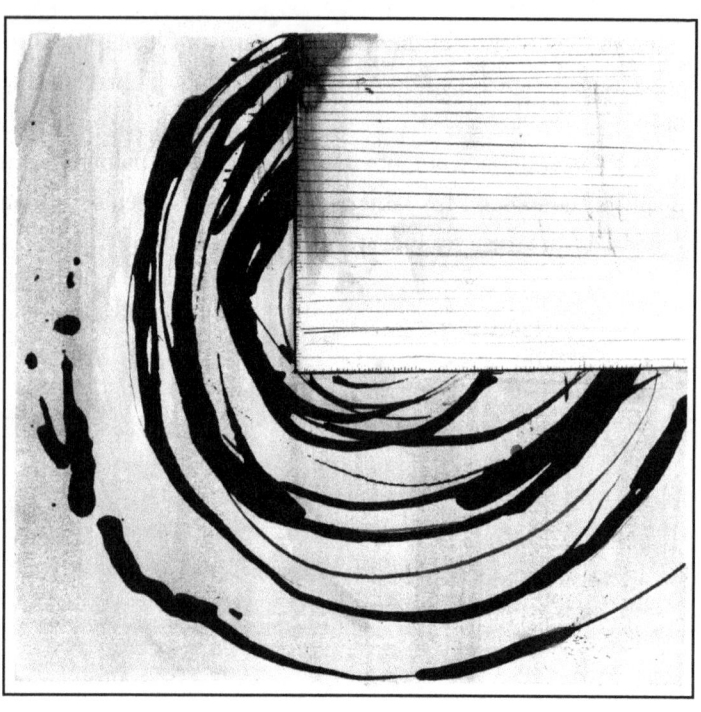

CHAPTER FORTY-FIVE
SILVER IONS

L ooking at his hefty key ring, Ndusen took a moment to reflect the consequences of what might lay ahead if he found something tangible, something that might solidify his darkest anxieties. For so long he had convinced himself he was not a collaborator, but simply a byproduct of the dishonorable system his employer increasingly spent his time devising. But with each progressive immoral undertaking, Ndusen knew he was more an involuntary accomplice, and less the principled bystander.

His thumb moved across the jagged metal teeth of the key to apartment 9.

"We've gotta look," Dorian said, standing in the third floor hall behind him.

"Yes, I know," Ndusen bristled.

Ndusen was quite sure if he did not act now, he might never be able to convince himself to take action. He finally unlocked Mioko's apartment and stepped inside.

The two men walked the space, scanning the elements of Mioko's insular life: the smashed bedside lamp on the floor, the broken lensed camera on a shelf. Ndusen peeked beneath the ancient legs of the tub. Charred wood he had missed in his slapdash painting. *What else had he missed?* The scorched spiral pattern snaked from under the corner of a new floor mat. His eyes didn't miss that.

He watched Dorian pick the black smartphone off the kitchen table. He pointed the lock screen at Ndusen: a black and white of three intertwined kids inside a dive bar stall.

"If this is indeed a crime scene, you ought not touch anything," Ndusen said. He was not even convinced he should have opened the apartment in the first place, but he had to be sure.

Crossing the hall and unlocking Mioko's second dwelling, they pulled back the inky curtains, letting daylight spill into the darkroom for the first time in years. The residual silver ion particles lining the countertops and floors—remnants from thousands of sheets of photographic paper—were suddenly energized, transforming back to atoms and creating a galaxy of imperceptible black pinpoints.

Ndusen was struck by the images hanging from the lines. He glanced at the Lamerica prints, noting their similarity to the photo on her phone, but that wasn't what interested him. Ndusen stepped past to a second line of hanging photos and pulled down one of a dozen prints of Rube. He studies the image closely.

'WARNING. This is Rube Carbia and he is stalking me.'

What did a Hispanic street punk and an Orthodox Jew from Long Island have in

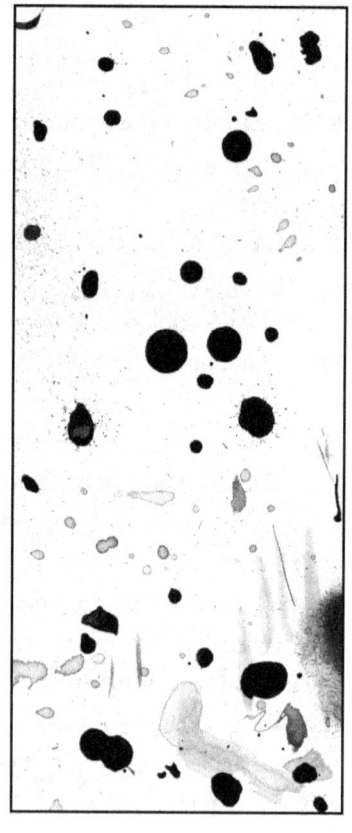

common, Ndusen wondered. Then it occurred to him, as little as the landlord had with the Malawian super who turned his head at every unethical infraction on the building's tenants; simply put, he was on the payroll.

As Dorian walked rapidly down the bustling Delancey sidewalk towards the 7th precinct, Mioko's black and white photographs swinging from Ndusen's hand next to him, he felt quite sure he was part of something important. Maybe even a truly selfless act. He still couldn't quite believe the sheer arrogance of it all, but he had to admit the Landlord's murderous enterprise fit nicely into Dorian's take on modern living; poor folks lived in the shadows of the elite in Manhattan, in America, across the world. Axlerod had just taken survival of the richest to its natural endgame. Dorian had pooled the entirety of his energies into flipping his own trajectory towards fortune and prominence, so he understood this hunger well. In the landlord's darkened depths, power and money had come to take precedent over fellow humans. Simple as that. Dorian wondered if this act of symbolic amends might clean his own dark depths.

They slowed as they reached the precinct.

"Are you ready?" Dorian asked.

Ndusen's father's words reverberated in his head, 'Not to know is bad; not to wish to know is worse.' He was frightened of what lay ahead, his life was already in such upheaval, but his legs had carried him this far, envelope in hand. He could feel the adrenaline pumping his body like an *Inyanga's* elixir; the village witch doctor's spirit powders, which she would razor-blade directly into the skin to ward off sickness. The slim keloid scars from the treatments still lined his legs from childhood.

Scars of healing. Ndusen didn't know what would come next. His employer held so much power over his livelihood, his home, even the safety of his family.

Ndusen pushed open the precinct doors.

As they stepped into the maw of American justice, their free will abandoned, Ndusen was surprised to feel the pressure on his ribcage uncoiling, the membranes in his central nervous system relaxing, internal fluids redirecting to find their appropriate biological domiciles, the rise and fall of his solar plexus.

The Axlerod virus was finally beginning to abate.

CHAPTER FORTY-SIX
JUST THE SLICE

Rube laid pepperoni on an uncooked pie, backing the counter of *Rosarita's* 'Loogie Hawks by da Slice.' He whipped it in the oven, and set the timer.

The bell chimed as a black female police and her Asian partner strutted their chunk asses inside.

Suddenly the after-lick of pepperoni turned against him, Rube felt nasty in the pit of his paunch.

"Let me get a slice," the Asian cop said.

"Anything for you, mam?" Rube said, wheeling to the partner, pleasant as pastry. "Pepperoni slice?"

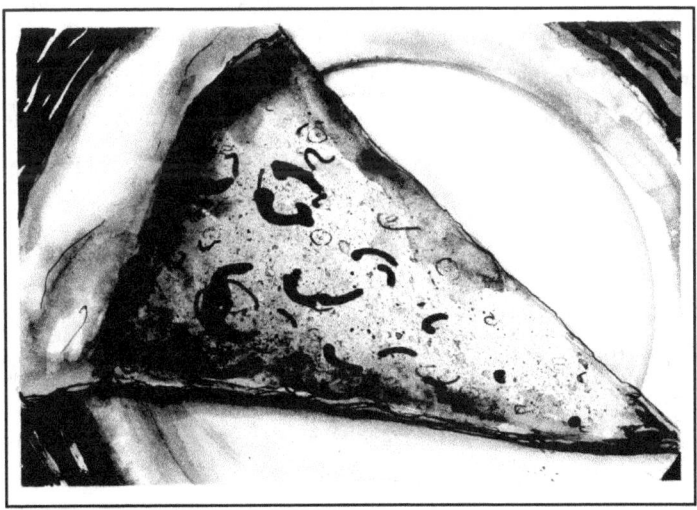

The female police shook her head, no. Slowly.

Rube whipped a cheese slice in the oven, eyes on the pigs.

"Beverage?"

Usually, a couple of bacon strips in the joint, Rube was ice cool. This morning, it was all he could do to keep from jumping out of his pelt.

"Just the slice."

Rube nodded. He tried to decide if he'd do better pretending to look busy, maybe start on a fresh pie. Try and dish up some casual pizza man blather. His eyes wandered over their belts: the guns, the handcuffs.

The female police grinned.

"Never seen a police officer before kid?"

"Wass that?" Rube asked.

"That's quite a cut you've got on your head, there," she said.

How was he supposed to respond to that?

"Right."

Rube opened the oven, boxing the pig's slice and handing it over. *Take your goddamn slice and leave.* The female police eyed Rube as he rung the order. Her partner flipped the box lid, took a nice slow bite, not looking like he wanted to go anywhere. He wished the pig would third degreed the roof of his mouth, but Rube knew the mozzarella was lukewarm at best.

As they finally turned to the door the lady porker took a real lingering staredown. Rube didn't flinch. Least he didn't think so.

He was sure happy to see the pair's potato sacks swishing down the sidewalk. Rube ducked and hit his vape to get back to the business of relaxing behind the counter. It was just a breakfast slice and a random ball bust so they could start the day walking the beat with their asshole foot forward.

But why were they slowing? Stopping at a parked yellow cab a half block down. The telltale yellow E-ZPass toll transponder a dead giveaway it was an unmarked. The female police leaned next to the front window, real casual.

Way too casual.

He could just make out the beefy reamteam inside.

Fuck.

Detective Emil "The Razor" Rozycki craned his tattooed neck out the window with a friendly grin, sitting shotgun next to his partner, Jared Serilo.

"So, what'd ya think?" Rozycki asked the female officer leaning against his counterfeit cab.

"He's good for it," the officer replied.

"It was me, I'd bring him in," her partner chimed in, mouth full of pizza.

Inside the car, the detectives flipped through the printed photographs from Mioko's darkroom, then at Mioko's handwritten note, now sealed in an evidence bag.

"But what kind of a genius extinguishes a victim with evidence like this taped to the front door of her building?" Rozycki asked.

"I didn't say pizza boy was a genius. Just he seems good for it."

"In the age of kids livestreaming murders in realtime," the Asian cop said through a mouthful of pizza.

"The state of crime in this country." Serilo mumbled, more to himself than the rest.

"What about building a case? You think he'd roll?" Rozicki asked Cochran.

"Like a bunny in a bear trap."

"Poor li'l rabbit," Rozycki said, winking at her as he closed his window.

Rube watched the cruiser continue to idle as the beat cops turned their radios back up and strolled along Stanton. He pulled the pepperoni pie. Before turning back, he willed that phony taxi gone, but Neck tattoo's eyes wouldn't quit.

CHAPTER FORTY-SEVEN
SHABBAT SHALOM

A fter the blessings over the wine and challah, Moshe Axlerod sat down to Shabbat dinner with his family. The thin shell of his father took up his usual spot at the far end of the table, pulling back his respirator mask to fork in Moshe's wife's apricot chicken, spilling the prized sauce all over her pristine tablecloth.

But for once Moshe didn't care. This celebration was for him, and him alone. Having just closed the lease on the seventh renovated apartment he'd liberated over the last year. His crowning achievement: the emancipation of the junkie photographer's third floor pair, which he'd just rented for nearly six times their fixed leases.

He stared at the inept old man across from him. The dunce who'd squandered such vast wealth. He had to wonder how long this *alter kaker* would be gumming at mushroom blintzes in the head chair of Moshe's table.

It didn't matter. He'd finally established himself downtown, where it counted, and he was already starting to reap the rewards. He couldn't help but smile from ear to ear every time he logged in to check on the accounts. It wouldn't be long now before the old man was underground and they were living half the year in Aruba. Sipping Myers Coladas under their beachfront *palapa*.

Maybe he'd even take the young Venezuelan waitress with braces, who'd served them so attentively last Hanukkah, as a lover on the side. Put her up in a modest apartment by the lighthouse peninsula. Hell, he'd buy the whole apartment block for her. Teach her how to run it. She was bound to have the braces off by now.

The doorbell rang. His daughter, Alexis, stood and politely excused herself to answer. Certainly she hadn't inherited her gracious ways from her mother.

"Who's that now?" his wife asked in her shrillest timbre, "a little late for the UPS truck."

Moshe leaned back in his chair to glimpse past the dining room towards the entrance hall, but the angle wasn't right.

"Some men want to talk to you, daddy," Alexis said as she returned to the dinner table.

He could hear a gentle rain from the open doorway, and his heart was no longer cooperating with his ventricle chambers, which were now pumping at a raging pace. Moshe stood up lightheaded. An ardent pressure in his chest he could only hope was indigestion.

Crossing the floor, he could see a pair of smug looks framed on cheap blazers in his doorway.

"Moshe Axlerod?" the big one with the neck tattoos asked.

"Yes."

"You're the landlord of 168 Ludlow?"

"I am."

"You're under arrest in connection with the murders of Sal Agnelli and Mioko Kimura."

"Who?"

Perhaps he had as limited an understanding of the laws of physics as he did the human heart, but from this reverse angle Axlerod was surprised to find he could clearly see his wife, children, and the feeble old man anxiously ogling him from the dining room.

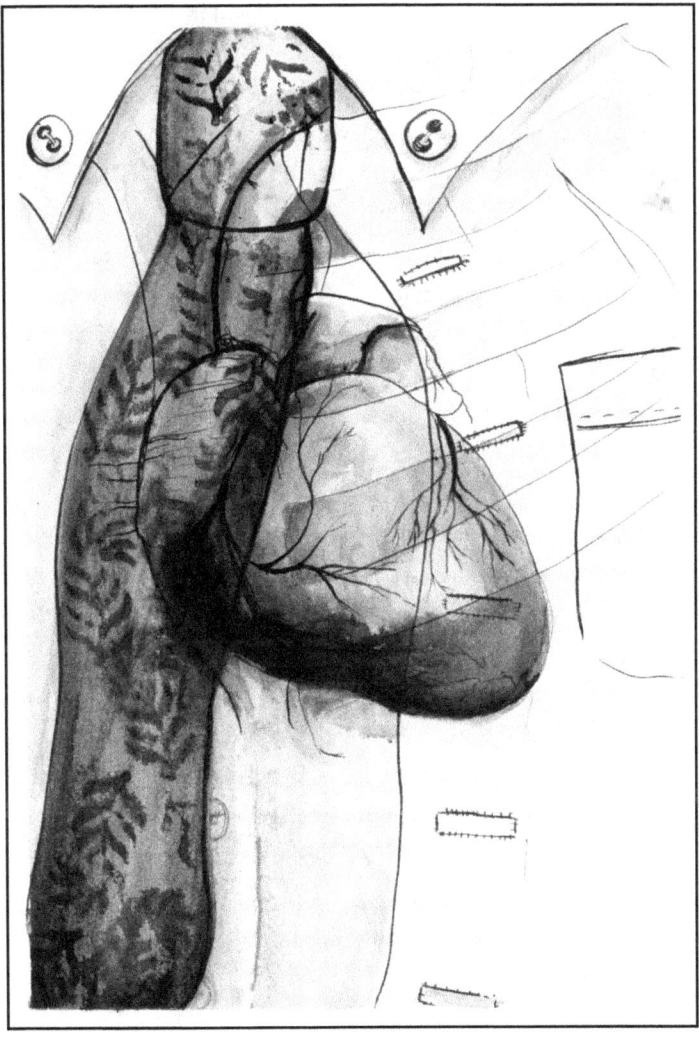

As he sat in the station with the untouched apricot chicken his wife had pushed on him, congealing in a tupperware box on his lap, Axlerod wondered what exactly they might be able to pin on him. He'd been fifty miles from the tenement on both dates.

Far as he knew, that old fart Sal had died in his sleep and the junkie overdosed. They hadn't mentioned anything about arson, or the laundry list of infractions he'd enacted on his lifer tenants. Not that he could be connected with any of that either. He had his ground-level lineup of superintendent fall guys for that.

This was just a shakedown. All he had to do was keep his composure. It would all just go away. And besides, he knew a lot of these guys. He'd grown up with them. He had three "Friend of the Patrolmen's Benevolent Association" cards in his wallet for God's sake.

He smiled more for show than for himself, and made an extravagant gesture of cracking the apricot chicken and sticking the plastic knife Eliada had furnished him with deep into the thigh. Cooking had never been his wife's strong suit and tonight's meal was no exception, but the box condensing onto his slacks now was a welcome distraction from the midnight bustle of the 7th precinct.

That's when his jaw fell to rubber, the cloying saccharine fowl lying dead on his tongue. Through the shifting prostitutes and thieves, he spotted an odd trio if ever he'd seen one in the adjacent room: the Malawian super, pizzeria rat, and the washed up painter sitting together at a detective's desk, fingering evidence. And upon sighting them, Moshe Axlerod ended the longest Shabbat dinner of his life, spitting a mouthful of coagulated orange flesh onto the precinct tile.

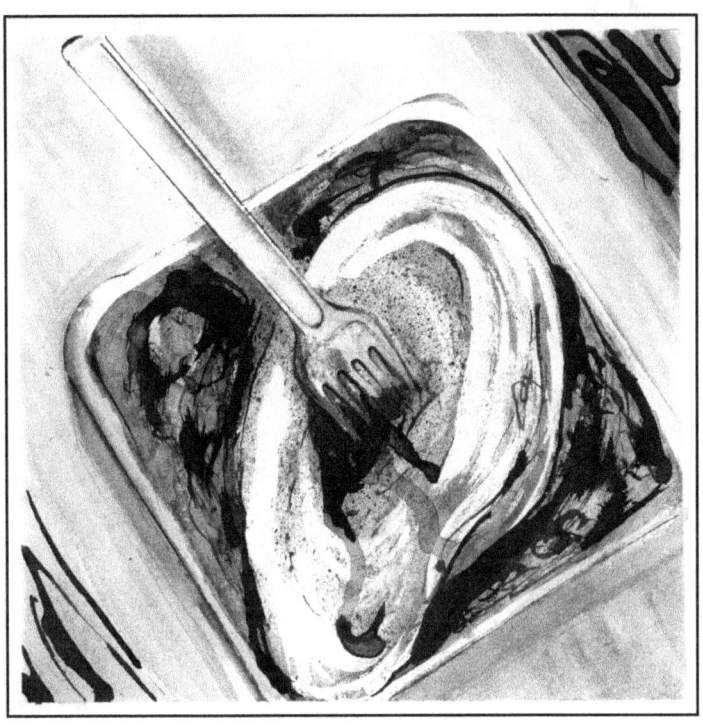

CHAPTER FORTY-EIGHT
PRIVATE GALLERY

The glow and crackle of the TV comforted Morris along with the whistling radiator. His ass sweated in his prized ancestral chair, the popcorn was popped, smoothie made, the start of the show.

But as one film bled into the next, the canvases behind his head took him over. Three discarded abstracts of a lonesome tenement that would just as likely sink into waves and silt the next hundred years as stay erect for more souls to find themselves stuck in. No doubt about it, the paintings hung handsomely on his wall. Repaired and dusted off, they were his own private gallery.

The new corporate umbrella company that had taken over the building after the pigs had come for Moshe seemed decent enough, and they weren't hassling him for the back-rent he owed. At least for now.

Many had come and gone from the crumbling tenement, gussied with expensive fixtures, but the artist who'd crafted the three prized paintings of his gallery remained above his head, just where he belonged. Quieter now. Finally. No longer hauling a pageant of sex and trouble home at all hours.

He'd spent eight solid months being paraded round as the next big deal in the art world of that fabled city at the mouth of the Hudson River: cocktail parties, paintings sold, models splayed, his name prominent in the pages of art rags and newspapers. Even beyond with orgiastic trips to Switzerland, Miami, Abu Dhabi. It was so much more than Dorian could ever have asked for, and yet, after months of cash grabbing and backslapping he'd found himself skipping out on one feting after another.

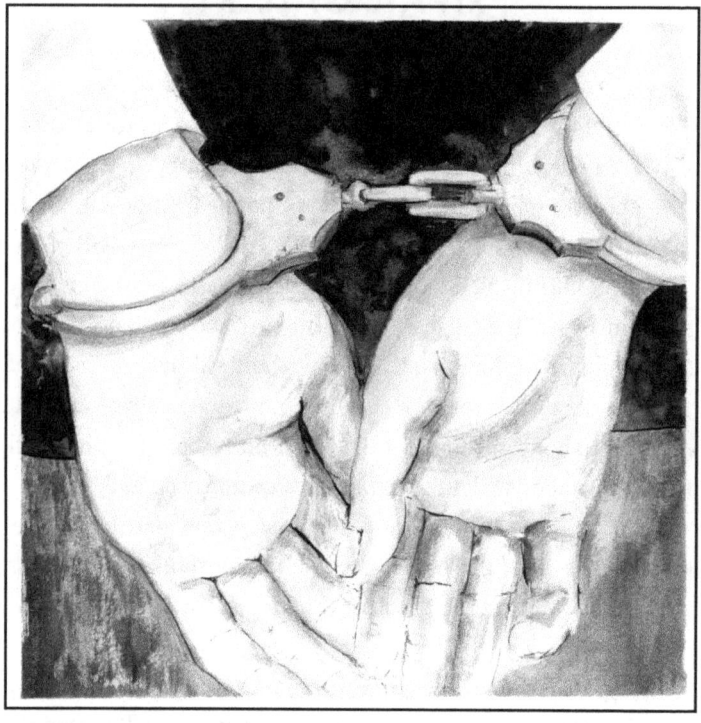

Sucked instead into a wooden bench at the back of Moshe Axlerod's trial room. And for once his interest in something other than himself had not even revolved around scheming the entire affair into a new project. In fact he hadn't picked up a brush since he'd begun cleaning the apartment that morning. His moment on the stand testifying to the ladies and gentlemen of the State Supreme Court wasn't exactly the high point Dorian had hoped— he'd gotten muddled on some of the dates, and didn't much like the bulldog defense lawyer's none too subtle character assassinations—but he was satisfied he'd told his piece.

Fourteen years lock up. Didn't seem much for a guy who'd torched his own building and paid a hit man to take out two of his tenants. Originally the district attorney had been talking 25 years, but without any priors, Axlerod weaseled into pleading out. Well, even fourteen years got the landlord choked up, talking about having no one to blame but himself, before they carted him out of the courtroom.

In truth, Dorian had barely known his two murdered neighbors, but doing something to help them—even post mortem—somehow felt more tangible than all the praise and glory his work had wrought.

He'd spent the better part of his adult life chasing it. Whatever *it* was. That illusive spark that would bring the world to his feet. The framework for an idea so seductively complex, yet somehow broadly accessible at the same time. A unique artistic thumbprint that would magnetize everything he'd ever wanted.

As he rubbed pigment out of his horsehair brushes, he noticed something beautiful around the plughole of his living-room bathtub. Something unplanned, that he could never recreate on any canvas. An explosion of built up colors, intermingling, worn by water into soft droplets clinging to the edges of the enameled bath, kissing the ring of scum and limescale.

Quite by accident, the vision conjured in Dorian something even more desirable than ripping the fixture out of the floor and putting it on display. The tub sitting here more meaningful than sharing the work--Dorian Teasdale's *Unwashed Bath* on display next to Tracey Emin's *Unmade Bed* at Turner Contemporary.

When he'd painted his comeback, he'd found a stillness borne of silence that opened the galactic pathways of his mind and steered him towards a wealth of imagery to paint. A stillness you could neither bottle, nor sell. But no sooner had he found it, he'd lost it again. He'd tried so hard to work backwards, to remember exactly what it was that had led to that spark in the first place. Sitting in the empty bathtub in the middle of the night, suffering from the most dreadful fit of self-loathing, was what he'd come up with. But why would an empty bathtub planted in the center of his kitchen and an interminable shit mood give him cosmic insight?

The harder he'd tried to grasp, the more elusive it grew, and his reclaimed star status had just filled him with an inexhaustible desire for more triumph, for even larger successes—along with unquenchable fear of failure, value judgments, pettiness, and all the unbearable mountains of nonsense in between.

He'd finally stumbled on the fact that perhaps the answer lay not in the peaks and troths of success or failure, but in the emptiness itself. By the time he'd gotten truly inspired, he had felt so completely empty; he'd more or less given up. And it was in that very act of giving up he'd found solace. He hadn't needed to escape his box on the sixth floor of the Lower East Side tenement after all; he needed something else.

To stay in the moment.

Which he was starting to realize was perhaps an artistic expression in and of itself. And when he put the brushes on the rack to dry and just sat there dwelling, and did very little else, the tenement walls and floor dissolved away and all his limitless desires and repulsions no longer seemed to matter.

Brooklyn based film director and writer, **Doug Karr**'s films have screened at over 50 international festivals including Sundance and won multiple awards, among them 3 Cannes Lions for his commercial directing. *Dwelling* is Karr's first novel.

UK based mixed media artist and blockchain bohemian **Ophelia Fu** works globally with other artists and writers with projects and connections formed, or shared, on the blockchain. Her work explores themes through digital drawing and a variety of traditional drawing media.

dougkarr.com
opheliafu.co.uk